THE
WORLD
BETWEEN
BLINKS

THE
WORLD
BETWEEN
BLINKS

AMIE KAUFMAN & RYAN GRAUDIN

Quill Tree Books
An Imprint of HarperCollinsPublishers

Quill Tree Books is an imprint of HarperCollins Publishers.

The World Between Blinks
Copyright © 2021 by Ryan Graudin and LaRoux Industries Pty Ltd
All rights reserved. Printed in the United States of America.

Library of Congress Control Number: 2020944584
ISBN 978-0-06-288224-0

Typography by Catherine San Juan
20 21 22 23 24   PC/LSCH   10 9 8 7 6 5 4 3 2 1
❖
First Edition

FOR TRACY GRAUDIN AND PHILIP KAUFMAN.

WE REMEMBER OUR ADVENTURES WITH YOU EVERY DAY.

THE WORLD BETWEEN BLINKS IS ALWAYS THERE.

It is everywhere and it is nowhere.

It is in every wreck, every abandoned lot, every city block, every scraggly patch of woods. It's the place you glimpse out of the corner of your eye, reflected in rain puddles and car windows. Blink. There and gone. Shoved just out of the streetlight's reach.

People see it every day, but they rarely pay attention. The grown-ups are too busy doing grown-up things—like ordering coffee or picking up dry cleaning—to stop and look, really *look*. Most kids are too distracted to examine it for long. They see the boarded windows and the DANGER: KEEP OUT sign posted by the entrance, and they shrug and go on with their lives.

Most kids.

But there are those who pause a little longer. The daydreamers—kids with burrs on their socks, who name sticks after legendary swords and call out the names of lost cities in their sleep.

They stare into the dark places: blink, blink.

They see.

1

MARISOL

MARISOL LOVED THE AIR AROUND THE OCEAN.

It smelled mostly of salt, yes, but there were so many other things happening inside it too. Sunscreen and crying seagulls and driftwood discoveries and waves washing castles back into sand. One breath held all of this.

When Marisol was younger, she used to think that's why her lungs felt so crowded whenever her family traveled to South Carolina, but now she knew the reason was more scientific. Something to do with altitude. La Paz, her home city in Bolivia, was surrounded by mountains, and Folly Beach was, well—a beach.

Every summer when Marisol Contreras Beruna went to her grandmother's house, her body had to adjust. This summer, the very first one after Nana's death, her heart was a big part of that equation.

"We're almost there!" Her mother's accent changed too, shifting to fit the southern Lowcountry around them. It always did, as soon as the drive from the airport became green marshes stretching forever. "Are y'all excited?"

Victor, her thirteen-year-old brother, grunted.

"¡Contesta! Tu madre no está pintada," their father chastised from the driver's seat.

Victor's second grunt at least sounded like a word. "No."

"No?" Dad protested.

"I'm creeped out," Victor replied. "Do you think the beach house is haunted now?"

Her mother's lip trembled in the rental car's side mirror, just above its printed words: OBJECTS IN MIRROR ARE CLOSER THAN THEY APPEAR.

There were almost tears in her eyes, which Marisol hadn't seen since the funeral last winter. Victor, looking out of the opposite window, had no idea.

Brothers are treasures—that's what Nana always told Marisol whenever she got mad at hers—*though some days you have to hunt a little harder to see the gold.*

Marisol had to hunt a lot when it came to Victor.

"If Nana were a ghost, she wouldn't stay in the beach house," she pointed out. "She'd be off having more adventures! Diving with sea monsters! Having a picnic on top of Mount Everest! Flying to the moon!"

4

"Ghosts can't fly to the moon."

"How do you know?"

"Because—" Victor caught himself, remembering like he always did that he was too important to argue with his little sister about ridiculous things. "Never mind. Do we really have to pack up *all* of Nana's stuff? It's going to take forever."

"Only the personal items," said their father.

"But . . . ," her brother faltered. "That's everything."

Mom's almost-tears turned into a laugh—though it was sad still. "You're right, but the realtor told us the house will be easier to sell if someone else can see themselves living in it."

The marsh outside the window had changed into ocean. Blue, blue, blue and a glitter of sun. It looked larger than Marisol remembered. Nana's house, on the other hand, seemed smaller. There was no FOR SALE sign yet, but that didn't stop Marisol's teeth from tightening. She didn't *want* to imagine a name besides Beruna on the mailbox, couldn't think of some strangers nailing a HOME SWEET HOME sign over the screen-porch door.

"Looks like we're the first to arrive!" Their father announced as he pulled their car into the driveway. "You have the keys, right, amor?"

"I *did*," Mom said, frowning in confusion as she dug through her purse. "I thought I did."

"Marisol?"

Both parents turned in their seats, not to blame her for the missing keys but to ask for help. Marisol was good at finding things. Keys, socks gobbled by the washing machine, even once a friend's escaped guinea pig.

It wasn't that she looked harder than other people. In fact, she barely had to search at all. It was almost as though lost stuff had a way of finding her. . . .

Marisol closed her eyes and felt for the *tug* that often prickled her fingertips. Sometimes the sensation was so strong it seemed as if her hand was pulled, though she'd never admitted this to anyone. She knew how it would sound. This time the force made Marisol reach for her mother's purse. "They're in the side pocket, with the zipper."

"So they are! Thank you, reina."

The porch looked the same as it did last year—lined with conch shells and sharks' teeth, wind chimes singing in the corner. Sunlight flashed through their strung sea glass, speckling the wood with blues and greens. This pattern had always made Marisol think of a fairyland, which had often led to Nana telling a story about the time she stumbled across Icelandic elf folk inside a cave on a beach much stranger than Folly, with black sands and icy tides.

Victor never believed the tale, but it wasn't much more

outlandish than any of the other things their grandmother did. To Nana, life had been one big adventure. There was photographic evidence all over the beach house, which Marisol studied as soon as she followed her parents inside. The oldest pictures—black and white—dated from Nana's days as a nurse during World War II. Her smile was young and brave, matching her friends' who wore the same khaki uniforms. Grandpapa was there too, saluting alongside Nana's brother, who'd been lost in the war.

As the hallways wound and stretched, so did the years. Nana's library held the adventures she'd shared with Grandpapa: riding camels through the Sahara, dog-sledding in Alaska, canoeing on the Amazon.

The photos often had maps framed next to them—yellowed with age, filled with Nana's travel notes. Sometimes she marked spots with an elaborate curling ✕. Other times she recorded the sights: *Pink dolphins. Aurora borealis. Sandstorm.*

Every time Marisol studied the landscapes—using a magnifying glass her grandmother had bartered off a Parisian bric-a-brac vendor—she found something new.

Today, it was *White reindeer*, written on a map of Sweden that was hanging in the kitchen. Marisol had been in here hundreds of times, chatting with Nana over glasses of sweet tea, but she'd never heard about that adventure.

Maybe she never would. . . .

"Mom?"

Her mother, who was already packing some silverware into a KITCHEN-FRAGILE box, paused. "Yes, reina?"

"Do you know when Nana saw a white reindeer?" Marisol pointed to the map and its adjoining photo, where her grandparents stood in knee-deep snowdrifts— bouncing a two-year-old between them.

"Well, let's see. . . ." Mom squinted at the photo. "Your uncle Matt's in this picture, so . . . 1956. Maybe?"

Marisol's chest ached, until even the ocean air couldn't fill her lungs. It wasn't the *when* she was asking for, so much as the story Nana would've told.

Nana would have said something about how the reindeer moved like a ghost, and maybe it was one, for all she really saw was the outline of horns scraping the snow-spun air, and eyes trapped like coal in the white of everything.

For a moment, Marisol could almost hear her grandmother's voice speaking the words. Imagining the scene was better than nothing, but it was worse too, because it reminded her that the true story was now lost. Too lost for even a girl who could find things others couldn't.

"You should ask Uncle Matt when he gets here," her mother went on. "He'd have a better idea."

Marisol rescued a sugar spoon when she passed the KITCHEN-FRAGILE box, sneaking it into her pocket. She kept following the photos up the beach house's main staircase, toward the bedrooms. More and more people appeared with Nana in each picture. By the time color film rolled around, turning Nana's hair auburn, she had five children—Marisol's mother the youngest by a minute— and they were all adventurers.

Mom's adventures had taken her to Bolivia, where she'd met Dad at the nonprofit where they both still worked. Her twin sister, Kate, traveled the world as a diplomat, constantly moving to new cities.

Then the adventurers had *more* adventurers: Marisol had plenty of cousins on the Beruna side, most of them much older. Their family portrait—taken last summer, before Nana got sick for the last time—sat in the living room, alongside pictures of their ninety-one-year-old grandmother hot-air ballooning in France.

Here Marisol paused, listening to the nearby wind chimes and Victor's heavy footsteps as he hauled luggage up to the porch. The beach house didn't feel haunted . . . but it did feel strange. Full of Nana's life, empty of *her*.

It made Marisol want to cry.

It also didn't help that all of her grandmother's things were about to be packed into a storage unit none of them would ever visit. The suitcases her brother wrestled down the hall were big enough to make him complain, but they couldn't fit Nana's shadowbox collection. Or the giant piece of driftwood she'd converted into a coffee table.

Marisol took a wobbly breath and walked to the nearest bookshelf. It held lots of knickknacks—a paperweight with a four-leaf clover, a white peacock feather, sand dollar doves—smaller things that fit neatly next to the sugar spoon.

She stuffed what she could into her pockets.

Her fingers started to tingle.

Qué raro. She wasn't looking for anything lost, but the buzz grew stronger when Marisol picked up a picture frame covered in macaroni. Maybe she was hungry? That didn't seem right. Besides, the pasta wasn't very appetizing, uncooked and coated in gold spray paint.

"Hi, Mari."

That voice didn't belong to her brother! Marisol turned to see a different boy in the doorway, with a shock of blond hair and a shy smile. "Jake! I thought you weren't coming until tomorrow."

"The embassy let Mom off work early. We caught the first flight we could out of Madrid. Didn't want to miss a day here." Her cousin's smile rearranged his freckles. "You're taller."

"So are you." It'd been six months since the cemetery— where the Spanish moss spilling off the oak branches matched the winter sky. Jake's hair was much brighter now that it was June. "You're blonder too!"

"Y más inteligente," he said.

It was Marisol's turn to grin. "¿Estás aprendiendo español, primo Jake?"

"Poco a poco. Slowly," her favorite primo emphasized in English. "I figured, you know, what with some of the family speaking Spanish, and us being posted to Spain this year—they said maybe even for a couple of years—it's about time I tried to learn some, don't you think?"

"¡Sí!"

Marisol was still holding the frame when she gave Jake a hug. He let go, studying the picture inside. It showed Nana standing with the two of them at the far end of Folly Beach, where dead trees twisted from the sand and a lighthouse jutted straight out of the water and the wind tangled their hair like seaweed.

"It's weird, being here without her," he whispered.

"I know." Marisol cradled the frame with both hands. Its macaroni suddenly felt extra brittle. "I hate it. But I hate selling this place even more. Mom's already packing up stuff in the kitchen. . . ."

Jake cleared his throat. "We have to, Mari. Beach houses cost a lot of money to keep, and Mom says this one needs a new roof, plus, like, a hundred other repairs."

Marisol's parents had offered the same explanation. Now that Nana no longer lived here, it didn't make sense to pay so many bills for a place the family only visited once a year. Marisol knew they were right, but this didn't

11

make her any less sad. If only the macaroni elbows were made of *real* gold . . .

One of the noodles snapped under Marisol's buzzing thumb as she offered the frame to Jake. Those were his initials on the back, after all. "Do you want this?"

He shook his head. "I don't have room to take it back to Spain."

No room? Marisol knew this was just an excuse. Her primo liked to travel light. After a day at the beach, when she was lugging buckets of broken shells back to the house, he'd race ahead empty-handed.

"It's nothing special," he continued with a shrug. "Just a bunch of pasta and paint. A six-year-old could make it."

"A six-year-old *did* make it!" She pointed out his shaky signature. "Nana told you it was the best Christmas gift anyone could ever give her."

Jake's face went very still at the edges.

"I can't," he said.

Marisol's fingers felt like fireworks as they popped open the back of the frame. "What about the photograph? There has to be room in your suitcase for—"

A folded sheet of paper fell to the floor by Jake's feet. He blinked with surprise and knelt down to pick it up.

"What is that?" she asked.

"It's a map!"

But this one wasn't as old as the others; the creases

didn't tear when Jake unfolded it. Nana's handwriting still smelled like ink when Marisol leaned in to read. As usual, their grandmother had written what she'd found on the map: *message in a bottle, pod of dolphins, home.*

"Not just any map!" Marisol breathed excitedly. "Jake, it's a map of Folly Beach!"

"Looks like there's gold nearby!" Her cousin was mostly joking. Nana had drawn ⊃⊂s all over her maps, but whenever they'd asked about them, she'd always had a tease in return. *Treasure,* she'd said, eyes twinkling. *They lead to treasure!*

Marisol had never been sure whether she meant the same kind of treasure that was allegedly hiding inside Victor or real treasure.

"Can I see it?" Her hand stopped humming as soon as Jake handed her the map. Her stomach flipped instead. Maybe . . . just maybe, this frame *did* hold gold. Marisol had never been close enough to explore any of Nana's ⊃⊂s before.

"It's right in the middle of the ocean!" Jake pointed to the mark: so deep it tore the blue paper. "The treasure must be some sort of shipwreck."

"No." Marisol squinted to read Nana's curly handwriting beside it: *Morris Island Light. Door.* "It's the lighthouse! Nana must have taken the fishing boat out there. Mom said it's all closed up now, because they don't use it anymore. I wonder if she got in through the door?" She stopped as the strangeness of Nana's absence washed over her again. "I'm going to miss her adventures."

"Me too." She could hear her own sadness echoed in Jake's voice, but his expression was calm. Jake didn't give away a lot on the outside, except for smiling, but Marisol had had practice over the years at understanding the things he didn't show.

He studied the map, and she studied him, wondering if she should say something. "Jake?"

"Yeah?"

"I think we should search for Nana's treasure." Marisol tapped the ♋. "Let's go on an adventure of our own!"

2

JAKE

JAKE LOVED GOING ON ADVENTURES.

You kind of had to, when your mother was a diplomat and your passport was so full of stamps it couldn't close and you knew how to say *thank you* in seven different languages. He wasn't sure what to say now, though. Something jingled in Marisol's pocket as she bounced on her heels, talking in the same excited tempo.

"Uncle Todd taught you how to steer the boat last summer, right? We should take it out to the lighthouse! What if Nana actually left something there for us to find? Like gold? What if it's enough to keep our parents from selling the house?"

Jake bit his lip. If Nana *had* buried anything, it probably wasn't gold. And it definitely wasn't enough gold to keep up something as costly as a beach house. Besides, he'd only ever taken the Berunas' dinghy on tidal creeks, and the Morris Island Light was almost out in the ocean. Dangerously blue.

"I don't know, Mari."

"Well, I do." Marisol's fist tightened. The map's edge began to crumple, and so did her lower lip. "Trust me, Jake. We need to go."

Still, he hesitated. Couldn't they just enjoy the time they had left, before they had to go? Head down to the beach, dig their toes into the sand, run along the edge of the water as the waves chased their feet?

Then tears started rolling down Marisol's cheeks, gathering onto her chin.

Jake grabbed the map before any of them could pitter-patter down and ruin Nana's handwriting.

𝓧. *Morris Island Light. Door.*

Why would their grandmother write that? He wished he could sit down and ask her, wished so hard it made his chest feel achy.

"The lighthouse is pretty far away."

He pointed at the photograph in Marisol's hand, where Morris Island Light jutted out of the waves. For a while, he'd saved pictures of all the places he'd been, recording details on the back just like Nana did. But he'd never had her gift for telling stories about them afterward, and it had ended up feeling like a collection of lost things, a reminder that the people and places in his life would be taken away. Replaced. Lost again.

Eyes ahead, don't look back. This was the best thing Jake could do. The only thing, really, which was why he threw away his photographs during the move to Madrid. It was one less box to lug.

"Por favor," Marisol sniffed. "I think Nana would want us to go, and this will be our last chance before . . ."

She trailed off just as Jake's mom appeared in the doorway.

Aunt Cara hovered behind her. Their mothers looked like the identical twins they were—their brown hair pulled back in ponytails, their noses dusted with freckles like his. Marisol got her warm brown skin and her black hair from her dad—Uncle Mache—and Jake got his blond from his dad, though he only knew that from photos. His father had been gone since before Jake remembered, and he'd long ago decided not to care.

When his mom saw them gathered around the picture of Nana, her expression softened. "You miss her, don't you?"

"Yeah," said Marisol.

Jake slipped the map into his pocket and shrugged, then immediately felt like a jerk. He just preferred not to talk about people and things that were gone.

And then Uncle Matt and Aunt Jayla's car pulled

up, and that was the end of the peace and quiet. Soon there was a flood of uncles and aunts and cousins hauling luggage and exchanging *Hey Y'all!*s, stampeding up the stairs, causing so many floorboards to creak that the house felt on the verge of either collapsing or waking up from a long slumber.

Mom and Aunt Cara and the rest of the grown-ups convinced Uncle Todd and Uncle Pierre to sleep in Nana's room.

"She wouldn't mind!" Aunt Cara insisted. "And look at the twins. Veronica and Angeline must be a foot taller than last year! Give them their own room, and you take Nana's." The girls agreed, even looking up from their phones to join the debate.

And then there was a cookout in the backyard as dusk drew the golden sky into velvet blue. Burgers sizzled and cicadas serenaded the Beruna clan from the surrounding marsh. The family made almost as much noise, exchanging stories both old and new. Tales of their recent adventures—hikes in the Andes and scuba diving with sharks in the Bay of Biscay—soon migrated into memories of Nana. Jake found Marisol beside him again, and the two of them sat in silence as smoke drifted up toward budding stars.

Eventually Mom caught him yawning—the flight from Madrid had been a long one, all the way to Dallas, and then to Charleston—and he got sent to bed. He shared a little room with his mom off the rambling, winding passageways of the beach house.

As he lay awake, listening to bugs bat against the window screens, his narrow bed tucked underneath a bookshelf crowded with old encyclopedias, he thought of his clean, white bedroom in Madrid. The apartment the American embassy had given them was airy and neat—exactly like the apartments all the other diplomats had. Someone who worked at the embassy had lived there before them, and someone else who did just the same would live there after them. The beach house, though—every inch of the place, from its dusty knickknacks to the rickety crab dock, was undeniably *Beruna*.

It was the closest thing he'd ever felt to home.

Jake woke to discover a ticklish gray light coming in through the windows—it was probably somewhere a little after six in the morning. A breeze whispered through the screen, and outside the window it caught at the frayed edge of the sunshade so it fluttered back and forth.

Ticka-ticka-ticka-tick.

Perhaps the sound was what had woken him. He glanced over at his mom's bed, but the only thing waiting for him there was a set of rumpled sheets. She was up already. He decided he'd shower later—he'd only get sandy and salty today anyway—and climbed out of his own bed to grab the clothes he'd dumped on top of their suitcase.

He pulled on the same pair of blue shorts he'd worn yesterday, and found a white T-shirt that said *International School of Paris* on the front and *L'École Internationale de Paris* on the back. It was from Mom's posting in France a few years ago, and it was starting to get snug. He should probably throw it out. He shoved his feet into his sneakers and turned for the door.

He met Marisol on the landing, and she offered him a huge yawn and a sleepy grin by way of good morning. One of the things he liked best about Marisol was that she didn't try to fill silences that didn't need filling.

They made their way down the stairs in one of their companionable silences, past Nana's many pictures and maps, all jostling for space, only ever allowing glimpses of the splashy wallpaper behind them. Jake could see more flowers now, since Aunt Jayla had started unhooking frames from their nails, revealing squares of unfaded wallpaper beneath.

"Morning!" she greeted them at the bottom of the stairwell. "Watch your step! I think these boxes multiplied in the middle of the night. The study is a maze, and I can't even remember how to get to the kitchen from here!"

"We can find it," Jake assured his aunt. "All we have to do is follow the smell of Uncle Pierre's famous biscuits!"

Aunt Jayla inhaled, her face lighting up at the golden-bready-butter scent. "Ah, yes! Bring one back for me, will you? I'm going to need some serious fuel to start stripping this wallpaper."

"You're tearing down the wallpaper?" asked Marisol.

"It's too bright for most people's tastes." A sad sigh left their aunt's lips. "But that was Nana for you. . . ."

Marisol's lip quivered as she looked down at the pile of photographs. Jake grabbed her hand before she could start distributing frames again.

"Come on, Mari," he said softly. "Let's hunt down some breakfast."

Aunt Jayla was right—there were so many boxes. Too many. Piled so high they looked straight out of a page in a Dr. Seuss book.

Jake walked past these towers on tiptoe, waiting, just waiting for one of them to fall. His heart felt so heavy. His throat cluttered. He rounded his shoulders, pushing his hands down into his pockets . . . where the fingers on his right hand brushed something unexpected. Paper. *Huh?*

He pulled whatever it was out and turned it over.

Oh. Jake hadn't thought twice about his grandmother's map since stuffing it into his pocket—out of sight, out of mind—but now that it was here in his hand again,

Marisol's words from the day before returned.

I think we should search for Nana's treasure. Let's go on an adventure of our own.

Suddenly being on the open ocean didn't seem like such a bad idea.

In fact, it seemed a lot better than tearing up Nana's wallpaper or watching Marisol's eyes get misty.

He paused by the door to the kitchen.

"¿Qué?" Marisol tilted her head. "What is it, Jake?"

"I think we should take Uncle Pierre's biscuits to go."

Fortunately, the family dinghy was already tied to the crab dock. Uncle Todd and Uncle Pierre had rescued the boat from its off-season tarp in the yard last night, and it now floated in the creek's muddy waters. All around marsh grass swayed, a vivid green Jake never saw anywhere else. Between that and the fingers of rust streaking the dinghy's battered tin, he felt as though they were about to set off into the unknown, instead of across the water they'd swum in all their lives. The orange life jackets he and Marisol strapped on only strengthened this feeling, wrapping around their chests in tight hugs, filling their nostrils with the faint, musty scent that came with years of being put away damp.

The sky was a clear blue, without even a hint of a cloud, and the morning air was almost still, save for that same breeze that had set the blinds outside his window fluttering.

He tossed a shovel and a bag of biscuits into the dinghy first, then hopped in himself, one hand on a piling for balance, another offered to help Marisol, who instead chose to sit and wiggle her way off the dock. If she got any splinters she didn't show it.

"Untie the mooring line, will you?" Jake asked, because she was closest. "I'll get the engine ready."

Marisol worked the knot free, and Jake turned toward the heavy black engine strapped to the stern, currently raised so the propellers sat above the creek. He unclipped the motor, lowered the blades into the water, and nodded to his cousin. Marisol gave a tug on the rope, and it slithered off the horn cleat just as the boat nosed out into the water.

They were loose.

Jake couldn't help feeling nervous, even though he'd taken out the boat with Uncle Todd countless times last summer. He knew how to push the catch into place. He knew where to grip the ignition cord. He also knew that none of the adults would be happy he was doing these things by himself.

Well, *he* wasn't happy they were selling Nana's house. . . .

Jake shoved these thoughts aside and grabbed the

cord. The trick was to pull as quickly as possible, like starting a lawnmower—not that he'd done that many times, moving from place to place, mostly apartments.

He grit his teeth and counted down: *Three, two, one, pull!*

The engine coughed twice, spluttered, then fell silent.

"That was close!" Marisol sat on the edge of her seat, staring toward the house. "Do you think the grown-ups heard?"

No, Jake thought, his frustration finding a voice inside him. *They won't notice we're gone either. They're too caught up wrapping Nana's dishes in newspaper and stuffing them in boxes.* His jaw clenched again. He squeezed the starter handle. *Three, two, one . . .*

This time his pull was enough. The engine coughed hard, then roared to life with a throaty spluttering, before it settled into its usual soft *putt-putt-putt.*

"¡Vamos!" Marisol squeaked.

Jake pushed the lever to move the engine into first gear, steering carefully along the banks of thick pluff mud, where fiddler crabs waved uneven hellos. These creeks were a maze, weaving in and out and through the bright grass, but he'd navigated them enough with Uncle Todd that he could find his way to the ocean without thinking twice.

The waterways grew larger and larger, until they

reached the inlet. Bleached ghost trees—the same ones from Nana's photograph—twisted out of the sand behind them, and the abandoned lighthouse lay dead ahead. Murky waves lapped around the little dinghy as the cousins motored toward it.

Long ago, according to Nana, the structure had stood watch over an island much like Folly.

"Morris Island went all the way out there," she'd said. "And you could walk straight to the lighthouse. That's what it was for, of course—shining a light to make sure ships didn't hit the beach."

"But what happened?" Marisol had asked. "Now it's all the way out to sea, just sticking up out of the water."

"The currents shifted. The shoreline moved," Nana had said. "The sand slowly washed away. But the lighthouse was made of stronger stuff, and it held firm. It's guarding a lost land now, if you like, a place that used to be there."

The idea had sent a delightful shiver down Jake's spine, as so many of Nana's stories did. Now, he looked ahead to the lighthouse, which stood tall above the sea. It was a deep red brick, and about halfway up he could see a faded white band, where once it had been painted, and another above that. At the very top was the light itself, like a giant iron lamp, a guardrail around the edge.

"Any guess on what the treasure might be?" His

cousin leaned into the breeze, her curls blowing every-where. "Pearls? Bolivianos? Rubies? Chocolate?"

"Chocolate! Definitely!" Jake hoped she wouldn't be *too* disappointed when they unearthed nothing. Other-wise he'd have to figure out how to distract her from *this* distraction. "There's some back at the house for later. You know, just in case . . ."

Marisol's expression reminded Jake of a feeling he'd tried so hard *not* to feel at Nana's funeral—like his heart was a soda can inside a fist. Every drop squeezed out, every side crushed.

"I know this is silly," she said softly, "but it feels like something Nana would do. And if she were going to bury treasure, it would be somewhere near the house."

The wind was picking up, he realized, the waves choppier beneath the boat than they had been before. But the cousins weren't far from the Morris Island Light now, and Jake carefully steered into the lee of it, the waters a little calmer where the lighthouse's bulk protected them from wind.

Marisol grabbed the rope tucked into the bow, hold-ing it in one hand with a big loop at the ready. The base of the lighthouse was shored up with a rusty wall designed to keep sand in and curious people out. In fact, there were two red-and-white signs above the lighthouse entrance, each reading DANGER: NO TRESPASSING. The door itself was a forbidding metal grate.

26

This wasn't enough to deter some previous visitors, who'd left large hooks hammered into the wall. Marisol stretched out to loop their rope over one.

Jake cut the engine, and the boat bobbed in the sudden silence. The cousins both tilted their heads back, taking in the crooked bricks and streaked iron above them.

Above and above and above.

The sun made Jake's eyes smart as he craned his neck back, and suddenly reaching the lighthouse felt more dangerous than exciting. The hooks leading up to its base looked slick with salt water. How were they supposed to climb without hurting themselves? And even if they reached the door, what would they see? Rust? It had probably been very different when Nana had visited all those years ago.

Even if she had *left chocolate it would've melted by now,* Jake mused.

Abruptly the boat pitched, and he almost fell backward off his bench. Marisol grabbed his arm to keep him steady, and he felt his cheeks redden. But the little dinghy was rocking properly now, the waves gathering in speed and size.

The sky above was still a clear blue, but the wind had picked up much, much more than either of them had expected. Jake's stomach twisted uneasily, but it had nothing to do with the rocking of the boat. If the waves kept growing like this—their tops starting to break, shivers of wind wrinkling them as they rose and fell—he and Marisol would be in real trouble.

Marisol's hair had turned into a snarl of knots tangling across her face.

"Maybe we should come back when it's calmer," she said uncertainly.

Jake was already scrambling for the engine.

"Be ready to cast off the mooring line as soon as I get it started," he called over his shoulder. He could see the whitecaps chopping across the inlet, and he was beginning to wonder how he was going to steer the little boat safely through the surf.

And what their parents were going to say if they found out he and Marisol had taken the boat out on their own.

He pushed that question aside, grabbing for the engine cord and giving it a quick, clean yank as a burst of spray hit the back of his neck with a cold splash.

The engine coughed and fell silent.

He yanked a second time, and it felt like pulling the cord through molasses. His muscles strained and his shoulder ached, but the engine didn't make a single noise.

The boat rocked again, and Marisol gasped behind him. Then: "Jake, hold on!"

He grabbed for the bench at the back of the boat, just as the bow surged in against the rusty iron barrier with a loud, echoing *clang*.

"Mari! Are you okay?"

"I'm okay!" But her voice had a shake to it, and he was pretty sure his had as well. He grabbed for the cord and tried again, and then again, ignoring the burn in his arm, the sharp line across his palm where the cord dug into it. But the engine wouldn't so much as cough, let alone sputter to life.

The boat rocked dangerously. He'd never gotten seasick before, but his stomach lurched again as he turned to Marisol. "Mari, I can't start it, and I think it's going to flip over if the waves get much bigger."

As one, they turned their gazes to the towering wall above them.

There was nothing for it.

They had to climb.

3

MARISOL

TREASURE HUNTS WERE SUPPOSED TO BE ADVEN-
TUROUS, RIGHT?

Already this felt like something out of Nana's stories.
The stolen boat, the lashing waves, the lighthouse windows gaping with shadows too dark for daytime. Marisol
shivered when she stared at them, but that could've had
something to do with the wind that was whipping her hair
around her face, splashing waves against the boat with
loud slops.

"We have to climb." Jake sounded shaky. She couldn't
blame him. There were seven hooks between the mooring and the top—a bad fall, if either of them slipped.

Marisol didn't mind heights. Rock climbing with Dad
in La Paz was one of her favorite weekend activities. She
loved swimming too, but the combination of water and
footholds was no good.

She stretched to grab the second rung, which was as slippery as she feared, slimy with green algae beneath her fingers. But the soles of her outdoor sandals held firm when she pulled herself up.

One hook, two, three.

When Jake left the dinghy to follow she could hear the boat colliding with the barrier. Tin on iron: *BANG*. Saltwater mist stung Marisol's eyelids, urging her to hurry to the top, and she might have but for her father's constant climbing advice: Tranquilo con la ruta.

She passed the English version down to Jake. "Just be calm on the route."

"Eyes ahead, don't look back!" he yelled in reply.

Marisol wasn't sure this meant the same thing.

She pushed forward anyway.

By the final hook, she could no longer hear the *crash-crash* of metal. A glance below revealed Jake's face, pale enough for her to count every freckle. Their boat—along with their picnic and their shovel—was half under the waves, which kept growing angrier, spitting foam higher and higher.

She pulled herself over the barrier, landing in silky sand. Jake clambered up after her, and Marisol used his life jacket to tug him over, grabbing at the straps and throwing her weight back to *heave*. Both cousins were breathing hard: inhale, exhale, terror, relief.

They were safe.

They were shipwrecked.

"Oh, Jake . . ." Back at the dock she'd been afraid of getting caught, but that was nothing compared to what Marisol felt now. "What did we do?"

He didn't answer, going wordless the way he always did when something was too hard to talk about.

"We're trapped." As far as Marisol could tell, they were stuck in the middle of the blue, no treasure in sight. She *could* see Folly Beach across the inlet. What was left of Morris Island was closer, but it was still too far to swim. "¡Vamos a estar trancados aquí para siempre!"

"Not forever." Jake walked toward the lighthouse door. It was nothing more than a gate, really, with bars and a lock that belonged in an old-fashioned prison cell. "Maybe we could climb up to the light and find a way to shine it to let someone know we're here."

Up close the building looked even shabbier—filled with cracks and holes and dents, bricks crooked enough to crumble. But nothing moved when Jake shook the gate. The sound startled some birds, who spilled out of the nearest window, sailing off on stark white wings.

Jake rattled the lock again.

Marisol swallowed back the sob building up in her throat—the one that had been growing since yesterday, when the beach house's emptiness seemed too much to bear. She'd give anything to know that she could stay there. To escape this island safely and have something of

Nana's to go back to each summer.

"Any other ideas, Mari?" Jake's tone was encouraging, and perhaps he was pretending not to notice how upset she was. "What would Nana do?"

What would *Nana do?* She'd been out here before, after all. The thought helped Marisol breathe easier. This wasn't the end of the world. It couldn't be, if their grandmother had returned from it.

"She would collect rocks to write a message in the sand for passing planes, or she'd hang the bright life jacket off the side for sailors to see. Or . . ." Marisol paused. A new feeling had just washed over her, tugging for her attention.

There was something *lost* here. Something that needed finding. She knew because she was still shivering, but only in her fingertips.

"Good thinking." Jake began unclipping his life jacket. "I'll hang mine on the Folly side, you hang yours toward Morris."

There was something buried by the door. The *door*! Just like Nana's note . . . Marisol absently pulled off her life jacket and handed it to Jake, and then with her heart dancing in the roof of her mouth, she knelt down and started digging. For all her talk of treasure, the wish only now seemed possible. As if the next scoop of sand might reveal gold.

What if there was something valuable here?

What if the Berunas didn't have to lose the beach house?

Lose their last piece of Nana?

Marisol's fingers flared as she dug, urging her deeper.

Shells, sand, more shells, more sand . . .

Something shiny.

It wasn't gold but a key. When Marisol brushed it off, she found that there was an ✕ etched into the side. Its soft edges matched the map's handwriting, curling like a pair of back-to-back Cs, as Nana's always did.

"Is that . . . ?" Jake blinked at her discovery. "How'd you find that?"

The buzzing feeling had vanished. She'd never explained the details of her talent to Jake, just as she'd never told anyone else in the family. Not even Nana, though her grandmother had somehow known anyway. Whenever they walked the beach together she'd tell Marisol to "flex her magnet fingers."

Had she left this key for her grandchildren to find?

It sounded like the fairy tales Victor teased her for believing.

It sounded exactly like Nana.

"The map said *door*, so I started digging beneath it," she explained, and handed the key to him. "Jake, I think . . . I think this belonged to Nana."

He didn't laugh at her the way Victor would have. He studied the key so intently his eyebrows almost collided.

Then he pulled out the map and compared the two Xs—sure enough, they looked identical.

The sight made Marisol feel better. Braver. As if Nana were standing there next to them.

"Try unlocking the door," she told Jake.

When he did, the key fit perfectly and the gate opened with one easy twist.

The two of them stared into the darkness, eyes struggling to adjust. Slowly, the lighthouse interior took shape: a wrought-iron staircase twisted up the pale brick walls. Rust had found its way in here too—eating some steps all the way through.

"Does this mean there's really a treasure?" Jake asked.

"I hope so."

"We should've eaten Uncle Pierre's biscuits when we had the chance," he mused, peering up at the staircase. "Treasure would be nice, but what I'd really like to find up there is a bakery."

But Marisol knew better. Something *was* up there. The pins-and-needles *find me* feeling sparkled all over, calling her inside. Now that her vision had adjusted it was easy to see, and even easier to imagine what the place had looked like with a fresh coat of paint—Marisol could almost catch this sight in the corner of her eye.

Jake started for the stairs. "We should try to reach the light, at least, to see if we can signal. Or find doughnuts."

The steps felt sturdier than they looked, though

Marisol was careful to follow her primo at a distance in case the extra weight made a difference. She pressed down on each corroded metal ledge before she stepped properly onto it, feeling the crunch of sand beneath her sandals, the steps flexing a little.

Their climb coiled like a shell's insides—round and round. Jake called out whenever he came across a hole, which was good, because it took her an extra blink to spot them.

"Careful!" he said from above. "This step is gone!"

Marisol paused, but not because of his warning. The first window opened up across from her, and its view wasn't at *all* what she expected.

Palmetto trees swayed where there should be water. And beside these sat a *house*, with chimneys and shingles and a pristine picket fence.

"Jake?" She gripped the railing, dizzy. The stairs felt more solid and then suddenly less, depending on where she looked. "Jake!"

"Huh?"

"Look outside!"

A flop of blond hair appeared at the overhead banister. "Um, where did the ocean go?"

The water wasn't completely gone—the sea still sparkled through the window on the other side of the lighthouse—but it wasn't where it was supposed to be.

"I think we'd better head back down," she said.

The steps shook less as the cousins descended. Somehow the walls seemed just as shivery as Marisol's skin.

She'd never found anything as big as a house before.

When they reached the bottom of the stairs and peered outside, the building was still there. It sat only a short walk away, looking like a dollhouse rescued from an attic and turned life-sized.

"Whoa. . . ." Jake paused in the doorway. "Did it just drop out of the sky? Where did it come from? There's supposed to be water here, not land!"

"I don't think we're in South Carolina anymore, Jake."

The more Marisol looked around, the more she believed this. Nana's hidden key was gone, along with the gate it had unlocked. And the sand. And the barrier. In their place was a stone staircase, which led down to a boardwalk, which then led into a neat yard with white flowers bobbing in the breeze. The blustery wind that had sunk the boat was no more, and though Morris Island seemed to have moved, it had also shrunk. Ocean hugged them on every side.

This must be where the lighthouse keeper lived . . . but how could he have? Why was there land all around the lighthouse now?

"Maybe the *door* Nana wrote about wasn't the gate at all," Marisol reasoned. "Maybe we slipped through a door into the past."

"You mean time travel?" Jake should have laughed at

her, but instead he sounded interested. It was a little hard to mock the idea when a house and garden had appeared where only water was supposed to be. "There's only one way to find out." He cupped his hands over his mouth and shouted, "Hello! Anyone home?"

Waves whispered.

Palmetto fronds prickled the air.

The curtains in the windows stayed still.

"Guess not," Jake said. "Come on! Let's investigate. Maybe there's something to eat down there, even if there aren't any people."

There were no handrails to grip, but Marisol felt steadier once she stepped outside the lighthouse. She followed Jake along the boardwalk, noting every detail she could. There were no footprints in the surrounding sand—only marks made by birds. An old-timey car was parked nearby, but it didn't look like it had moved in a *long* time. A chicken was pecking its steering wheel.

They both stopped to examine the bird. Up close, it was clear the vehicle was completely rusted out, and the hen was nesting inside it.

"Maybe she'll give us a ride out of here if we get the engine started," Jake suggested as the chicken clucked what was clearly a warning to stay out of her car. The porch's rocking chairs tilted with the breeze.

She smiled for a moment at his joke, but this place

felt . . . creepy. If Victor were here, he'd make another joke about the place being haunted, the way he had with Nana's house. This time he might've been right.

"Jake, wait!" Marisol halted. "I don't know if we should just walk up to the house."

"Why not?" Jake turned. Then his eyes went wide. "Um, Mari . . ."

She turned too, and right away she knew why he looked so shocked.

The Morris Island Light had faded. No . . . *faded* wasn't the right word, but Marisol couldn't think of a better one. Most of the lighthouse was gone, except for a few bricks floating in midair. Stray steps from the iron staircase hovered with nothing to hold them in place.

It wasn't a lighthouse, but the suggestion of a lighthouse, like a jigsaw puzzle just starting out.

"We're *definitely* not in South Carolina," Jake said softly. "I don't think we're in the past either. Unless things used to float back then and they forgot to mention it at school."

Marisol looked to her right, where Folly Beach was supposed to be. But it was gone, vanished more completely than the lighthouse.

This wasn't some past version of their world.

It was a different one altogether.

Marisol and Jake waited for the Morris Island Light to *un*-fade, counting the bricks over and over to see if any reappeared.

They didn't.

And they didn't.

Not even when the cousins climbed the front steps to where the lighthouse door should be. Marisol stretched both arms as far as she could, trying to *find* the key. Her fingers stayed dull. All she grasped was air. Jake tried leaping off the stairs, but whatever portal they'd entered through remained shut.

He tumbled to the sand below, a sheet of it flying up as he rolled down a small hill, coming to rest on his back in the sunshine.

"I'm okay!" he called up. "It's okay! We're okay!"

The more Jake said the word, the less Marisol believed him. Tears began blurring everything. Nothing had been *okay* since Nana died, and this felt just as unreal. This was much worse than losing the dinghy.

"We're *really* trapped this time."

She punched at nothing, then sat, unable to hold back her sobs.

"Hey, hey!" Jake circled the staircase, climbing up to her, still trailing sand. "Chin up! We'll figure this out. I promise."

Putting on a brave face, like always. Marisol wished

her cousin would admit how he really felt. The only thing worse than crying was crying alone.

"All we've got to do is get our bearings. First thing I do in a strange place is study a map!" Out came the paper, edges more crumpled than before. It danced in the breeze after Jake's unfolding. "Let's see here. . . ."

"That's *not* here!" she sniffed.

His finger landed on the ☾. "This is."

The sight of their grandmother's handwriting anchored Marisol: heavy but calm. Had Nana meant for them to find this world? Had *she* been here? The beach—with ribbons of sand rippling on and on—seemed too deserted to imagine it.

"Everything's inside out," Jake announced. "There's land where there should be ocean. Ocean where there should be land."

"This makes *no* sense," she wailed. "Where's Nana's house, Jake? Is it ocean now too? Is this some kind of reverse world?"

"We'll figure it out." Her cousin's smile faded as he spoke, and though a moment before she'd wished for him to cry too, now Marisol just wanted Jake's confidence back.

She glanced back where the door should be. There was something new on the water past the lighthouse's invisible walls. The longer she stared at the speck, the larger it got, until the shape took a clear ship form. The vessel looked like it belonged in a museum, with white sails billowing out in front, square-edged and stacked one atop the other, the sun gleaming off its dark wooden hull.

"Someone's coming," she warned Jake.

He peered over the map, eyes narrowed against the sun. "Pirates?"

"I don't see a skull flag," Marisol said, relieved.

There was a long strip of white along the bow, as if the name of the ship had been roughly painted over, but the crew milling about on the deck didn't look particularly pirate-y. One of them—a woman dressed in a long pale gown—was waving.

At this, Jake shifted his assessment. "Maybe they're ghosts."

"They look pretty solid to me." Solid enough to come to shore.

Indeed, when the boat drew closer, its sails began to quiver and shake. The long tangle of ropes reaching up to their corners slowly slackened, letting the wind spill out. A huge chain rattled deafeningly as the anchor dropped with a splash, and then the boat was stationary, slowly swinging around to face into the wind.

As the cousins stood watching, mouths open, a rowboat was lowered with pulleys, and the white-clad woman climbed down a rope ladder and into it, followed by four sailors. She took a place in the bow, and they sat down to fit their oars into the rowlocks on either side of the little boat.

They were coming ashore.

As the rowboat neared, Marisol could see that the woman in its bow was squinting through a monocle. She smiled and called out to the cousins, "Ahoy, foundlings!"

"That sounds like something a pirate would say," Jake whispered.

Marisol's heart started pounding when she spied a pistol in one of the sailor's belts. Pirates or ghosts or not, these people were strangers. "Do you think we should run?"

"We're on an island," Jake reminded her. "Without a ship or a magic door, the only place for us to go is in circles."

When the boat scraped into sand, the lady climbed out, hoisting her dress so it wouldn't dip into foam, and marched toward them. "I do hope you haven't been waiting long. Winds can get tricky in the World Between Blinks. They slip in from all sorts of places."

Marisol looked at Jake.

Jake looked at Marisol.

Neither of them could find anything to say.

"Ah, forgive me. Where are my manners? I'm . . ." The woman trailed off, turning to one of the sailors by the rowboat. "Would you happen to remember my name?"

"You had so many of them." The man grunted and pulled his own monocle out from his pocket. It made his eye look like some starstruck planet. "Says here you're the daughter of the US vice president Aaron Burr, who incidentally happens to be the villain of a very popular Broadway musical. You slipped into the Unknown with the good ship *Patriot* and her crew in 1813. It was a cold January day—"

"My name, dear sir! You are boring these children with such dross."

Marisol was anything but bored. *1813?* That explained the woman's strange accent and flowy dress, but it also opened up *so* many other questions. How was this possible, if they hadn't time traveled? What was the Unknown? And what, exactly, was the sailor reading? What did he mean, *says here?*

The sailor squinted through the monocle's clear glass. "It says Theodosia Burr Alston."

"Ah, yes! Of course! Theodosia! That was my name!"

Theodosia Burr Alston seemed strange and certainly forgetful, but now that she was up close, Marisol didn't think she was dangerous. "Shouldn't it still be your name?" she asked.

The lacy edges of Theodosia's neckline twitched as she shrugged. "We let the Curators worry about labels.

They're the ones who keep everything sorted: doing all of that dreary paperwork and situating new arrivals. They're going to want to examine you two at once."

"Examine us? Hold on a moment," Jake interrupted. "Where in the world are we?"

"Yes, that's right!" the woman said, beaming approvingly. "You're in the World."

"The what?"

"The World Between Blinks," Theodosia explained.

"The World Between Blinks?" Marisol repeated. "But what does it *mean*?"

"Yeah, how do you fit a whole world between blinks?" Jake wondered.

"Well . . ." Theodosia's eyelashes fluttered. "Have you ever blinked twice in a row, quickly, and between the two of them—just for an instant—believed you saw something?"

"Maybe?" Jake screwed up his forehead. "This one time when I was seven, Mom was working in Australia. And we were down at the beach playing pirates, and . . ." He paused, looking almost . . . embarrassed? Marisol had never seen his cheeks flush like that before, except from the wind. "I saw an old ship flying a Jolly Roger flag. Everyone laughed and said my imagination had gotten the better of me. But for a moment, just for a heartbeat, that boat was there. I *knew* it was there. Somehow. Magically."

45

"Indeed!" their new friend agreed. "Though, technically, the ship you saw would've been *here*. Blinks in the other world reveal this one, and vice versa."

"I think that happened to me today!" Marisol offered. "When we climbed the lighthouse, I saw the missing bricks mixed in with the ones in our world! Everything looked whole."

"That would be the overlap," Theodosia said. "Our worlds sit alongside one another. In fact, they'd mix together if it wasn't for the Unknown, but your Curator can explain the mechanics much better than the crew of the *Patriot*. Personally, I find the Unknown incredibly mysterious."

"Huh?" Jake glanced at Marisol. "I mean, the unknown is mysterious to everyone, isn't it?"

"No, no," Theodosia corrected him. "The *Unknown*. With a capital U! It hovers along the border between our worlds like a fog. Sometimes it leaks into your world— lost people, lost places, lost things seem to draw the Unknown like a magnet—and then . . ." The way the woman's hands waved reminded Marisol of a bird's wings.

"And then?" she prompted.

"You're here," Theodosia replied helplessly. "In the world just next to your own. Lost."

The world just next to your own? The words sent a chill down Marisol's spine. She'd had enough of this adventure, and treasure or not, she was eager to get home before her parents became too worried. "We just need someone to tell us how to return to Folly Beach."

"Ah . . ." Theodosia hesitated. "I'm afraid it's not as easy as all that. Once you're in the World Between Blinks, only the Curators have the power to let you back out again. You'll have to take it up with one of them, but I must warn you, they're very stubborn."

Marisol's throat cinched tight. What if the Curators didn't listen to them?

What if she and Jake were stuck here forever?

"I'm sure once we explain our situation, the Curators will understand." Jake tilted his chin, confident. "Can you take us to them?"

"Of course! That's the *Patriot*'s job! We're part of a fleet that patrols thin spots in the Unknown, looking for foundlings. Anyone who spends time on the water is liable to stumble over new arrivals. Lostness tends to accumulate in certain places, back in the old world. Anywhere there's a war or a flat horizon—like a desert or an ocean or a sky, for example—more people get lost and slip through."

"¡Claro que sí!" Curls scattered when Marisol nodded. "It must be the same with couch cushions and washing machines!"

"Just so, I'm sure," Theodosia agreed, with an

expression that clearly said she had no idea what a washing machine was. Her brows lifted until her monocle popped out. She pocketed the piece and gestured toward the waiting boat. "Climb aboard."

There was little else to do, seeing as the lighthouse was still half disappeared. Its door gone. Marisol reached out for the missing key—again, just in case—but it didn't call back.

She was the lost one. Lost on a deserted island in a sideways world. . . . If she and Jake passed on Theodosia's offer they'd end up marooned, walking in circles with only the automobile hen for company.

Marisol really, truly didn't want to eat that chicken.

So she stepped into the boat.

Jake squeezed onto the seat next to her, his legs bouncing nervously as the sailors shoved off, and slipped his hand into hers.

It seemed their adventure was only just beginning.

4

JAKE

AHOY, MATEYS!

Jake had to keep biting his tongue to avoid speaking in a pirate accent. There was a notable lack of cutlasses and an abundance of teeth on board the *Patriot*, but these were the high seas all the same. The ship's deck was a gleaming dark wood, crusted with salt where waves had splashed over the sides and dried in the sun. Jake and Marisol took up a position near the bow with Theodosia, whose white dress fluttered in the wind. Her hair did the same, chestnut wisps escaping her bun. The longer Jake watched her, the more he sensed she was both very old and not aged at all. There was something about her—she seemed like she was both here and elsewhere. If everyone else's memories anchored them in one place, Theodosia seemed . . . free.

"Was this your ship in the real world?" he asked.

"The *other* world," she corrected him with a smile. "Yes, I think so. I'm almost certain. We must have been lost over on that side."

"Do you . . ." Marisol's voice almost drowned in the wind. "I don't mean to be rude, but you don't mean you *died*, do you?"

Theodosia looked shocked. "I certainly do not!" she said. "Can you imagine how crowded it would be, if those who died ended up here? This isn't heaven, child. If you die, I can't say for sure what happens, but you don't come to the World Between Blinks. Only people or things or places that are *lost*, one way or another, arrive in the World."

Jake was relieved—he wasn't ready to be dead yet—but also a tiny bit regretful. When Marisol had asked the question, his heart had leaped, wondering if somehow Nana had marked the door on the map because it led to the place she would come after she died.

But no. Nana wasn't here, and it was better not to think about it. Right now, he had a problem to solve. *Eyes ahead, don't look back.*

"What do you mean, lost things or places?" he asked. "How do you lose a place?"

"All sorts of ways," Theodosia replied. "There are whole cities that sank beneath the waves or were buried by deserts. People who wandered from the path and became so lost that the Unknown found *them*. Things slip away all the time, my dear foundlings. And this is where they go."

"What, *all* the places that don't exist anymore?" Jake's eyes widened. "Every single person who gets lost?"

"No . . ." Theodosia trailed off, thoughtful. "No, not all. Just the ones the Unknown takes."

This answer didn't seem to satisfy Marisol. "But what makes the Unknown take something? And why did it choose *us*?"

"The clue is in the name, my child," the woman said. "It's *unknown*. Some places vanish from the old world because they are now here. Others simply disappear. Some things—a penny you thought was in your pocket, or indeed, an entire ship such as this very vessel—are able to pass through the Unknown to the World Between Blinks. The Unknown takes what it will. Your Curator might be able to explain the selection process more thoroughly. They do so enjoy making sense of such things. . . ."

"What's a Curator?" Marisol wrapped her arms around herself. It was colder than it'd been at the lighthouse, for though the sun was shining it seemed farther away here.

"The Curators keep the World in order," Theodosia replied. "They have lists upon lists in their great repositories. Everything you see here might be lost, but that doesn't mean it's disorganized. Indeed, the Curators are swathed in so much red tape, one could knit uniforms for an army with it."

She paused, her brow creased, and she mouthed the word again: *army*.

Then she sighed and shook her head. "Never mind, I thought I had it there for a moment, but it's gone."

"What's gone?" asked Jake.

"My memory of the other world," she replied. "It all begins to slip away. The lostness accumulates around one, like barnacles growing on a ship, until one is completely caught up in it. Perfectly happy, but forever lost."

"H-how—" The word wriggled in Jake's throat, the idea was both scary and also . . . interesting. Was it really possible to leave behind his memories the way he'd always left behind his photos? "How long do we have?"

She looked at their faces and threw up her hands. "Oh my, what a thing for me to say! Don't worry, we'll have you to a Curator soon, and they may be able to help you."

May. Jake had never liked that word. From his experience with adults, saying something *may* happen meant it almost certainly *wouldn't*, and the thought of never escaping this place pitted his stomach. What would his mom think when the Coast Guard found their capsized dinghy?

His lungs gave a quick, tight squeeze as he imagined her face. They had to get back before she and Aunt Cara knew anything was wrong.

Theodosia jolted him from these thoughts when she spoke, raising her voice cheerfully over the breeze. "The winds have slipped in our favor! It shouldn't be long before we reach port. In the meantime, I advise you take in the view. It's rather spectacular. Perhaps you'd like to try my monocle? The Curators lent these charms to the *Patriot*'s crew to help us find foundlings! They reveal many unseen things."

She held out the eyepiece—a circle of glass about the size of a silver dollar. Jake automatically extended his hand, and she dropped the little monocle into his palm. It didn't look like anything special. He wasn't sure if he should try it out or not. Would he forget something if he did?

Theodosia bustled away to check on the crew, and Jake and Marisol kept to their place in the bow, letting the breeze turn their cheeks pink. The water *swish-swish*ed beneath the boat, and sunlight winked off indigo waves, and on the shore they saw a pyramid go by, and then an ancient castle, complete with battlements. A creature much too large to be a bird winged over the sails, covering the schooner in triangular shadows.

"Is that a pterodactyl?" Worry mixed with wonder, and Jake felt the same way he did that time he and his mom treated themselves to a tour of the ten best gelato shops in Rome—like this was one of the most amazing things that had ever happened to him, but he suspected it was going to end badly. Still . . . "Cool!"

"Qué raro . . ." Marisol pointed at the castle. "Dinosaurs definitely didn't live in medieval times, Jake."

Would the monocle explain how a pterodactyl came to be flying above a castle? Unable to resist any longer, Jake lifted the glass disc to his eye, squinting the other one closed. Immediately, words began to appear above the castle, as if some invisible hand was writing huge curling letters in the sky.

Tintagel Castle, Cornwall, built by Richard, First Earl of Cornwall, thirteenth century.

He tipped his head back to look at the creature flying overhead. The writing appeared again.

Pterodactylus, roamed the Earth approx. 150 million years ago. Not a dinosaur, do not misclassify.

"Jake?"

He lowered the monocle and found Marisol gazing at him. "This thing . . ." He didn't know how to describe what he was seeing. He wasn't sure *what* he was seeing. Things that had gone missing from their own world and appeared in this one? He passed the monocle to her instead.

She lifted it to her eye and went silent, twisting around to examine the shoreline, her mouth open. Then, with a squeak, she rose up on her toes. "Jake, look at that pyramid! The writing says *Pyramid of Djedefre*! I learned about pyramids at school; there are mummies in them. And . . ." Her voice dipped to a whisper. "And treasure."

"Treasure?"

"Just think! Jake, if everything lost ends up in this world, it must hold all kinds of treasure! Maybe Nana's been here before. Maybe that's what she was talking about. Maybe we can pay for her beach house roof with Egyptian gold! Or a chest of pirate loot!"

"Maybe." His stomach kept wobbling, and he wished Marisol would let go of the idea. Keeping the beach house didn't matter if they couldn't get home. "Let's see what these Curators have to say before we do any more hunting."

"Claro." She nodded, but Jake could tell by his cousin's smile that she wasn't giving up on this treasure idea any time soon.

Eventually a long pier came into view, and Theodosia fetched them as the schooner drew near to it, taking her monocle back.

The sails were let out once more so the ship slowed, and when it became clear they meant to dock, a figure at the end of the pier, clad all in white, waved enthusiastically.

"Very energetic, for a Curator!" Theodosia sounded impressed. "Must be new. Keep to the side, now, let the crew throw out the mooring lines."

The *Patriot* was soon made fast, and with a loud scrape the sailors pushed out the gangplank, so Theodosia could walk the two children down to where the Curator was waiting.

The man didn't seem nearly as serious as Jake had imagined. He had a tousle of blond hair, suntanned skin, and a dimple in his chin—he looked like he might be younger than Mom and Aunt Cara. There was something mischievous about his grin—a glint in the eye, a gleam off the teeth—and perhaps because Jake was thinking of her, for a moment the Curator's smile reminded him a little of Mom's.

"Greetings, new arrivals!" he said cheerfully. "My name is Christopher Creaturo; welcome to the World." He turned to offer Theodosia a bow, which seemed to please her. "Thank you for their safe passage, ma'am."

"I'm afraid I have brought you a challenge, sir," she said.

"We're not lost," Jake added, unable to wait any longer, "just shipwrecked! We knew exactly where we were when it happened, so the Unknown shouldn't have swallowed us."

Christopher's smile slipped. There was the seriousness that'd been missing before. "Yes, we already noticed the mistake. Never fear. I've been investigating the best way to send you home, and I think I have it. But we must hurry."

He nodded to Theodosia, already reaching for the children's shoulders to steer them down the pier.

Relief rushing through him like soaking summer rain, Jake let himself be ushered along. "Thank you, Theodosia!" he called over his shoulder, looking back.

She was still standing on the dock, but her frown made her seem adrift. "Curator, don't I need to sign the delivery papers?"

"No time!" Christopher called back as Marisol skipped a couple of steps to keep up with his pace. And then it was just the three of them.

There were several other ships moored along the pier, all different shapes and sizes—a big steel battleship and then a paddle steamer, its wheel turning lazily as steam spun from its chimney and it prepared to depart. Next came a sleek white yacht, then a vessel with a dragon's head growling at the prow. Beside this floated a long wooden boat that had no mast but places for rowers and a stag for a figurehead.

Between the ships, Jake caught glimpses of a town set into a hill, but just like everything else they'd seen so far, it was a hodgepodge of styles, as if someone had thrown all of history up in the air and let it land wherever it wanted. As if to underscore the point, a bronze-skinned man in what Jake was pretty sure was a Roman centurion's uniform walked past. The plumes in his helmet rippled—a hearty red—when he nodded hello.

Jake waved back. This was so awesome! He only wished he had Theodosia's monocle, so he could find out more about the man. Now he was hurrying along with Christopher to where he'd return them to their own world, he felt like he could admire the wonders around him a little bit more—after all, it would be over soon.

"Where are you taking us, Mr. Creaturo?" Marisol asked.

"Christopher, please," he corrected her. "We're going to the Crystal Palace."

Jake looked to where Christopher was pointing. On one side of the harbor sat an enormous building made almost completely of glass. He could see the metal framework that held it up, but where there should have been stone or brick or wooden walls, and a tiled roof, there was only one soaring sheet of glass after another.

"That has to be from a fairy tale!" Marisol gasped. Jake thought she had a point—with so many clouds reflecting from its panes, the Crystal Palace belonged in a sky kingdom, or perhaps a land of never-ending snow. "I thought everything here disappeared from the *real* world."

"Oh, but it did," Christopher replied, still walking. "The Crystal Palace was built in London in 1850. When it burned down, Winston Churchill himself said it was the end of an era. Turns out he was right."

"Who's that?" Jake asked.

"I like his name," Marisol added.

"Who's Churchill?" The Curator blinked, sidestepping a dog that looked like every picture Jake had ever seen on a LOST: REWARD poster. "I really have been here a long time."

"The bakery near our apartment in Paris burned down," Jake mused. "Is it here somewhere?"

"Why would it be?" Christopher asked, his brow creasing.

"The Crystal Palace burned down," Marisol pointed out.

"Yes, but . . ." Christopher waved one hand in a way that didn't actually explain anything. "End of an era, children. Did tens of thousands, *hundreds* of thousands of people mourn your local bakery, Jake? Did they think of how it was lost, conjure up a sea of lostness to attract the Unknown?"

Jake considered this. "I mean, they made really good croissants, but probably not that many people, no. Is that how the Unknown chooses what ends up in the World Between Blinks?"

Christopher's mouth opened, then shut again, before he replied. "It's complicated. What you need to know for now is that the Crystal Palace is where Curators keep most of the records. We catalog everyone and everything and everyplace that enters through the Unknown."

"What about us? Do people like us show up much?" Marisol asked, glancing across at Jake. Worry turned her brown eyes darker. "People who don't want to be here?"

"Hardly ever," Christopher admitted. "And we have little time to reverse the problem. Your door to leave will be closing soon. Can you think of any reason this might've happened?"

Marisol lifted one of her hands, looking down at it as if her fingertips might hold the answer, and shook her head.

Jake shook his head too, though as he did so, he wondered if he'd somehow caused this mess. Everything around him always ended up lost—the places he lived, the friends he made. Maybe it was only a matter of time before *he* got lost.

"Perhaps . . ." Marisol hesitated. "At our Nana's house, there was a map. . . ."

"Your grandmother?" Christopher asked, his own smile fading. "I'm afraid I have no record of her being here."

"She wasn't lost. Not . . . that way." It hurt, sitting like a hard ball in the center of his chest, but Jake made himself say the words. "She died."

The crumpled-can look reappeared on his cousin's face, and he took her hand.

"I'm sorry." Christopher's voice was quiet now. "I

suppose we'd better focus our efforts on getting you home, rather than spend too much time wondering how you arrived. In fact . . ." He hesitated, then nodded. "Perhaps you can help me. I oughtn't let you, because you're not Curators. But desperate times call for desperate measures."

"How can we help?" Jake asked.

"I have a theory," said Christopher. "Everyone who arrives here is written down in a ledger. If your names were somehow put into the ledger, perhaps you could have been summoned that way, though I can't think why."

"So we need to check the ledgers," Marisol said.

"Exactly." Christopher nodded. "The problem we have is that if I'm right and we don't erase your names quickly, we won't be able to do so at all. And my fellow Curators are, ah . . . They can move a touch slowly at times. I think we may need to tackle this off the books. Er, with the books? Regardless, it's better for us not to be seen."

That was what Theodosia had said—that the Curators were always tangled up in red tape. If the window home was closing as fast as Christopher claimed, they couldn't afford to go the official route. Mom's face swam up in Jake's mind again, and he looked across at Marisol. She nodded, her mouth set in a firm line.

"We're in," he promised. "Whatever it takes."

5

MARISOL

MARISOL HAD NEVER STOLEN ANYTHING IN HER LIFE.

Well, except for the family dinghy, but that didn't count! Borrowing the Beruna boat was nothing like sneaking into a giant see-through castle and staying hidden long enough to find the book of names.

The task seemed impossible.

There were hundreds of thousands of books, for one thing. Shelves on shelves on shelves filled with large ledgers that looked as if they belonged in a church. Leather spines and gilded titles—all blending together. Marisol was in the garden outside with Jake and Christopher, hunched inconspicuously behind a row of bushes, but she knew the books wouldn't be any easier to tell apart up close.

"Which one has our names in it?" she whispered, because the closer they got to the Crystal Palace, the quieter Christopher's voice had become.

The Curator was currently peering between the branches of a bushy shrub as big as he was—dark green leaves jostled for space with yellow flowers shaped like tiny pom-poms. A fancy brass plaque on the ground beside it said:

ACACIA KINGIANA, WESTERN AUSTRALIA, 1950

Through the leaves, they watched a steady stream of Curators flow through the building's entrance. Every single official walked with the same clipped step. Busy, busy, in and out.

"Are you sure the other Curators are as slow as you say?" Marisol asked.

"Trust me, when it comes to paperwork they make a snail seem like a racehorse," said Christopher. "Now, the volume you want is in the farthest corner on the second-to-last shelf. There will be a number on the spine—341,069.512. It's tucked in the last place you'd expect. That's what's supposed to stop accidents like this from happening."

The other Curators didn't *look* very accidental. Like Christopher Creaturo, they were dressed in sharp white outfits—three-piece suits and boxy dresses. They each wore a necklace. When a Curator stopped just on the other side of their bush, Marisol saw that the strand held a monocle identical to the one Theodosia had lent them. There were other charms strung alongside: a tiny scroll, a key, an hourglass, a fountain pen, a feather, and . . . was that a fish scale?

When she leaned in for a closer look, Christopher shook his head. The chain around his own neck glistened. Its pendants were tucked too far into his shirt for Marisol to see, so she studied their guide instead, watching him grow paler and paler. By the time the other Curator finally wandered off, Christopher was as white as his wardrobe.

"Phew! That was close." He sighed. "Now remember, under no circumstances can you two be seen."

"It's a glass palace!" Jake pointed out. "Everyone can see everything!"

"That's why I'll be staying behind to provide a distraction. You two grab the book and meet me under the St. Helena olive tree by the Aral Sea. If I'm not there yet, you'll know the tree because it will have a nameplate like this one. It's on the other side of town. You'll know you've reached it when you see the Loch Ness Monster. And yes, before you ask, Nessie is real."

The Loch Ness Monster! It sounded like another fairy tale, but if it was here, then it must have been at home, once upon a time! Proof, thought Marisol, that the world was as weird and wondrous as Nana had claimed. Christopher even stated it with the same matter-of-fact tone their grandmother favored.

"Are you two ready?" Christopher asked.

Jake nodded, eager. Marisol's *yes* was more cautious. Nerves wiggled like worms in her belly, but home was close enough to see—sitting on the second-to-last shelf in the farthest corner.

They could do this.

They had to.

"Wait here," Christopher instructed. "I'll release the decoy and distract the other Curators. That will be your signal to enter the Crystal Palace."

"What's the decoy?" Marisol asked, in case they missed their window.

"You'll know when you see it."

With a wink, Christopher Creaturo disappeared deeper into the bushes, and the cousins found themselves alone. Minutes passed. The worms in Marisol's stomach turned into snakes. Jake seemed fidgety too, peering through the branches every few seconds. She wanted to apologize, to tell him she was sorry for dragging him here, for being foolish enough to believe they'd find Nana's treasure when it turned out their grandmother hadn't even been to the World Between Blinks. Marisol's gift had never led her so astray before, but there was a first time for everything.

"Jake, there's something I have to—"

Before she could admit anything further, there was an explosion. Well, not an explosion, exactly, as explosions tend to involve fire and this one was all water.

And tentacles.

A massive creature writhed in the harbor they'd just left. Not a fairy tale but a monster! One that looked as if it'd been ripped straight from an ancient map's deep-ocean drawings. The animal's limbs thrashed, suction cups pulsing as they began wrapping around nearby ships.

Marisol clasped her hands over her mouth.

"A kraken!" Jake was too excited to muffle his yell, but their hiding place remained intact.

Every Curator near the Crystal Palace's entrance had paused to study the harbor, their blinks intensified by the monocles they each popped over their right eye.

"Oh dear," one of them said. "There's an unsorted arrival. Does anyone have a clipboard on hand?"

After a brief scuttle of suits, three clipboards appeared.

"We'll need a customs form as well as permanent residency papers." The Curator squinted as the kraken latched on to a battleship. "Toss in a damage claims packet as well. This will get messy."

None of the Curators ran. Their pace stayed steady as they sorted the papers and proceeded in a straight line down to the harbor. This was exactly the point Christopher had been making—if they weren't going to hurry for a kraken on a rampage, they certainly wouldn't rush for two lost children.

The Crystal Palace was clear.

Marisol felt her heartbeat all over her body. It thrummed through her spine when she stood; it pounded the ground when she dashed for the door. It made her feel small and fluttery beneath the vaulting glass, like a butterfly inside a greenhouse.

The palace *did* look like a greenhouse: fountains bubbled in the central aisle and there were even trees stretching over the stacks. Limbs twisted alongside shelves three times taller than the cousins. The books themselves were arranged down to the decimal, and it gave Marisol a thrill to see these flowing, growing numbers. The Curators had clearly spent a lot of time cataloging this place.

"I hope Theodosia's crew left already." Jake glanced back at the harbor, where the monster's tentacles had developed a taste for fine dining, rocking the yacht as if it were a bath toy. "Krakens are no joke. I wonder how Christopher found one."

"I don't know," Marisol answered. There were a lot of things they didn't know about Christopher Creaturo. . . .

"Hello?" A voice leaped from the stacks. "Who's there?"

Someone was still in the building.

Marisol's pulse stuttered, but Jake was fast on his feet, pulling her between some shelves just as the Curator emerged. They spotted the woman through a break in the books—her bun wound tight with a frown to match.

"Hello?" She paused.

It was quiet enough to hear dust falling, a silence that stretched and stretched until it became almost unbearable. Marisol's skin prickled with the pressure of waiting.

Eventually, the Curator sighed. "Someone must have lost their voice . . . another entry for the laryngitis book."

She stepped back into the stacks. Marisol watched the woman's bright strip of clothing ghost over the ledgers. Back and forth, making the rounds—how were they supposed to reach the farthest shelf without getting caught?

Jake nudged her, nodding toward the nearest tree.

¡Claro! They could climb! Most people—adults especially—never looked up, because they were as tall as they were going to be, so why bother?

Marisol gave a thumbs-up and crept toward the trunk. Rough bark and sprawling branches made it easy to scale—much easier than the rock climbing she did with her dad—and they reached the shelf tops in no time. Laid out, these looked like a series of long wooden roads, the gaps between aisles bridged by tree limbs.

Now came the hard part.

The book they needed was a building's length away—there were countless routes in between, and almost as many dead ends. Marisol and Jake didn't have time to test them all. Every passing second made their entries in the book more permanent, closed the door back home to Mom and Dad and even Victor. . . .

Tranquilo con la ruta, her memory whispered. *Be calm, be calm on the route.*

The stomach snakes stopped slithering, though a few still hissed.

She and Jake crept along the shelves, keeping their feet light. The Curator walked below, humming a song that sounded unfinished. Just as Marisol had suspected, the woman didn't look up, not even when the cousins shimmied across a branch directly overhead.

A hop, a crawl, a tiptoe, a skip . . . at last, they reached the farthest corner of the second-to-last shelf. Jake leaned over the edge and reached for their book: 341,069.512. His fingers strained for the golden numbers on its spine until it seemed as if he had an extra knuckle.

He caught the edge and tugged.

The ledger came free. But so did the neighboring book. Marisol watched in horror as 341,069.511's shiny pages tumbled to the ground.

WHUMP.

The Curator stopped singing. The Crystal Palace held

its breath, sunshine glittering with dust. Jake clutched his prize, eyes wide enough to sharpen each eyelash. Heels sounded against the floorboards: *tap, tap, tap, tap, tap, tap*.

They had to run!

Marisol and Jake scrambled for the nearest tree. Because of the book, her cousin was slower, navigating the branches one-handed. They had a better chance of escaping on the ground, so she shimmied down the trunk and gestured for Jake to toss the ledger, so he could do the same.

Tap, tap, tap.

Marisol caught the book, pressing its cover to her chest to keep her heart from falling out. The Curator would appear any moment now. . . .

Jake showed up first, landing on catlike feet.

Together they ran for the entrance. Shelves blipped past, one holding an extra flash of white. Had the Curator seen them? Marisol couldn't be sure, and she wasn't about to pause and double-check.

She ran and ran and ran, stopping only when Jake did—well outside the Crystal Palace gardens.

"Phew!" Her primo panted. "That was a close one!"

Marisol nodded and studied the book she was holding. It was too big to fit into a pocket—about the size of Nana's *National Geographic Atlas*. The binding was thicker than her arm, not to mention heavy. Hopefully Christopher would know which page their names were on.

Hopefully there was time to erase them.

Hopefully there was a way to get home.

The Aral Sea was exactly where Christopher Creaturo had promised it would be. So was he, lounging against the trunk of the St. Helena olive. Cobalt water tickled the shoreline, though several yards out its color stretched thin, giving way to the gliding green length of today's *second* sea monster.

"I can't wait to tell Victor that Nessie's real," Marisol said. "Then again, I've seen his laundry hamper. He probably already knows monsters exist."

Christopher had spotted the cousins, and he started waving as though they were an aircraft coming in for a landing.

"Excellent job, you two!" he said, once they reached the spot of shade under the tree. "I hope things didn't go too haywire on your end."

"One of the Curators stayed behind," Jake explained, "but we still took the book without getting caught."

"May I?" Christopher nodded at Marisol.

She handed him the ledger, feeling relieved. Soon they'd be safe and this would be nothing more than a tall tale told over sweet tea on Nana's screened porch.

Centurions and krakens and Nessie, oh my! Getting in trouble for taking the boat didn't seem nearly so bad anymore.

"How did something as big as the Loch Ness Monster get lost?" Jake watched Nessie's neck periscoping out of the water.

The monster was *awfully* tall. And splashy. Spray from her fins misted over the trio, creating a rainbow that stopped right on top of the ledger. Marisol had never seen the end of one before. Maybe they all landed inside the World Between Blinks. . . .

"That's a good question, Jake. A very good question." Christopher waited until the shower subsided, then opened the book. "I suppose Nessie was never really found in the old world, and when people stopped believing in her in the 1940s the Unknown brought her here. That's the Curators' theory at least. They labeled her as *quasi-mythical*. See?"

Sure enough, he was pointing to the entry: *Loch Ness Monster. December 10, 1944. Quasi-mythical.*

Marisol frowned. Something wasn't adding up. The dates especially . . . all of them were from the same time period, written in tidy chronological calligraphy. *1944. 1945. 1945* again. These numbers barely changed as Christopher flipped through the pages.

"Where are our names?" she asked.

"What?" Christopher looked up. For a second he seemed surprised to see the children still standing there. "Oh. We'll get to them! Have patience!"

"I thought we were supposed to hurry." Marisol crossed her arms. Now that the book was in Christopher's hands, he didn't look nearly as rushed.

"I've never actually sent anyone back to the other world before," the Curator explained, "so it's in everyone's best interest if I perform a few test runs first. Now let's see. . . ."

Christopher pulled a pen from his jacket. It was nothing like the elegant writing utensils the other Curators wore around their necks, and much closer to the ballpoints Marisol often rescued from the bottom of her backpack.

Why was it different? And why had Christopher sent them into the Crystal Palace to get a book he could've accessed with far less trouble? And why hadn't he let Theodosia sign the delivery papers if they weren't *truly* in a hurry? And why hadn't he said *we* when he talked about the Curators categorizing Nessie?

Slowly but surely, she began to realize that all these questions could only be solved by one answer. . . .

"You're lying!" Marisol's voice shook with the accusation. "You aren't a Curator at all!"

"Mari!" Jake looked shocked.

Christopher, however, didn't seem upset. He smiled—

his chin dimple deepening, his eyes twinkling blue. "I should've known you'd see through my ruse."

"Wait . . . Mari's right?" Her cousin's expression hardened. "Can you even send us home, or were you lying about that too?"

"Watch." Christopher flipped to the previous page and pointed out at the Aral Sea, where the Loch Ness Monster kept splashing and swirling, stirring sky into waves with her tail.

Pen scratched across paper. A word was struck through.

Nessie vanished.

Ripples shuddered through the water, but the monster that caused them was nowhere to be seen. Christopher Creaturo gave a triumphant laugh and snapped the ledger shut. "It worked!"

But something strange was happening. . . .

Marisol's vision flickered when she blinked. She swayed, fighting off the same dizziness she'd felt while climbing the lighthouse. *The overlap*, Theodosia had called it. *Blinks in the other world reveal this one, and vice versa.*

Only this time things didn't look whole. A crack split through the Aral Sea, as jagged as a lightning strike. The water seemed to be pulling itself apart, and right in the center of the tear sat . . .

Their world.

There was a lake with a crumbling castle on its misty shore. Dozens of tourists crowded the edge, holding their cameras and phones up to the spot where the Loch Ness Monster splashed, just as playful she'd been a few seconds ago.

"Whoa!" Jake's eyelashes fluttered. "Whoa! It's gone!"

Marisol kept her own lids open as long as she could, but soon her eyeballs stung too much. The overlap vanished with her second blink and didn't come back.

She turned toward Christopher, determined. "Now you need to send *us* home!"

"Yes! What about us?" pressed Jake.

"About that—" Christopher paused, glancing toward the town. "Oh, hot dog!"

With the way this day had been going, Marisol wouldn't have been surprised to see actual hot dogs trundling down the road. But no, when she turned it was a herd of white suits she spotted.

The real Curators had found them.

They did not look happy: eyebrows scrunched over monocles, clipboards tucked beneath arms, *tap-tap-tapping* steps.

Everything about this spelled trouble.

Big trouble.

"Uh-oh," Jake said.

"What should we do?"

But when Marisol looked back, she discovered things were even worse than she'd feared.

Christopher Creaturo was gone. And so was the ledger.

6

JAKE

THEY WERE IN BIG, BIG TROUBLE.

"Mari," said Jake. "This is bad. *Really* bad."

"The Curators don't look happy," she agreed.

"Why would they be? We only just arrived, and we're already wanted criminals."

"But we didn't want to be criminals!" Marisol wailed.

"I'm not sure that matters," he said as the white-clad crowd drew closer. "We'll have to try and explain, if they're the ones in charge."

She nodded, lips pressed together hard, expression grim.

With Christopher gone, the Curators were the only ones they could ask for help. So they stood under the St. Helena olive tree, and Jake reached for Marisol's hand, giving it a squeeze as they waited for the oncoming storm—then he had to let go to dry his damp palms off against his shorts. Nerves ran through him like a buzzing electric current.

In some ways, the Curators were identical—each wore a white suit or a boxy white dress, each wore a monocle, each had the same necklace around their neck, the same charms threaded onto it.

But now Jake got a better look, it was clear they were all different as well. At the head of the pack was a short man with dark brown skin and a magnificent droopy black moustache. The top of his head was bald, polished to a shine.

Beside him was a tall lady who walked with a businesslike stride. Her skin was almost as white as her crisp suit, setting off the fiery red of her hair, which was scraped into an unforgiving bun.

Her voice sounded equally harsh when she spoke. "You have not been cataloged!"

The other Curators nodded in agreement as they stopped behind her, a forest of white.

Jake's heart fluttered harder. A breeze blew past them, sending the leaves of the olive tree shimmering with a *shush-shush-shush*. He wished he could shush too, but he had to try and say something.

"We know," he agreed, reaching for the calm tone he used when his mom was in another meeting, and he was trying to convince the receptionist to pass on a message for him. You always had to sound calm when dealing with adults who had the power to give you something, or not. "We were with a man who said he was a Curator, and we thought . . ."

His voice trailed off as her thin brows lifted. Straight, unsympathetic lines framed her face, reminding Jake of the Renaissance paintings he'd seen with his mom at the Louvre. No one smiled in those. *All* of the Curators looked like portraits, actually. Grumpy and ageless and not one bit like Christopher Creaturo.

"The man you were with was *not* a Curator," Droopy Moustache said.

Marisol scrunched her nose, as if she were having trouble concentrating. "You sound funny. . . ."

"Funny?" Droopy Moustache sounded *horrified*. "On the contrary! We are very serious, foundling. Christopher Creaturo is a rogue. An agent of chaos! Why, just yesterday he broke into the Public Record Office of Ireland and ripped a page out of our most current ledger! He is a fraudster of the highest order, a scalawag, a scoundrel, a—"

"We know that *now*," replied Marisol, shifting in closer to Jake. "I guess that's why he sent us in to get the book instead of going in himself."

The Curators' eyes all snapped across to focus on

Marisol at the same time, like one giant white creature with twenty eyes, or like those pictures at a gallery with gazes that followed you around the room.

"You took a ledger?" the woman asked sharply. "Where is it now?"

Jake and his cousin exchanged a long look.

"Um . . . ," Marisol said.

"I'm afraid Christopher Creaturo ran off with it." Boy, this was epically bad, Jake thought, taking in their expressions. End-of-the-world bad, even. "Look, we came here accidentally in the first place."

He explained as quickly as he could about their arrival through the Morris Island Light, about Theodosia and their meeting with Christopher. He instinctively left out the fact that Christopher had sent the Loch Ness Monster back to their world. That would only cloud the Curators' mood, and they looked pretty unhappy already. He only hoped they hadn't arrived in time to see that terrible glimpse of Nessie splashing for the tourists.

The Curators listened: ten sharp white shapes cut out against the green of the grass and the cobalt blue of the Aral Sea.

"So we were wondering," Jake said as he concluded, "whether you could send us home, please? We were never meant to be here."

"Yes," said the woman with the bright, tight bun.

"Certainly. This chaos cannot be allowed to stand. We can send you home."

Marisol snatched Jake's hand in excitement, and he squeezed her fingers.

"But *not*," said Droopy Moustache, "until you have undone the damage you have caused. As my colleague said: this chaos cannot stand. You must find Christopher Creaturo and retrieve the ledger. Everything must be in its right place. You are the ones who caused the disorder, and you must restore the world to the state in which you found it."

There was a murmur of agreement from the Curators behind him, like a whisper of wind going through a forest.

"Everything must be organized."

"Everything must be correct."

"But—" Jake hesitated before stating the obvious. "It's just a book."

"Just a book? Just a . . . ?" Red Bun fanned herself, her expression sterner than ever. "Foundlings, I don't think you understand. If our ledgers fall into the wrong hands—such as Christopher Creaturo's—objects might be displaced from one world to the other."

Jake glanced across at Marisol with a quick flush of guilt—now he *really* wasn't going to say anything about Nessie.

"If too many objects are displaced," continued Red

Bun, "then the fabric between the worlds starts to rip. Why . . . it could even unravel! Everyone and everything would be lost!"

End-of-the-world bad times *two*, it seemed.

"So you see," Droopy Moustache concluded, "you *must* find Christopher Creaturo and retrieve the ledger."

"Don't you think an adult should do it, if it's that serious?" Jake ventured.

"By which you mean us, I suppose," Red Bun sniffed.

"Well, um . . ." *Yes?*

There was a long silence, and the Curators flocked together like seagulls—heads swiveling, feet shuffling, everyone waiting for someone else to speak. What was it? Why wasn't one of them answering?

Then Red Bun's reply burst out of her, as fast as floodwaters breaking past a barrier. "We cannot hunt him down ourselves! If we abandon our posts to chase that miscreant all over the map, the Administrator will demand to know why we are shirking our duties!"

"And then," said Droopy Moustache gravely, "we will have to tell him what has happened."

Understanding lit Marisol's eyes as she glanced from white suit to white suit. "You'll have to explain to your boss how you let someone steal a ledger."

There was another jittery silence.

"The Administrator takes breaches of the rules very seriously," said Red Bun. "You must retrieve the ledger."

"But how are we supposed to do that?" Marisol protested.

"That," said Droopy Moustache, "is your problem. You certainly showed enough ingenuity in stealing the ledger the first time around. I suggest you employ those same brains to acquire it again."

"And you're wasting time," the woman with the red bun pointed out. "As we speak, Christopher Creaturo is no doubt moving farther away. We won't send you back until you have the ledger, so you should get started."

Jake studied the town behind them. Their savior-turned-thief must have disappeared somewhere into its rabbit-warren streets. It was a mishmash of buildings from different times and places, rough-hewn stone slabs sitting alongside curling patterns in elaborate balcony railings. Judging by the way the Curators were talking about organizing and cataloging things, there must be some system to which building ended up where, but Jake couldn't tell what it was.

How could they possibly find Christopher inside that maze? All the worry that had started to fade at the idea of going home was back with a rush, squeezing the breath out of his chest.

Then a voice sounded from the back of the group of Curators. What did you call a group of Curators anyway? A collection? A catalog?

"We can't just send them off to chase the rogue down

with nothing." It was a younger Curator speaking. His expression was more understanding than the others'. Sympathetic, even. He had longish hair, and in looks, he reminded Jake of his South Korean friends.

This made Jake wonder. Had the Curators come from his world too? Or had they always lived in the World Between Blinks?

"They don't even have language charms!" The man's hand rose toward his necklace. "We should at least give them money to buy some at the marketplace."

Jake studied the necklaces with new interest. The monocle on each, he recognized. But it seemed the pen, key, scroll, and hourglass also served a purpose. Interesting.

"What are they for?" Marisol asked, voicing his question.

"They serve sundry purposes," said Droopy Moustache.

"Sundry?"

"It means many," he replied, with an air of flagging patience. He lifted the little scroll on his necklace. "This one's a language charm. Everybody speaks their own tongue in the World Between Blinks, so if you wish to travel here, you'll need to be able to understand them. Nobody in the World is without one, it would be utterly impossible!"

"But we can already understand all of you," Jake protested.

Red Bun dismissed him with a quick shake of her head. "When you enter the World, you travel through a thick barrier of Unknown. Just now, a little of its magic is still clinging to you, which is why it sounds like we're speaking your language. But we Curators alone are speaking in four *different* tongues. Without a charm, your understanding will soon fade. The charms themselves are made from the Unknown, mined from the border between worlds."

"Oh." Marisol scrunched her nose again. "That's why you sound so funny . . . I'm hearing you speak two languages at once!"

Droopy Moustache nodded. "Exactly."

This time Jake heard the Spanish version too—exactamente—but only because he knew it and only because he focused. It must be very loud inside Marisol's head right now.

"The monocle is a vision charm," the young Curator started to explain. "We use it as a reference tool. It also helps us see through the Unknown—"

Red Bun cleared her throat; a reminder that they were on the clock. The young Curator blushed and began digging through the pockets in his suit. Grudgingly, the others did the same.

Soon, Jake was holding a handful of coins, each from

a currency no longer used in his world. There was a small silver coin with a man's head on one side and a five-pointed star on the other. The edges were crinkled, dipping in and out like the crust of a pie, except they were flattened.

"That one," said the young Curator, "is a Ghanaian three-pence. This one here is an Australian sixpence." He was pointing now to a silver coin with a man's head on one side and a crest held up by a kangaroo and an emu on the other—both creatures Jake had met when his mother was posted to Australia. The edges of the coin were worn smooth, but its symbols had stayed crisp.

Marisol was holding a thin, orangish paper note up to the light. It was covered in intricate writing Jake didn't recognize and had beautiful, circular designs around the edges.

"That's a Georgian maneti!" The young Curator told her. "And these are staters." He deposited several well-battered coins—not even proper circles—in Jake's hand. Each showed a horse with wings: a Pegasus. Did *those* live in the World Between Blinks too?

The Curators laughed when he asked, as if this question was absurd.

"Of course not!" said Droopy Moustache. "Pegasi are purely mythical, not *quasi*-mythical. I mean, they don't even meet the first three criteria for a quasi-mythical beast, and the question of aerodynamics . . . Pegasi never existed, child, not like Nessie or the Yeti. The ancient Greeks made them up."

He looked at Jake and Marisol as if he'd just made things perfectly clear. The cousins looked at each other.

Did you understand that? Marisol's eyebrows asked.

Nope, but I'm not volunteering to listen to him try again, Jake's nose-scrunch said.

The friendly young Curator came to their rescue, changing the subject. "Staters originated in Greece, you know. I used to collect currency from all around the world before I came here."

"Here?" Jake echoed. "So you're from home?"

"I'm from Busan in South Korea," he replied with a smile. "Min-jun's my name."

"Did you arrive in the World Between Blinks like us?" Jake asked, his heart fluttering. "By accident?" If lots of people had fallen through, then it couldn't be his fault, could it? Wishing he could forget things from his past couldn't have pulled them into the Unknown.

"Oh, I doubt it was an accident! Every one of us is an avid collector. Zuzanna over there had the largest stamp collection in Poland." A round, blond woman with two braids wiggled her fingers *hello* as Min-jun continued. "But there's an even stronger similarity: we all had such good collections because we had a knack for finding things nobody else could. That's why we belong here."

Beside Jake, Marisol squeaked, but when he looked over, she was busy making room in her pocket for the Georgian maneti, rearranging a sugar spoon and several other knickknacks he recognized from Nana's shelves.

"Do you miss your collections?" Jake asked as Min-jun produced a few more coins.

"Not really," the Curator replied, pausing to gaze down at one admiringly. "We have larger collections here to tend than we ever had before. We left those things behind to focus our attentions on what's in front of us."

Jake felt like he'd been punched. Min-jun could have been describing Jake himself—all he ever tried to do was leave his memories behind, so he could deal with the next new place and forget the loss of the people who had gone before.

Eyes ahead, don't look back.

"Speaking of things we should be paying attention to," Red Bun interrupted, sounding cross that she'd been sidelined, "we need that ledger back. The sooner, the better."

Min-jun pressed the last of the coins into Jake's hand, and as Jake glanced down, he realized there were two little discs among the others that weren't made of metal at all. They were glass. They were monocles! The Curator closed Jake's fingers over them firmly, and since they were clearly supposed to be a secret, Jake slipped the charms into his pocket.

"You'll need hourglasses," Droopy Moustache said, producing two from his suit pockets and threading them onto chains, which he offered to the children. Each was no larger than Jake's pinky.

"These are strange!" Marisol exclaimed.

She was right. All the sand stayed at the top, and no matter how many times it was turned, none slid through to the other half.

"You must wear them at all times," warned Red Bun.

"Is this how long we have to find Christopher?" Marisol asked.

"Not exactly. You'll need them to see if you can still go home," she told the cousins. "Although unless you hurry, you might not have a home to go to."

"But what do they *do*?" Jake studied his, giving it a shake. Still not a single grain of sand shifted.

"The sand represents your memories." Droopy Moustache seemed weary of explanations, his facial hair wilting more with each word. He kept on doggedly. "When the first grain falls, that means your memories are starting to leave you."

Red Bun pursed her lips. "If this were by the books, we'd catalog you two and call it a day, but that would turn you into permanent residents of the World Between

Blinks. To honor our agreement, we'll hold off doing so for as long as we can, but if you lose too much sand, those forgotten memories will catch the Administrator's attention and we'll have no choice but to make your arrival official."

"How long do we have?" Marisol's voice rose in alarm.

"Impossible to say," Red Bun replied. "But I wouldn't let more than two or three grains slip."

Suddenly a cry went up from the back of the group. Zuzanna, the stamp collector, was holding her monocle up to her eye and staring through it, pointing with one trembling finger. Every other Curator whipped around, lifting their own vision charms to squint through them.

"Great pages!" Droopy Moustache exclaimed. "Is that . . . ? But . . . she's supposed to be in the World Between Blinks! Is it really . . . ?"

"The Loch Ness Monster. Christopher Creaturo must have returned her to the old world," Red Bun finished, sounding grim. The cousins had seen her back home between blinks—the Curators must be using their monocles to look through the Unknown too.

"This is so unexpected!" Marisol's eyes were as wide as she could make them, her voice a notch too loud. "We had no idea Christopher was doing such things!"

But . . . the word bubbled up. Jake bit down on it quickly. If they'd known Nessie would be spotted, they'd have told the Curators straight away. But they'd been hoping not to make matters worse.

"Oh yes," he said, hearing how wooden and weirdly cheerful he sounded. "What a shock!"

Red Bun squinted at him for a moment. "Are you quite all right?" she asked, but she didn't wait for an answer. "We'll have to file every outstanding report we can lay our hands on to keep the Administrator from noticing *that*. And if the fabric between the worlds starts to unravel . . ."

"We understand," Jake said, feeling a bit sick. "Get the ledger back before we lose more than two or three grains of sand, or you'll have to catalog us, and we're stuck here forever. Get the ledger back before Christopher Creaturo uses it to send anything else home, or the fabric between the worlds might unravel, and there won't be a home to return to."

"That's about it," Red Bun agreed. "If I were you, I'd get moving."

"One moment!" That voice came from the middle of the group.

Another Curator stepped forward, studying Jake and Marisol over the top of his glasses. He lifted his clipboard and brandished his pen, speaking in a quick singsong voice, running his words together as if they were all one. "Thank-you-for-interacting-today-with-members-of-our-Curator-staff. We-appreciate-your-time." He paused for a breath, then continued. "Please-rate-your-customer-satisfaction-on-a-scale-of-one-to-ten."

Jake and his cousin exchanged a long, confused glance, then turned back to the Curator.

"Um, ten?" Jake tried. It didn't seem sensible to upset the Curators.

"Much better than that old fake, Christopher," Marisol assured them.

This seemed to please the man, and he made a note on his clipboard.

"Go," said Min-jun. "Hurry. The marketplace is on this side of the city—just turn right as you make your way in through the gates. Good luck."

It didn't take the children long to find the marketplace, and Jake kept hold of Marisol's hand while the crowd thickened. The jostling elbows were as pushy as the worries inside Jake's head.

Had they been missed back home?

Had anyone found the boat or their life jackets?

Was Mom freaking out? How about Aunt Cara and Uncle Mache?

What would happen if they couldn't find Christopher?

What if their memories started to fade as badly as Theodosia's?

Would that be so terrible? asked a tiny part of his brain. *You wouldn't ever have to feel the way you do when you leave everything behind. You could just . . . forget.*

But Marisol didn't want to forget—she wanted to go home. So did he, really, which was why Jake let his cousin pull him through an arch into the marketplace. The street's stones—massive and gray—were worn smooth by an uncountable number of feet over an uncountable number of years. Along the edges tiled signs were set into the ground, pointing to all kinds of businesses. Stalls lined both sides, crammed close, graffiti scratched into the rock between them. Even as Jake stared, the letters of DONKEY FOR RENT began to change, English rearranging into a language he couldn't read.

The Unknown was wearing off.

Marisol pulled him behind a large statue of a wrestler wearing a carved stone sheet (and not much else), where they could take shelter from the crowd.

"This must be some place on Earth that was lost," she said, watching the endless stream of figures hurry by, clad in colorful clothes, from places far and wide and all over history.

"It looks kind of Roman," Jake thought aloud. "I saw ruins when my mom and I were posted there."

And in fact, the longer he looked, the surer he was. When a gap in the crowd opened up, he ducked over to the nearest stall. Its stone countertop held portions of roasted vegetables on little clay plates, with a big jug beside them. There was a mosaic at the back, hundreds of tile pieces fitted together to depict a glittering fish leaping out of a river.

Jake's stomach reminded him that he hadn't eaten breakfast yet, and he rose up onto his toes to smell what was inside the jug.

A pungent wave of fish and salt punched his nose.

"That's garum!" The stall keeper turned to them. He was a weathered man with thinning brown hair and skin of almost the same shade, clad in a tunic. "Fish sauce," he elaborated. "It adds flavor to anything. Welcome to Ostia Antica! You have the look of foundlings. Can I fill your bellies, perhaps?"

Jake glanced across at his cousin, but they were both thinking the same thing. No matter how hungry they were, they should wait and see how much the language charms cost before they bought anything else.

They thanked the stall keeper and made their way along the road, looking for a stall that would sell them charms. Vendors clamored for their attention on both sides, shouting their wares.

"Socks for sale, never together!"

"These dentures belonged to George Washington himself!"

"Over here for keys to forgotten doors! Perhaps that lost door is right here in the World!"

Marisol kept dragging him over to different stalls— filled with bins of buttons; cell phones that had no service;

and even, strangely, with jars of baby teeth. She stopped by a bowl of wedding rings, her eyes sparkling at the sight of dozens of diamonds.

"I don't think those are language charms, Mari," he said, tugging at her hand. They couldn't spend *too* much time here.

"No," Marisol agreed, but she also pulled back. "I was just thinking that maybe . . . well, maybe we could find something valuable here to take home. Something that could help pay for a new roof on Nana's house. That way the grown-ups won't have to sell it!"

Jake didn't reply. He always told himself the same thing at difficult moments: *eyes ahead, don't look back.* That was because he had learned it was better to let things go, no matter how much it hurt—because whether he fought it or not, they'd end up lost anyway. He thought for a moment of the friends from his international schools, who meant to keep in touch but never did. Of the places he and Mom planned to visit again but never returned to. He didn't want to lose the beach house—his only *true* home—but wanting never made a difference in the end. The FOR SALE sign would go up, boxes would be packed, goodbyes would be said.

A diamond ring couldn't change that. Not even a whole bowlful of them.

"We should keep going," he said instead. "I guess the charms are farther in."

Marisol held out her hand, not to grab the jewelry or for any other reason Jake could see. She wiggled her fingers, frowning. "I guess."

Farther up and farther in . . . Ostia Antica sprawled in all directions, the roads running along lines so straight, it seemed they had been laid down by an invisible ruler. Or, Jake supposed, by some very hardworking Romans, centuries ago. While the market itself looked ancient, most of its stall keepers didn't keep to the theme. A few—like the garum hawker—wore tunics. Some sported mismatching shoes and socks. Others looked like they'd walked straight out of old movies with their costumes on, cries echoing through their helmet visors. But they weren't actors. They were all real.

"Swords! Get your lost sword of legend right here! Excalibur not guaranteed . . ."

Did time move the same way here as it did back home? Had these Romans and knights stepped out of their own moments in history into this one, or did people never age in the World Between Blinks? Jake hadn't thought to ask Theodosia whether she'd been here one year or one hundred and one.

They passed stalls filled with suitcases. Sunglasses. Bus tickets. Stuffed animals. *Real* animals too! Cats and dogs and parrots and more. Jake couldn't believe how many things they discovered as they walked.

But they still hadn't found the charms. . . .

The children stopped to ask directions every so often, but most of the vendors were only interested in selling their wares, and after the first few conversations, they replied in languages Jake and Marisol couldn't understand. The Unknown magic that had been clinging to them must be gone. Once they caught a glimpse of bright blond hair just like Jake's, and they chased it all the way down the street in case it was Christopher, but it turned out to be a completely different man, who spoke Scandinavian-sounding words in a friendly voice.

Hunger gnawed at Jake's stomach, and the worries in his head had gotten stronger too. On top of all this, he was suddenly shivering. Cold enough to wish he had a sweater to go over his T-shirt.

"Are you freezing?" Marisol asked beside him. "Yo también."

A moment later, the ground crunched under their feet. When Jake looked down, it wasn't sand, but glittering white particles that his sneakers were breaking. Frost! Through another stone archway ahead, an iced-over river was visible.

"Oh no." Marisol shook her head. "¿Estás bromeando? No way am I going somewhere that cold."

"Let's ask for directions again," he said, without much hope.

They stepped back, away from the fingers of frost that grabbed at their feet, but Jake came up short when he collided with someone. He turned around—apology on the tip of his tongue—and was met by a friendly smile.

He'd bumped into a tall, strong woman whose grin showed off a gap between her front teeth. She wore a leather jacket and a matching cap. A few auburn curls peeked out from under it, as well as a sliver of paler skin—she was suntanned, and freckled too.

"Well, hey there." The woman gave a little wave, and Jake was relieved to find that they could understand each other. Her English sounded very American. "Are you two okay?"

He shook his head.

"We're looking for language charms," Marisol said. "Do you know where they are?"

"No problem," their companion replied. "You'll need one of those, for sure! Every citizen of the World does. Look carefully and you'll spot scrolls next to the hourglasses on everyone's necklaces. You'll have to go to the Frost Fair to buy them. Come! I'll walk you over there."

His cousin made a sad sound—clearly she didn't like the idea of venturing into the cold. The lady laughed, peeling off her jacket and settling it around Marisol's shoulders.

"Here," she said. "This'll help. The Frost Fair is

great, you'll love it. I'll get you a hot drink. Cocoa's my favorite!"

The three of them headed for the archway, and the plunging temperature turned Jake's breath into white-cloud puffs. Marisol must be even colder—he had sneakers on, but she was stuck in sandals.

"I didn't catch your names," the lady said cheerfully.

"I'm Jake," he offered. "Thanks for helping us."

"I'm Marisol." His cousin wrapped the jacket around herself a little tighter.

"Pleased to meet you, Jake, Marisol," the lady said, like finding them was the best bit of luck she'd had all day. "My name's Amelia. Amelia Earhart."

7

MARISOL

MARISOL TRIED NOT TO SHRIEK AT THE INTRODUCTION.

"Amelia Earhart? *The* Amelia Earhart?" she gasped instead, nearly dropping the jacket. *Amelia Earhart's* jacket!

This time when Marisol shivered, it wasn't because she was cold. Meeting a famous pilot was weird and wonderful and so much like one of Nana's stories it gave her goose bumps.

Jake's mouth formed a perfect, shocked O.

Amelia kept walking into the wintry wonderland, steps punching through the frost. "So you've heard of me?"

"I had to write a report about you last year!" Marisol volunteered. "You were a famous pilot! The first woman to fly all the way across the Atlantic Ocean by herself! You loved tomato juice and hard-boiled eggs and Chinese food!"

"I still do," their new friend replied with a wink. "That's wild that you learned about me in school! But it's nice to know I've stood the test of time. I have a theory that people remembering you on the other side of the Unknown helps your memories stick longer. Of course, there's no way for me to prove it. . . ."

"Do you remember what it was like coming through the Unknown?" asked Jake. "Did you do anything to make it happen?"

"Golly! That was over eighty years ago." The famous pilot paused, her breath pluming out ahead. "There were lots of clouds that day. So many snatches of sky and shadow and sea. I was flying over the Pacific Ocean with my friend Fred. We didn't come through the Unknown on purpose. . . . Our plane veered off course, and right as we realized we were lost, we had this strange sense that up was down, and down was up. All of a sudden we were in brilliant sunshine and flying over the World Between Blinks. We've been here ever since!"

"Eighty years?" Jake's brow furrowed.

Marisol did some quick math in her head. "You look very good for someone who's more than one hundred, Ms. Earhart!"

"No one ages here!" Her laugh was as silver as bells and wreathed in frost. "And it's Amelia! Please! You can even call me Meeley if you want."

Jake seemed at a loss, so Marisol leaned in to explain. "That was her childhood nickname."

"You really *did* do your homework, didn't you?" Amelia gave another gap-toothed smile and waved them forward. "C'mon! Let's go get that cocoa!"

Cocoa sounded heavenly, especially since the road started ribboning into a frozen river. Marisol was a little chilled at the thought of never turning thirteen, but she decided to let the surrounding sights distract her, since there was nothing she could do about it for now. Instead she marveled at the ice beneath her feet: so solid an elephant could walk on it. The proof was only a few yards away, the large beast curling its trunk over a juggler, whose brightly colored balls flew higher than the elephant's head, whirling past its flapping gray ears. The performer was really very nimble for a guy wearing at least three coats.

They followed Amelia Earhart through a maze of snow-laced tents.

Unlike other fairs Marisol had been to, the Frost Fair didn't have a Ferris wheel or a merry-go-round, but there was plenty of entertainment. Acrobats performed backflips off barrels, and horses pulled sleds of shoppers. They even passed a man who swallowed swords. Had he bought them from the knight in Ostia Antica?

It felt almost impossible that they'd seen him, on a perfectly warm day in a Roman marketplace, just a few minutes ago. . . .

Marisol trotted up to Amelia and tugged her elbow. "Where was the Frost Fair in our world?"

"London!" the pilot answered. "This used to exist on the Thames back when the river got cold enough to freeze. It was so much fun, they still put on the festival here sometimes."

Now that Marisol knew the Frost Fair's origins, it was easy to see. Union Jack flags hung from some of the tents as well as signs written in English—advertising everything from gingerbread to skittles, not the fruity candy, but a game that looked similar to bowling.

"So why is it next to a place from ancient Rome?" Jake wondered. "The geography doesn't make sense."

"It can get confusing," their new friend agreed. "The Curators are in charge of arranging things, and they don't think quite the same way as the rest of us."

Hard to argue with that!

Amelia went on. "They love putting everything into categories, but this *is* where lost things appear, so lots of people and things and places have a way of popping up where they're not supposed to. Of course, this makes a mess of the Curators' system, but they do keep trying. Both Ostia Antica and the Frost Fair are lost markets, which is why they ended up close together. Shopper's convenience! Imagine if you showed up in one place and discovered the thing you needed was all the way across an ocean?"

This made Marisol think of their journey on the *Patriot*, passing coasts filled with castles and pyramids. "How big is the World Between Blinks?"

"Very, very big. And still growing! Every time something disappears from our old world and appears here, the World stretches to fit it. Ah! Here's the cocoa shop!"

The three of them ducked into a toasty tent, where groups gathered around tables of steaming mugs. Chocolate and coffee and something silvery scented the air. Amelia ordered drinks from the vendor, waving the cousins' hands out of their pockets when they reached for change.

"This round is on me." It wasn't a coin or a banknote she used to pay but gold! The piece was no bigger than their pinky nails, shinier than the lost wedding rings.

"Where did you get that?"

Jake shot Marisol a sharp look, and she suddenly feared her question had been too rude.

Amelia didn't seem to mind. "I run a taxi service with my Lockheed plane," she explained. "Lots of pilots here do! Wings make it easier to travel the World's distances."

Good to know, thought Marisol, although as she watched the gold disappear into the vendor's pocket, she doubted they'd be able to afford a ride. She'd been hoping Amelia would say that there was lost treasure to be found all over the World Between Blinks, and she'd just scooped this gold up herself. But of course if that were true, the Curators wouldn't have given the cousins money, would they?

Even if she could afford a ride, it'd help to know where they were going first. Her magnet fingers had failed to find the language charm stall, since every passing person wore a tiny scroll.

Hopefully locating Christopher Creaturo would be easier, since there was only one of him.

"Is there anything better than chocolate?" Amelia gave a happy sigh when the earthenware mugs were passed around. "Seriously? Is there? I imagine the old world's changed a lot since I left."

"Well . . ." Jake sipped the drink, thoughtful. "There are iPhones."

Amelia blinked. "Telephones with eyes?"

Marisol tried not to giggle.

"Kind of." Her primo stretched for an explanation. "I mean, they can certainly see things, and take pictures of them. But they don't use eyes. There were a bunch in the bin of cell phones at Ostia Antica. They look like flat glass bricks."

"I always wondered what those were! Telephones, you say? How swell!"

The cocoa helped warm them up, and so did the hunks of gingerbread Amelia bought at the next stall: treats wrapped in crinkling blue paper that opened to a smell like Christmas.

Marisol nibbled the edges, careful not to get crumbs on the borrowed jacket. Jake—clearly hungry—chomped into his slice. A piece fell to the ice, and an instant later it was snatched up by a stray dog, who dove for it in a blur of movement.

No . . . not a dog.

No un perro para nada.

She didn't know *what* the animal was. It looked like a tiger mixed with wolf—sandy brown with several dark stripes down the back. Despite a long snout crowded with teeth, the creature seemed tame. It sat up on hind legs, nose politely pointing out that they had more gingerbread to give.

Amelia obliged, throwing a piece. Jaws opened wide— as big as those great white shark bones Nana's neighbors had—and caught the bread with a *SNAP*!

"Hello, Oz! Long time no see!"

The animal's round ears perked up. Its bark sounded like a cough: *ah-ah-ah!*

"What is it?" Jake clutched his snack. "An Oz?"

Now it was Amelia's turn to chuckle. "He's a thylacine. Whenever a species is about to go extinct back in the old world, the Unknown seems to . . . well, to know. A few of each one slip through into the World Between Blinks—I guess extinction is a way of being lost. Our friend here is one of the last Tasmanian tigers."

"Pleased to meet you," said Jake, still keeping careful hold of his snack.

"Oz is what everyone in the World Between Blinks calls him," Amelia said. "And I do mean everyone! He gets around all over this place, Oz does."

"Oooooooh." Her cousin nodded. "Tasmanian tigers used to live in Australia!"

"Is that why he sits like a kangaroo?" Marisol wondered.

Oz grunted, returning to all fours, and for another wild moment she worried she'd offended the animal. Could the thylacine understand them?

Marisol tossed him another gingerbread offering.

Just in case.

SNAP!

"Feed Oz and he'll follow you anywhere," Amelia said. This seemed true, since the thylacine kept trailing them across the ice—nails clicking. "He's been on a few adventures with me in the *Flying Laboratory*. Er, my plane."

"I mew dat!" Marisol declared through a bite of confectionary.

Crumbs went everywhere. So did Oz, in an attempt to collect them.

The newest addition to their group wore a collar.

There was a plaque on it—much like the nameplates identifying the plants at the Crystal Palace, but its text didn't translate into either of Marisol's languages. All she could pick out were numbers: *1936*. That must be the year the Tasmanian tigers went extinct. It made her sad to think about such a weird but cute creature disappearing.

Oz stuck around, though, following the trio even after the gingerbread became nothing but wrapper. They strolled through the fair, past women with baskets of hot apples on their heads and more missing keys than Marisol could count. The keys reminded her of the set her parents had lost just yesterday. They reminded her of the key with the curling ƆⳄ she and Jake had found at the lighthouse. It'd vanished when they slipped into the World—and probably wouldn't be any help getting home, even if they'd somehow held on to it. She'd have liked to try, though.

When they passed some chests of golden doubloons—guarded by a watchful vendor—she even began to miss her brother, Victor.

We'll get back to the beach house, Marisol promised herself.

We'll find the treasure to keep it too.

Her fingers buzzed at the thought, though it would've been very hard to find the language charms without Amelia's help. The shop that sold them had no sign, its sail-like fabric shut tight against the frigid air. Oars supported the tent instead of poles, Marisol noted when they ducked under the flap.

Inside sat a woman with television-static hair—white and everywhere. The chain around her neck drooped with dozens of charms: a scroll, a monocle, a fish scale, a feather, to name a few. She was nose deep in a book called . . . Marisol tilted her head to one side. *Love's Labour's Won* by William Shakespeare, the spine said. The woman behind it was oblivious to her new customers.

Oz yipped.

She jumped, snapping the script shut. "Bonjour! Madame Earhart! Ça fait longtemps! Comment ça va?"

"Hello!" Amelia returned the greeting. "I'm aces, thanks for asking! My foundling friends here need language charms. Do you have any in stock?"

The shopkeeper kept speaking in what Marisol suspected was French, waving toward a basket filled with hundreds of miniature scrolls. With Amelia's help they negotiated a price: most of their pence, both Australian and Ghanaian.

"She wants to know if you're interested in buy-one-get-one-free T-rex repellent," Amelia added after the exchange.

"Maybe not today?" Jake answered diplomatically. "We shouldn't spend our money all at once."

"*Could* we get eaten by a T-rex?" Marisol asked. She wondered what else they should be worrying about—how many dangers lurked outside this tent?

"Eaten, no. Smooshed. . . ." Amelia hesitated. "Probably not. Jake is right. You'll need your cash for other things."

They untied their chains and added the scrolls next to their hourglasses.

"Hey, look at that," Amelia said, leaning in to examine the necklaces. "Not a single grain of sand has fallen! That's not a sight you see every day."

The cousins exchanged a fraught look, as Amelia's words brought their problems bubbling back to the surface. They had to keep moving, before sand *did* slip through their hourglasses—before any of their memories trickled away—and they were cataloged and stuck here. Twelve years old forever and ever . . .

"Better, yes?" the shopkeeper asked when they put their necklaces back on.

Marisol listened past the tent, catching the fair's frostbitten voices.

A certain music had faded: the same sort of melody she heard whenever Aymara and Quechua were spoken around her in Bolivia. Words you didn't understand were beautiful just for their sounds. This background of kaleidoscope syllables was gone, and two distinct languages were in its place.

English and español.

Spanish y inglés.

Overlapping.

Jake turned to her, frowning. "¿Cómo How's es it sound para to you ti, Mari?"

"Está bien." If Marisol focused, her concentration could shift from one automatic translation to the other. Like adjusting a radio dial. "It's okay."

Her primo nodded. "At least now we'll be able to ask around after Christopher Creaturo."

"Who?" Amelia wondered.

"This man dressed up as a Curator and tricked us into stealing a ledger for him," Jake explained. "We have to get the book back if we want to return to Folly Beach. To our family."

The shopkeeper *tsk*ed behind her explosion of hair, and at their feet, Oz gave a disapproving whuffling noise.

The look on Amelia's face needed no translation. "This Christopher just put you behind the eight ball, did he? What a twit! Not everyone in the World is trustworthy. . . . You need to take more care around its people than its dinosaurs."

"He's blond." Jake pointed to his own bright bangs. "Wearing a white suit and carrying a giant book. Maybe you've seen him?"

Both adults shook their heads.

"I'd like to help you search," Amelia began, "but I'm afraid I have to hoof it. It's time for me to pick up Glenn

Miller for his concert in the Hanging Gardens of Babylon. With all of his trumpets there isn't enough room in the Lockheed for you two."

"You've helped us so much already," Marisol told the pilot.

She started peeling off the leather jacket—reluctantly—but Amelia stopped her. "Keep it for now! We'll have an excuse to meet again. If you look inside its pocket you'll find a walking-talking."

¿Un qué? Marisol pulled out a walkie-talkie.

"It doesn't have eyes, like those telephones, but it does patch in to the *Flying Laboratory*'s radio. You can use it to reach me if you need a quick lift. Take care of these kids, okay, Oz?"

The thylacine sat on his hind legs and barked.

They said their goodbyes. Marisol felt a pang when Amelia ducked out of the tent. Jake turned his back to the exit, studying the nearest basket, which held dozens and dozens of shining scales.

"Bubblers," the shopkeeper told them. "Underwater charms make ocean breathing a breeze! I'll give you a three-for-one deal!"

Marisol shook her head. They'd spent enough time shopping.

Now they needed to find Christopher.

The Frost Fair felt bigger without a friend to guide them through it. Colder too.

"Where do we even start?" Jake asked as they followed the flow of ice past yet another sock vendor. "If the World Between Blinks is as big as Amelia said, Christopher could be anywhere!"

He could. It was true.

Good thing Marisol was good at finding things. . . .

She needed to focus to "flex her magnet fingers," which meant pausing between two tents—out of the crowd again—and closing her eyes. Hands came out of her pockets, reaching into the frozen air.

"What are you doing?" Jake sounded impatient.

"Thinking."

Marisol pictured Christopher, with his sunshine hair and chin dent. Cold shivered into something else: the tug, the pull, the *find me* feeling. Her fingers swung like a compass needle, pointing back toward the Roman market.

"We should go this way." She opened her eyes, still pointing.

Confusion squished Jake's face. "Why?" he asked, and Oz echoed the question with a soft whine.

Outside the Crystal Palace, she'd been ready to tell Jake about her talent, but they were in a hurry and it would take too much explaining. Besides, if Marisol could use it to get them *out* of this World, she wouldn't have to admit it was her fault they got stuck here.

"It's just a hunch," she said, and started walking.

Oz and Jake followed.

Her fingers pulled them back the way they'd come, past the elephant, through the archway, back into the clamoring dust of Ostia Antica's market. The garum vendor waved hello again. But Christopher Creaturo wasn't hiding in the colorful crowds. The cousins soon found themselves navigating the wider, jumbled cityscape— past Viking longhouses and sleek office buildings. Jake gasped when they walked past a huge round building, though the noise was nearly drowned out by a roar from a crowd somewhere inside.

"Mari, that's the Globe! Where Shakespeare performed his plays! It must be the first one. I saw the replica when I was in London."

"Was it the same?" she asked as Oz paused to salvage a sausage in bread someone had dropped near the entrance.

"The replica was cleaner," he said. "Pretty close, though. But where are we going, Mari? Shouldn't we start asking people if they've seen him?"

No. They shouldn't stop now. The buzz beneath Marisol's fingernails grew stronger. . . .

She shuffled forward. Arms out. Reaching.

"Mari!" Jake trailed, exasperated. "Will you at least tell me why you're walking like a zombie?"

Stronger . . . Closer . . . Almost there . . .

Marisol turned onto yet another mixed-up street— where extinct flowers bloomed from window boxes and gas lamps were planted next to torches. At least the buildings had a theme: they all looked like residences. Igloos. Sod houses with grass growing from the roofs. Sturdier structures with doors as bright as songbird wings and shiny, out-of-order numbers. *Probably not gold*, Marisol reasoned, but her fingers flared all the same. *Here! Here!*

She halted.

Jake stumbled into her.

Here! Sunlight beamed off Christopher's hair as he stood across the lane, studying one of the tidy brick houses. The ledger sat open in one hand, a pen in the other. He looked from page to postal address. Double-checking. Triple.

"It's him!" Jake gasped. "Mari, how on earth did you find—"

Christopher struck a line through the stolen book.

Marisol knew what would happen next, but that didn't make seeing it any less jarring. There was a house. Then there was NO house. Her heart skipped when she saw the empty lot, and when she blinked . . .

Things started to rip.

Through this new tear in the fabric between the worlds Marisol could see a street where cars had quickly braked, almost as if she were watching it on TV. Horns blared. A double-decker bus, painted a signature London red, had passengers pointing out of its windows. Marisol followed their fingers, expecting to see the un-lost house and finding . . . *more.*

Christopher had struck this address from the ledger, sending the building back to their world—never mind that a new one had been built in its place since it disappeared. Because there was no room, the structures mashed together instead. A pair of doors jostled beside overlapping windowpanes. Some of the wall was built out of brick, while other parts were constructed from granite, as if two architects had fought over the plans and decided to call it a tie. Pieces of both materials scattered the road, which was why traffic had piled up, but there was no obvious damage to the building.

"Oh!" Jake was clearly seeing the same thing. "I hope nobody was hurt!"

"Yo también."

Marisol blinked without thinking. The London scene vanished, but there was a traffic jam forming here too. A penny-farthing bike wobbled to a halt, its rider tumbling, while cars of old stacked bumper to bumper ahead. Drivers were getting out.

"Did you see that?"

"I'm sure that Curator was just rezoning the house...."

"I meant the fissure, good sir! The enormous crack! That was the clearest glimpse of home I've ever seen!"

Marisol's pulse drummed hard in her throat. They had to stop Christopher before it was too late! Before too many objects were displaced and the Unknown unraveled! Before everyone and everything was lost!

"Stop!"

Her yell wasn't loud enough to reach the other side of the clogged street, and even if it had been, Christopher probably wouldn't have listened. There was a grin on the man's face as he tucked the book under his arm and strolled smartly down the sidewalk, toward the harbor. The Crystal Palace shimmered from the other side of sapphire waters. But . . .

Christopher wouldn't be going back to the scene of the crime?

Would he?

"Jake!" She gripped her cousin by the arm, jolting him into his second blink. "Christopher is heading for the docks! If he gets on a boat . . ."

Jake understood well enough to take off running, but when her primo tried climbing over the hood of a canary-yellow sports car, its driver scowled, laying on the horn. The Viking in the cart behind that hurled an ax into its bumper. The dodo being carried in said cart leaped out, landing with a flightless *plop* and startling a sled team of huskies who'd begun howling in tune with the horn.

"This way!" Marisol narrowly avoided tripping on the big wheel of the penny-farthing bicycle. So many spokes!

She and Jake ran the long way round, forced to double back when they finally crossed the street, and slowed down again when they had to pass the newly vacated lot. Christopher's stunt had attracted quite the crowd. The cousins pushed through as quick as they could, running down to the marina.

Its docks were messier than before, splintered by the kraken's tentacles, boats all tumbled together. The Curators must've contained—and cataloged—the offending beastie, since there was no sign of it.

Most of the white suits were gone too. Only one remained, climbing into a submarine. Christopher's gold hair flashed a final time in the sunlight before he disappeared into the hatch.

"Hey!" shouted Jake. "Wait for us!"

Oz gave a loud cry as they ran down the dock, dodging broken boards and disgruntled sailors. Marisol's fingers seared. Her calves did too, burning all the way to the slip.

They were too late.

The choppy gray waves closed over the body of the submarine as it cut a path through the water, away from the dock. Then it vented water up into the air, like a whale or a fire hose aimed straight at the sky, huge jets streaming high, then falling to the ground in silvery showers.

For a long moment the periscope was visible, and then it slipped into the sea. The submarine and its passenger were gone, vanished beneath the waves.

8

JAKE

NO!

They couldn't come so close only to lose Christopher! Jake stared at the swirling, marbled waters, stomach churning, hope sinking faster than the submarine had. Marisol looked ready to dive in after it—so ready that he grabbed her hand to ground his cousin on the dock.

"No worries, mates!" A big man waved from down the dock, sporting a legendary blond moustache and a sea captain's hat. His accent sounded Australian. "There's another ship headed to the underwater cities in a few minutes. Mine, in fact! Better views, better price, and you *don't* feel like a sardine marinated in strangers' armpit juice at journey's end!"

While this did *not* help Jake's queasiness, it did lift his spirits. "The underwater cities?"

"Yep! Biggest collection of sunken civilizations this side of the Unknown! Popular destination. Are you two aiming to go?"

Jake and Marisol exchanged a quick glance, and she nodded. He wasn't sure *why* Christopher Creaturo would go to an underwater super-city, but whatever the reason, they had to follow.

Jake dug in his pocket for his remaining coins, pulling out a handful of the Pegasus-stamped Greek staters. The soaring horses made him think of Amelia for a moment. If only she were still here to offer a flight in her plane! But then again, she could hardly take them underwater.

"Is this enough for two tickets?" Marisol had her orange banknote out, the Georgian maneti, and it fluttered in the breeze like a miniature flag when she held it up for inspection.

"It is." The captain paused to squint at Jake's shirt. Or rather, Jake realized a moment later, at the necklace that rested on top of it. "But you'd best not come until you have your bubblers. Your underwater visit will be drastically shorter without them. Unless you both happen to have gills?"

Bubblers. That's what the wild-haired shopkeeper had called those shiny scales. If only they'd taken that three-for-one deal!

"I'll run back and get them," Marisol volunteered. "I remember the way."

Wind blasted across the dock. Jake shivered, his insides feeling as wild as whitecapped waves at the thought of separating from his cousin. But she shot him a significant look, flicking her gaze sideways at the captain. *Oh*, Jake realized. *She wants me to stay here to make sure he doesn't sail off without us.*

Pushing his worries down again, he nodded. "Go with her, Oz."

With a quick yip, Oz took off after Marisol as she tore back toward the Frost Fair. It made Jake think of how they'd left that market. Why had she had her hands out in front of her, like she was feeling her way in the dark? He'd have to ask her later. For now, he had a more pressing concern: stalling the captain so the boat didn't leave before Marisol returned.

"I'm Jake Beruna," he said, offering his hand to shake, like his mother always did.

The captain's hand was sun-warmed and hard with calluses, engulfing Jake's as they shook. "I'm . . ." He frowned. "I'm sorry, I had it a minute ago. . . ."

After a moment it was clear the man wasn't going to speak again, so Jake ventured a question.

"I don't mean to be rude, but what's it like? Not remembering things?"

"Peaceful." The sailor's voice drifted along. "Memories can be as heavy as an anchor. That's why I cast most of mine off soon after I arrived here. The only sand I have to worry about is the shoreline! My life's made of salt and sea and sunshine!"

"That sounds nice," said Jake. "But—what do you mean *cast off*?"

"There's some that cling to their memories, like a starfish to a rock! Keep 'em a long while too, but sooner or later the sand always falls." The captain nodded at Jake's hourglass. "I wanted to get the forgetting over with! So I forgot."

"Oh. . . ." Jake went silent.

It was zero fun leaving everything behind, as he'd done over and over. Would it be easier if you never had to think about it again? Of course, then you never *could* think about it again, even if you wanted to. But perhaps it'd be worth it.

"Don't worry!" said the sailor, interrupting his thoughts. "I still know how to captain this beauty!" He pointed to a big black-hulled boat with flags strung from the front funnel to the bow. "She's the *Baychimo*. Got stuck in ice in the Arctic, and her crew had to leave her behind. Floated around for thirty-eight years, if you can believe it, appearing and disappearing, popping into the World Between Blinks and then back again, never quite lost enough to get stuck. Eventually she lodged here, though. We had this historian on board the other day, a chap who spent so long with his books that he got lost in them, and strewth, was he excited to see her. Now, are you nippers about ready to go? We've got a delivery to make to the underwater cities, then on to Carthage, and I can't be late."

Jake's mind scrambled, searching for a joke or a story or anything to distract the captain a few minutes more. The best he could come up with? A retelling of his encounter with a shark while snorkeling at the Great Barrier Reef. So he threw himself into the performance as best he could.

"It was ten feet long!" Much longer than Jake's arms when he stretched them.

"Only ten feet?" The captain guffawed. "Wait until you see the critters in this ocean! You haven't truly lived until you've met a megalodon."

A megalodon? Jake wasn't sure he wanted to ask. Thankfully, he didn't have to: Marisol and Oz had reappeared.

The pair galloped down the rickety dock, both panting. "I got the three-for-one deal she offered us," she said, handing Jake a shiny scale to thread onto his necklace. Oz already had one dangling from a loop on his collar.

"You didn't happen to snag any of that T-rex repellent?" Jake wondered. Maybe it worked on sea monsters too.

"No." Marisol frowned. "Should I have?"

"All aboard!" The captain accepted the maneti note and led them onto the ship. Brine and engine oil tickled Jake's nose. Marisol snuggled deeper into Amelia's coat when they reached the wind-whipped deck.

"Over to the side there," instructed the captain. "Out of the way, until we've left dock."

The cousins and Oz pressed themselves against the rail as sailors scurried from port to starboard. Just like the market merchants, none of them seemed to be from the same time or place. They wore a dozen different outfits, from a lady in trousers and a coat with a woolen collar to a man in perfectly modern storm gear.

"Did you lodge the route paperwork with the Curators?" the lady called to the captain.

"Yes," he grumbled. "In triplicate. Not that it matters with all the phantom islands popping up out of nowhere. The official course we plot almost always ends up being a dead end."

The boat eased away from the dock, and at the very last moment, a white-clad Curator appeared where the final line had been cast off. Jake felt like he was going to have his seventeenth heart attack of the day. Had they taken too long to find Christopher? Had the Curators changed their mind?

The Curator drew a deep breath and called out to

the retreating ship. "Thank-you-for-interacting-today-with-members-of-our-Curator-staff. We-appreciate-your-time." He gulped for air, then continued. "Please-rate-your-customer-satisfaction-on-a-scale-of-one-to-ten."

"Seven-point-six-two-three-seven," the captain replied cheerfully, shooting the children a grin. "Working that out'll keep them busy," he muttered. "Then they won't waste my time micromanaging shipping lanes and trying to tame the seas!"

The sailors ran this way and that across the deck, seeming always on the verge of colliding. Eventually, Jake realized he was watching an intricate and complex dance, to which everyone knew the steps. Soon the boat was underway, chugging across choppy waters, leaving the hodgepodge city in its wake. It was time for the cousins to leave the rail and explore the ship a little!

They found the woman in the woolen-collared coat up near the bow. She must have been aboard awhile—her fair skin was covered in freckles from the sun, and a little salt too. There was a big smile on her face, framed by a sweep of straight brown hair down one side.

"Hey there, passengers," she said. "And I see you've met Oz."

"You know him?" Marisol asked.

"Oh yes! He's quite the social butterfly," the lady replied. "Oz here is one of just a few Tasmanian tigers who made it through to the World. Kaparunina, they called these animals, where he's from. That was their oldest name, the first name they were given. And you two, you look like foundlings. Bessie Hyde's my name."

"How did you get here?" Jake was still trying to wrap his brain around the Unknown. If he could learn why this magic had reached out for Bessie, maybe he'd understand why it had reached out for *them*. He had the stomach-squeezing feeling that all this was his fault, *his*, and it'd be nice to learn otherwise.

"Well, I seem to remember I was rafting with my husband, Glen," Bessie said. "That's him down in the stern with the captain. We were in the Grand Canyon to run some rapids, but I recall there was a smooth patch of water, and we got to gazing into each other's eyes—we were newlyweds, you know, very much in love—and we sort of got . . . lost in each other, I suppose. We reckon we must've pulled in enough Unknown that it swept us off here, though we don't rightly know. That's why it's called the Unknown, after all!"

Marisol pressed her hand to her heart. "¡Qué romántico!"

Jake glanced at his language charm. It must allow him to hear the Spanish his primo spoke, phrases he already knew. The scroll had let him learn a new word for Tasmanian tiger too. Clever magic!

None of the sand had slipped in the adjoining hourglass, and his stomach still felt tight. It would be so nice not to worry . . . to simply think only about the salt spray on his lips and the sun rays on his cheeks, like the captain.

"I suppose it is romantic." Bessie grinned. "Most people wouldn't opt for that sort of honeymoon, but—"

"Watch out!" A loud voice interrupted from the back of the boat. "It's the *Lyubov Orlova*!"

Bessie's smile vanished faster than Christopher Creaturo had. "Oh dear."

"What is it?" said Jake.

"Well . . ." Bessie hesitated. "It's a ship."

That much was obvious. He could see it nearing them—a neat blue-and-white vessel that looked straight out of a cruise commercial. Why was it making the *Baychimo*'s sailors so anxious?

"Go ooooon," said Marisol, suspicious.

Something on the *Lyubov Orlova* was moving. . . . Something big and brown and wriggly. No, Jake realized, when tiny pelts started splashing off the side. It was *lots* of somethings. . . .

"Oh dear!" Bessie's hand clamped over her mouth. "Ohdearohdearohdear."

Jake pointed at the dots in the water. "Those are rats!"

Oz hissed, his forepaws scratching the railing for a better view.

"Not just any rats, nippers!" the captain called from

the stern. "Those are cannibal rats!"

"What?!" both the children shouted in unison.

"Captain's right, I'm afraid," Bessie said. "The *Lyubov Orlova* broke free when it was being towed to a scrap yard in the old world. When the ship started drifting, there was nothing for the wharf rats on board to eat . . . except each other. They aren't picky diners, though. The Curators couldn't even get close enough to catalog the thing."

The captain put it more succinctly: "Full steam ahead if you want to keep all of your fingers and toes!"

Bessie ran to join the rest of the crew.

Jake shuddered and tucked his hands beneath his armpits. Marisol's toes curled at the edge of her sandals. Oz's hiss had become a deep, throaty growl. The rats—the *cannibal* rats—swam fast. Scores bobbed toward the ship, almost close enough to count their whiskers. Close enough to see their ragged teeth.

His voice trembled when he turned to his cousin. "Now might be a good time to use that walkie-talkie—"

WHOOOOOOOOOOOOSH!

More teeth appeared in a surge of choppy white water—but these teeth were much, much sharper and much, *much* larger—each the size of Jake's hand. The shark they belonged to was bigger than a school bus! Its massive jaws gathered the teeming rats in a single bite.

Everyone on board the *Baychimo* froze, except for Oz, who scurried between the cousins' legs—ears flat. Jake couldn't breathe until long after the dorsal fin vanished in a frenzy of foam.

"Ha-ha!" the captain crowed. "There you have it, foundlings! Your first megalodon sighting!"

Jake could have lived his whole life without seeing that. Marisol probably could have too: Amelia's walkie-talkie shook in her fist. He'd never seen her knuckles so tight.

"Are you all right, Mari?" His cousin didn't answer. Her stare was fixed on the waves, so Jake reminded her, "Eyes ahead, don't look back."

Even if there's a prehistoric fifty-nine-foot shark behind you. . . .

"Just be calm on the route," she agreed. "You're right. We have to find Christopher. We have to get home, no matter what stands in our way."

Oz chimed in with an enthusiastic bark.

The *Lyubov Orlova* became a speck on the horizon, and a while after it vanished, Bessie came to find them.

"Looks like it's been a long day," she said sympathetically. "Why don't you both bunk down for a little, and I'll wake you when we arrive. We'll be underway all night."

She led them downstairs and scrounged up something to eat in the galley—chowder made according to someone's lost family recipe, Ansault pears, and steamed Old Cornish cauliflower, followed by a handful each of light

130

brown M&M's for dessert.

"I've never seen M&M's like this before," Marisol said as the two of them snuggled down together in a bunk, pulling a thick quilt up to cover them. The scents of old cotton and salt tickled Jake's nose.

"I don't think they make that color anymore," he said, popping one into his mouth. "That's why they're here, I guess."

He wrapped his arms around Marisol, and despite everything that had happened since they'd left home that morning—their parents' discussion about selling Nana's house seemed a lifetime ago now—he drifted off to sleep.

The next morning Bessie woke them for breakfast, and they were up on deck by the time the *Baychimo* reached a large collection of buoys bobbing on the face of the ocean.

There must have been hundreds of them, maybe a thousand. They were orange and yellow and white, salt-stained and encrusted with sludgy seaweed. They jostled for space like seagulls at a picnic, seeming almost like a tiny island.

The captain walked over to check that their bubbler charms were threaded onto their necklaces. "You're good to go," he said. "Jump on in, and you'll find there are ropes running from the buoys all the way down to the bottom of the sea. Just grab hold and pull yourself down. You'll be able to breathe just fine, like regular air. Those are good, strong charms you've got, plenty of the Unknown magic in those."

"Jump in?" Jake gurgled. "Is it . . . is it safe?"

"Safe as anything in life!" The captain chuckled. "Don't worry. The rats are long gone, and Curators don't allow scary critters anywhere other people live. It'd create too much incidental paperwork."

"We'll get so wet," said Marisol fingering the leather of Amelia's jacket.

"You won't notice," the captain assured her. "And the things in your pockets will be fine, thanks to your bubbler charm. It'll anchor your necklace in place too, so there's no need to fret about the magic floating off."

There was nothing for it except to go. The cousins climbed up onto the edge of the railing, and the captain and Bessie helpfully lifted Oz so the three of them could jump together. They landed with a splash, and a momentary shock of cold salt water shot straight up Jake's nose and sent him spluttering.

He took a breath as best he could, even if he wasn't going to need it, and ducked below the water. Sure enough, a forest of ropes stretched down toward the seabed, which was only barely visible below, a patchwork of buildings and sand interwoven with brightly colored coral and seaweed.

Before he could pull himself down any farther, he felt

something tugging him back up. He surfaced once more, his hair plastered flat against his eyes.

"Oz can't dive," said Marisol. "He's trying, but he keeps floating back up. He doesn't have any hands to hold on to a rope."

In the end, Jake managed to anchor Oz under one of his arms and pull them both beneath the surface. Then gravity seemed to help, and after a minute he was half pulling them down, half falling. He held his breath at first, but when he finally let it out, he just exhaled bubbles, and found that somehow—impossibly—he could breathe just fine.

"Everything good?" he asked Marisol, who was descending the rope next to his.

"Sí," she said, giving her feet a little kick. "This must be what fish feel like!"

He could hear her voice perfectly.

They made their way down slowly and landed together in a large stone-paved square, with arches exiting in every direction. As Jake's feet hit the ground, he found he could stand normally, and walk normally, with just a little resistance from the water. These bubbler charms were really something!

The light was dim, dappled and filtered through the waves above, but he could see perfectly well. The square was cluttered with ropes' anchor points—with people and smaller fishes threading through them. A large signpost directed traffic from the center, its destination arrows pointing in every possible direction. He started to read them.

WANAKU

Thonis Heracleion

ΒΔΙΔΕ

Neapolis

Ꝃiᴛezh

Port Royal

And wait, did that faded, starfish-splashed sign at the bottom actually say . . .

ATLANTIS

It couldn't, could it?

"Oof," said Marisol beside him, reaching down to pet Oz. "This place is huge, Jake! Where do we even start? Christopher could have gone to any of these cities!"

Jake read the signs again, his heart slowly sinking. If they picked the wrong starting point, Christopher would get even farther away while they searched for him. But where to begin? He had absolutely no idea.

9

MARISOL

MARISOL HAD NEVER TESTED HER GIFT UNDER-
WATER BEFORE.

She'd never *been* this deep—period. Sometimes,
during Folly Beach summers or trips to Lake Titicaca in
Bolivia, she would put on her wetsuit and goggles and dive
down to explore the sandy floor, but she could only go so
far. The bubbler charm meant that everything around her
was blue, a blue so deep that her lungs wanted to burn
just because.

Breathe! Marisol reminded herself as she studied the
sign. She needed oxygen to concentrate, and she needed
to concentrate to flex her magnet fingers.

Jake tapped his chin in thought. She could tell he was
worried but trying to push it aside—he stood up a little
straighter, pushed his shoulders back. "We don't have a

lead, so maybe we should shut our eyes and pick one? The sooner we start, the sooner we'll find him."

Marisol gazed out into the deep blue, and the memory of the megalodon came gliding back into her mind, teeth glinting. Her hand shook a little when she held it out. Nana had never seemed frightened by anything. . . .

These thoughts cluttered her brain, made it impossible to focus.

There were too many cities. Too many directions.

Christopher Creaturo could have gone anywhere, and it was her fault they were stuck.

"Lo siento, Jake." Her arm dropped back to her side.

"Sorry?" Jake blinked. "For what?"

"Because I'm the reason we're trapped here! I wanted to find Nana's treasure so badly that I followed my magnet fingers and—"

"Your what?"

"My magnet fingers." Marisol sniffed. She couldn't tell if she was actually crying or not, since her entire face felt wet. "I—I've never told anyone about them before. Not even my parents. They just think I'm good at finding things, but it's more complicated than that. It's . . . it's like lostness pulls me. There's this buzz in my fingertips that leads me to missing items. People too, sometimes."

"Oh!" Jake's eyes went bright—matching the sea around them. "You mean . . . that zombie walk you were doing? You were using your powers to find Christopher?"

136

"Sí."

"That's *so cool*!" Her cousin was so excited that bubbles popped out with his shout. His worries about Christopher seemed forgotten.

Oz jumped at the shimmery air pockets, giving a cheer of his own.

This hadn't been the reaction Marisol was expecting. "You believe me?"

"Mari," he said, waving both his arms around like windmills to gesture to their surroundings, leaving ripples in their wake. "Look where we are. I'd believe anything right now. But if you can do it back in our world, that's *amazing.*"

"You think so?"

"Um, yeah? But why did you keep it a secret? I'd tell everyone if I had a superpower!" Jake said. "Can you do anything else?"

"I can breathe underwater!" Marisol grinned. "But seriously, Jake, you aren't mad that I got us stuck here?"

"Oh. . . ." His face fell. "That's not your fault. We're lost because of me."

She frowned too. This didn't make sense. Jake didn't find Nana's map or dig up the ✖-marked key, and without either of those items they would still be at the beach house.

"I lose things," he went on. "Every time Mom and I move I have to let go of friends and homes and schools."

He got quieter and quieter as he spoke, bowing his head. "And it hurts, so I guess I *try* to forget them all. You say the lostness pulls you. I think it follows me, and this time it finally caught up. Like . . . like I belong here, or something."

Was *Jake* crying too? If there were any tears, the ocean covered them.

"No, Jake! You belong with your family!" Marisol took hold of his hand. "And as long as I'm around, there will always be someone to find you. Lo prometo."

He looked down at their entwined fingers. "I guess we do make a good team, huh? Can you show me your superpower again?"

Marisol took a deep breath and held her free hand toward the signpost. It was easier to concentrate with that confession off her chest, even though she knew she was still to blame for this entire adventure. The Unknown had reached out for *her*, because she'd been reaching out for *it*. Wasn't that how all of the Curators had ended up in the World Between Blinks? Collecting and collecting, using their own magnet fingers one time too many?

We all had such good collections because we had a knack for finding things nobody else could, Min-jun had said. *That's why we belong here.*

Marisol's heart squeezed like a fist as the buzz beneath her fingernails grew and grew.

She didn't belong here.

And neither did Jake.

Her primo watched with glittering eyes. *Amazing.* He'd described her power with so much feeling in his voice, like the word was all lit up with flashing marquee bulbs. Maybe he was right. Her magnet fingers had helped chase down Christopher once already, and even if they *were* to blame for drawing the cousins here, Marisol didn't think there was any harm in using her powers to find their way home again.

Slowly but surely, her hand swung in the same direction as two of the arrows: Kitezh and Wanaku.

"Onward!" Marisol tugged Jake toward the proper archway.

Oz bounced after them—half jumping, half doggie-paddling, chasing every fish in sight.

The tunnel did not open straight into the city streets, but wound through a zigzag of lanyards that made Marisol think of an airport. A long line snaked between these ropes. People filed past countertops where their bags were picked apart by Curators. The giant sign above them read:

NO UNAUTHORIZED SPECIMENS/ ARTIFACTS PAST THIS POINT

Marisol hoped Oz didn't qualify. Or Amelia's jacket, for that matter.

"Welcome-to-the-great-sunken-city-of-Wanaku-lost-beneath-Lake-Titicaca-do-you-have-anything-to-declare—" The Curator paused when he realized his new subjects were shorter than the countertop. He leaned forward and started again. "Welcome-to-the-great-sunken-city-of— Oh, hello, Oz!"

"Ah-ah-ah!" The Tasmanian tiger really *did* know everyone.

"Found some foundlings, did you?" The Curator eyed the children and their necklaces in turn. "Do you two have anything to declare?"

"I'm not sure," Marisol admitted.

This was not a satisfactory answer. The Curator sniffed. "Well, we can't risk things being put where they shouldn't. If so, what would the World come to? Chaos! Clamor! Catastrophe! Pockets out, please!"

Marisol was beginning to get the impression that the Curators spent a lot of time trying to put things where they belonged, and that the residents of the World Between Blinks just filled out the paperwork and then moved things wherever they pleased. But both cousins started turning out their pockets as the Curator watched cautiously.

Items began piling on the table: a big chunk of lint, a Fini Gelatinas wrapper with gummies still stuck in the bottom, Jake's leftover staters, all of the trinkets she'd rescued from Nana's house, the walkie-talkie, a couple of dog-eared football cards, a tiny green bottle with a crown-shaped stopper from Marisol's—or really Amelia's—jacket, and two monocles from Jake's pocket that Marisol definitely didn't remember buying.

"*These* belong on your necklaces." The Curator slid the last items back across the counter and proceeded to uncork the glass bottle. He gave its contents a sniff. "What's inside—OOH!"

"Those are smelling salts. Amelia uses them to keep herself awake during long flights," Marisol explained quickly.

Jake's reply was low, so only Marisol could hear. "I hope she doesn't need them anytime soon."

"And then we have— Oh, hello there!" The Curator waggled his brows and picked up the football cards and turned them over. There was something reverent about the way he smoothed out one dog-eared corner. His eyes went hazy, and Marisol knew he wasn't looking at these cards at all, but was seeing some old memory from long ago. "I used to collect these, once upon a time," he murmured. "The thing about collector cards that you need to know is—"

"I'm so sorry," said Jake, in his politest tone. "We're in a really big hurry."

"Oh yes!" The Curator shook himself like a dog

coming out of water, and seemed to focus on them again. "Everything looks to be in order." He shoved their possessions back to them—lint ball included. "Thank-you-for-interacting-today-with-members-of-our-Curator-staff. We-appreciate-your-time. Please-rate-your-customer-satisfaction-on-a-scale-of-one-to-ten."

"Nine point nine!" Jake said.

The Curator waved them off, muttering. "You're losing your edge, Horace. Next in line!"

"What I want to know is, how did Christopher get through that line with the ledger?" Jake restuffed his pockets as they walked past a sign that said:

EXPORTS ALLOWED BY LICENSE ONLY: SEA TREASURES BELONG IN THE SEA

"Maybe he posed as a Curator again." Though—after having met several actual Curators—Marisol realized he wasn't very good at it. Christopher was much too chaotic. He couldn't fool a real official, even if he did find a monocle. Which reminded her! "Where did you get those vision charms?"

Jake handed one to her. "Min-jun slipped them to me—you know, that nice Curator who gave us the coins? I'd forgotten all about them until now."

It took Marisol a few tries to string on her new charm, because there was so much else to see when the tunnel opened up to Wanaku. The Curator had said the city was lost beneath Lake Titicaca, but she might've guessed, even if he hadn't. The *colors* felt like home. They splashed everywhere—blue, green, red, orange, yellow. Bright, bright walls lined the cobbled streets, setting off even brighter fabrics. Passersby wore wool tunics with flowers woven in slanted lines and tasseled hats sewn into a box shape.

There were llamas all over the city too: carved into walls and hammered into thin gold leaf. Living versions strolled past, a few spitting at Oz. Or . . . it would've been spit on land. The action was less rude underwater.

Marisol felt a swell of pride, seeing her homeland's history brought to life. Everything was so beautiful! So brilliant! She wished her dad—who loved visiting ancient ruins—could be here to enjoy it.

"I don't see Christopher anywhere." Jake paddled above the crowd for a few seconds before landing back on the ocean floor. "What do your magnet fingers say?"

"Um . . ." Marisol held out her hand. It sparkled—clear and true. "¡Por aquí!"

She pointed past the adobe buildings, where the seabed sloped into terraced crops. Christopher must've followed this path to Kitezh. The road kept going, and Marisol's fingers kept pulling to where the next city's silhouettes rose through the currents.

"Those buildings look like onions, don't you think?"

When Jake didn't answer, Marisol turned to find her cousin standing at the edge of a field. His hair floated alongside the crops, the same flaxen color. He was staring out at nothing with a worried expression. Oz sat next to him, whimpering.

"Jake?"

"Look, Mari!" He pointed across the terrace at a sign:

END OF RESIDENTIAL ZONE,
SWIM AT YOUR OWN RISK

Shadows shaped like beasts drifted in the water beyond, dragging long, long tentacles over a wild tangle of coral.

Marisol shivered. She was glad she couldn't see them *too* clearly. "Good thing the Curators don't let any monsters near here."

"What? No! Don't you see that crack? I think Christopher sent something else back. . . ." Jake frowned, blinking so many times she thought his eyelashes might fall off. "But I can't get a good view!"

"Why don't you just use your monocle? Isn't that how the Curators spotted that the Loch Ness Monster was missing?" she reasoned.

"That would make sense." Jake held the vision charm over his right eye.

Marisol did the same. There was a lot to see through

the glass. *Sections of the Great Barrier Reef circa 2016* colored the seabed past the residential border, and there were far more statistics about the *Kronosaurus* and the *Tusoteuthis* squid than she cared to read. Largest of the pliosaurs with three-inch-long teeth? Eleven-meter-long tentacles? *No gracias.*

Thankfully, these entries were interrupted by the tear.

Marisol hadn't noticed this split between blinks—ocean overlapped ocean, endlessly blue—but now it looked like a crack in her lens. A lightning strike underwater. Inside of that?

"Is that another submarine?" She squinted as the vessel pulled away, farther into their world. . . .

"The USS *Seawolf.*" Jake was reading the same text as she was. "October 4th, 1944. It must have been lost during World War II."

"But why would Christopher send back a submarine? Or a house? Or Nessie?"

Her cousin shrugged. "Why do evil villains do anything?"

"He has to have a reason. . . ."

The USS *Seawolf* faded, but the crack didn't, even when Marisol put down her monocle and picked it up again. She blinked through the glass. Her stomach fluttered. What else would Christopher try to displace? How many rips could the Unknown handle before it unraveled?

"Then we should go to Kitezh and ask him," Jake

said, determined. "If he's still there, of course."

Marisol turned toward the city. *Kitezh, Russian city lost beneath Lake Svetloyar in the thirteenth century. Quasi-mythical.* The monocle entry went on, in dictionary-esque detail, but she dropped it to concentrate on her magnet fingers instead.

They glowed, pointing toward equally bright rooftops. "He's there," she confirmed.

The closer the cousins and Oz drew to the city, the more solid it became, but Marisol couldn't help but think that Kitezh felt . . . ghostly. Maybe it was the church bells chiming with the currents, or the candlelit processions of women wearing nun habits. Fabric buoyed around their shoulders, and a few of the faithful were floating altogether, rising up past white walls and golden roofs that now looked less like onions and more like Christmas ornaments.

Jake pointed to the nearest building. "That reminds me of Saint Basil's Cathedral in Moscow!"

"It's so shiiiiny." Marisol took in the sight with gleaming eyes. There was enough treasure here to buy all of Folly Beach. Heck, the Berunas could even use gold on the beach house's new roof if they wanted!

Too bad she didn't have bigger pockets. Or an export license. The Curators would probably catch her even if she tried to take something small, and she didn't want to give them yet another reason to be upset.

"Christopher probably came here because it's the perfect camouflage," Jake said. "White suit, gold hair! He'll blend right in with these churches!"

Her cousin wasn't wrong—white churches washed together with white sailors' uniforms and white tunics. It was kind of like playing a game of *Where's Waldo?* Of course, Marisol always won those. She couldn't help frowning, though, when she glanced back at the gilded domes.

She wanted treasure to fix Nana's house so badly. *Too* badly. Was it possible her magnet fingers sensed that?

Had Marisol been searching for the wrong thing?

A frown started creeping onto Jake's face too. "What's the matter?" he asked.

"Nada." Her fingers felt as fiery as the passing candles, blazing a trail down the street. The only way to know whether or not they led to Christopher was to keep going. "This way!"

The road ended in a square, where vendors hawked their wares—*Socks for sale! Never together!*—beneath the city's biggest towers. Dozens upon dozens of people gathered to listen to the music of bells and women, as their melodies twined together. Some in the audience were even dancing.

Glistening trails of bubbles occasionally drifted up

toward the surface like rows of pearls, and there was a special grace to the dancers' movements, a swish and a flow that reminded Marisol they were underwater, their bubbler charms allowing them to walk and talk and breathe and dance. She'd grown used to the magic so quickly!

She let her gaze drift over the dancers, floating from one pair to the next.

Then she saw Christopher Creaturo.

Marisol's breath caught between her teeth. Surprise. Then relief. Christopher's eyes were closed, and he had his arms around a woman in a smart khaki skirt. There was a smile on her poppy-painted lips as they swayed.

"Jake!"

Her primo's gaze swung around to follow hers, and he grinned, his voice soft but excited. "Your superpowers worked! You found him!"

Marisol smiled back, wondering why she'd ever doubted herself.

"Who *is* he dancing with?" Even though the bells clanged loudly, she whispered. It felt like a quiet moment.

"No clue," Jake answered. "Where's the ledger?"

A quick scan found the book sitting on a nearby bench, set aside where anyone could grab it. Including them. As long as Christopher wasn't looking, he wouldn't notice they were stealing the ledger back!

Marisol held a finger to her mouth and motioned at the bench.

Jake's eyebrows shot up. He nodded.

Oz's tail quivered.

They tiptoed along the edge of the square, pausing every time the dancing couple twirled. Christopher kept his eyes shut. He was almost smiling too, Marisol realized, except his face seemed sadder than the woman's.

Her face, though . . .

It tickled the back of Marisol's brain. The closer she crept to the lady, the more familiar she seemed. Was she someone they'd learned about in history class maybe?

"Hello!" The dancing woman paused and waved.

Directly at Marisol.

Uh-oh. She'd stared too long, and now Christopher Creaturo was turning his head to see who his dancing partner was talking to.

"Jake! Get the ledger!" she screamed, because her primo was closer.

Jake broke into a run, but it didn't matter. Christopher's legs were longer. He lunged for the bench, snatching up the ledger just before Oz's teeth reached it. The fake Curator clutched the book to his chest. For a moment, it looked as if he wanted to say something.

Instead, he turned on his heels and disappeared into the crowd.

10

JAKE

THE CHASE WAS ON!

"After him!" Marisol shouted, and Jake didn't need telling twice.

The two of them plunged through the many dancers, Jake's "excuse me's" mixing with Marisol's "perdóns" as they ducked and dodged and doggie-paddled their way after Christopher's disappearing form.

But the crowd was unpredictable, swirling like the eddies and currents of the water itself, tugging the children in every direction. Including up. Jake tried taking long, loping steps, pushing off the ground and letting the water buoy him along as Christopher vanished through an archway of mixed-up stones.

A sign hung over the structure, its letters burned into wood by an uneven hand. *Port Royal*, it said. A crudely drawn skull and crossbones leered beside the script. Jake was pretty sure this was a bad sign—no pun intended—but losing the ledger would be even worse, so the cousins plunged through. Into a new, murky city.

Cobblestone streets clattered past white-plastered houses with terra-cotta roofs. The crowd here was just as thick as it had been in Kitezh, but it couldn't have been more different. Flowing white robes were replaced with tattered shirts and tilted hats. Jake dashed past eye patches, peg legs, knotted hair, and rough faces.

The skeleton on Port Royal's sign was starting to make sense.

They'd run into a town full of pirates!

Jake might have been excited, if the crowd wasn't so *smelly* and loud. Every third or fourth doorway seemed to be a tavern, raucous music spilling out, shouts and screams issuing from the windows. Amelia's warning echoed through his head as he listened: *Not everyone in the World is trustworthy. . . . You need to take more care around its people than its dinosaurs.*

A man with mossy teeth snarled at the children, the cutlass in his belt glaring bright. Jake didn't like how sharp it looked. His arm hairs prickled into needles while he and Marisol hurried away.

Oz's hackles rose too.

That sealed it. If the thylacine didn't trust anyone here, they shouldn't either.

"Jake," his cousin said uncertainly. "I don't like this place—"

Bodies burst out of the nearest door, almost knocking the children clean off their feet. It was a brawl! Fists flew all around, curses gurgling from pirates' mouths, while a huge raggedy parrot with a bubbler charm buckled to one leg screamed straight in Jake's face. Oz barked back at the bird, and Jake somehow found Marisol's hand. He pulled her away from the trampling boots, toward the other side of the street, where a pile of empty barrels provided temporary shelter.

"Now I *really* don't like this place," Marisol rasped.

"Agreed." Jake flinched when a shadow appeared in front of their cask, but it was only Oz. The Tasmanian tiger planted himself in front of the cousins, teeth bared, clearly ready to protect them. "We can't stay here. And it looks like Christopher's disappeared again. . . ."

A peek through the barrels showed nothing but pirates being pirates.

Marisol's hand trembled as she lifted it, fingers flexing. After a long moment, she shook her head. "Qué raro. I can't feel him."

"Let's go back and speak to that woman," Jake suggested. "Maybe she knows where he was going."

"They looked like they knew each other," Marisol agreed.

Jake held his cousin's hand as they made their way back toward Kitezh, and he was honest enough to admit to himself that it wasn't just to comfort her.

Back in the white city, all was calm. Church bells sang, and the dancers kept swaying in time to them inside the crowded square. The woman with the khaki shirt and the flower-bright lips waltzed on her own, though she seemed eager for company when they approached.

Her smile was sunshine at the bottom of the ocean. Her wave was warm.

"Hello," said Jake, uncertain where to start. Was this woman on Christopher's side? Did she even know what he'd done? She *seemed* friendly, but they'd just seen her dancing with the enemy.

"Hello!" she said, her voice low and delighted, as if there was nobody else she'd rather see than the two of them. Her gaze dropped toward Oz. "Why hello . . ." Her voice trailed off, unable to catch Oz's name. Jake got the impression that like everybody else, she knew the thylacine, even if she couldn't remember what to call him.

Jake felt better when Oz's striped tail quivered with greeting. The Tasmanian tiger seemed to be a good judge of character so far.

"Would you like to dance?" the woman asked.

"Sure," said Marisol.

"Mari, we don't have time for that," Jake reminded

her. "We're sort of on an urgent mission here."

Marisol gave him a firm look and raised one brow. "Jake Beruna," she said. "Sometimes it's all about keeping your eyes forward. And *sometimes* you have to stop a minute."

The woman held her hands out to them hopefully. Jake took one and Marisol took the other, and the three danced together, all linked up. Oz slid into the middle of the circle, winding in and out and around their legs. And though he should've tripped them up, somehow he was simply dancing too, releasing little bursts of bubble with the occasional excited bark.

After a few dizzying turns, Jake introduced himself. "My name's Jake. And this is my cousin Marisol."

"I'm so pleased to meet you!" The woman released their hands to execute a twirl before she claimed them once more. "I'm afraid my name is long lost. . . ." She spun again, then held up her necklace.

There was a bubbler on it—of course—and a language charm, plus two sets of military dog tags—the identification soldiers hung around their necks when they were on duty. But Jake's attention went straight to her hourglass. The timer's sand had settled completely to the bottom—a mirror opposite of what the cousins wore around their necks.

"¡Ucha!" Marisol murmured. "*All* the memories are gone?"

The woman shook her charm hard, but the sediment at the bottom didn't budge. It was as if a cold current of water swept through the square, wrapping up and down Jake's spine. The Curators had told them their memories would slip away with the sand, but to see it right in front of them—this woman was worse than Theodosia, worse than the captain of the *Baychimo*.

In time, Jake knew he and Marisol would end up like this: happy but unable to remember who they were. Basically, they'd be clams. *Happy as a clam*, that's how the saying went, right?

"The man you were dancing with before. He's a friend of ours." Jake didn't feel great about the lie, but it was an emergency, and Christopher *had* lied to them first. "You don't know where he went, do you?"

"He visits me sometimes," The woman's eyes fogged over, almost misty. "But I don't remember why."

For a moment, there was something so familiar about her expression that Jake was *sure* he'd seen her somewhere before. In a textbook, or maybe a documentary. A photo? This made Jake glance at his own hourglass. All of its sand stayed safe and snug at the top, but still he couldn't remember.

It bothered him.

It itched.

The woman didn't seem to mind her own lack of

memory, though. He'd told Marisol earlier that lostness simply came to him, gathering like the strands of seaweed that wreathed the square's pillars. For a moment, studying the woman's brilliant smile, Jake couldn't help but wonder again if it would be very bad to fade like this. She seemed carefree. Jake bet she never spent any time feeling sad about what she forgot. She wouldn't wallow in the bad things that happened in her past either. . . .

Happy as a clam.

Shellfish aren't selfish.

But choosing to forget now *would* be selfish. The Curators had warned them that if they cast off even two or three heavy memories, the mysterious Administrator would notice, and then he and Marisol would be cataloged—stuck in the World Between Blinks forever. It was bad enough he'd attracted the Unknown in the first place, with his knack for lostness, *his* need to let go of things, and even though his cousin was putting on a brave face, he knew she wanted to return home. That could only happen if they retrieved the ledger before Christopher struck out one woolly mammoth too many and broke both worlds beyond repair.

"Do you have any idea where he might have gone?" he asked, failing to keep the worry from his voice. "Any idea at all?"

The woman's frown looked sadder than most,

probably because of her bold lipstick. Her feet fell still while the others in the square kept spinning, spinning around them. Jake wished she would let go of his hand. Or say something.

When their dancing partner stayed quiet, he turned to his cousin. "What about you, Mari? Can you feel where Christopher is now?"

Marisol pulled her fingers from his, flexing them a few more times before giving a glum sigh. "It's just not working! I don't know why for sure, but I *think* it's because Christopher doesn't want to be found."

"He figured out we're chasing him," Jake reasoned. "And he obviously doesn't want us to catch him. Do you think that's messing with your superpower? Like, when a magnet gets flipped around, and it pushes away instead of connecting?"

"It must be." She bit her lip, fingers wriggling. "I can't feel the ledger either. I guess whatever Christopher's doing is protecting the book too. . . ."

"He was talking about a submarine," the nameless woman said suddenly.

"The *Seawolf*?" Marisol asked.

"No." The woman shook her head. "It was . . . Oh, darn. I can't remember. I think it started with a K? Or a C? Not *Sea*, mind you. He said he was sailing for the sands. He said . . ."

"What?" Jake urged.

Their dancing partner's cheeks turned pink. "He said, *I love you.*"

Both cousins fell quiet, letting the currents swirl around them. Jake didn't know what to say, so he looked ahead instead. Over on the edge of the square, Oz was begging from a man who was pushing a cartload of fish.

That guy must have the easiest job in the world, Jake thought, as he watched the thylacine snap up a silvery mouthful of scales. *Much easier than tracking down an agent of chaos.*

How many submarines left the underwater cities in a day?

How would they possibly figure out which vessel Christopher boarded?

"Jake!" Marisol gnawed her lip, half smiling. "If Christopher was leaving, he'd have to go back through a checkpoint, sí? We should go and ask if the Curators have seen him. Even if they haven't, their micromanaging paperwork could help us narrow down what route he took."

Of course! Jake had never been so thankful for customs before!

They said goodbye to the forgetful woman, called Oz away from the seafood vendor, and wound back through Kitezh's dreamy streets, past more candlelit processions and singsong bells. Jake could still hear their chimes when he and his cousin reached the edge of the city, could still feel the bells' joyous dance sweeping through his feet. This rush grew stronger when he spotted another customs point.

Marisol gave an excited squeak and ran up to the Curator who was staffing the booth.

"¡Perdón!" She stood on tiptoes, nose tilted toward the glass. "We're looking for a man who may have just hurried through. He has golden hair and a white suit. He was probably carrying a book. Did you see him?"

The Curator—a short, fat lady with very pale white skin turned almost bluish by the water and wavy brown hair cut into a neat bob—frowned and began riffling through her papers. Jake wondered how in the world she kept them dry.

"White suit, white suit," she murmured to herself. "Ah, yes. Your friend boarded the EML *Kalev*."

"It was a K!" Jake exclaimed.

"Is that a submarine?" Marisol asked eagerly.

"Indeed," the Curator replied. "Launched in 1936, presumed sunk in 1941, though in fact she strayed off course due to a navigation error, becoming so hopelessly lost that she attracted the Unknown and drifted through into the World. She's 59.5 meters in length, or 195 feet and two inches, if you prefer that sort of thing. It has Vickers-Armstrongs motors, and—"

"Thank you," Jake cut in. She was clearly just warming up, and they didn't have time to sit through the level of detail the Curators liked to provide.

"Christopher really likes submarines," Marisol muttered beside him.

"Has it left?" Jake asked.

"Yes, about half an hour ago." The Curator nodded. "I-hope-this-information-has-been-helpful.I-hope-you-have-enjoyed-your-stay-at-the-underwater-cities.Please-rate-this-information-provision-and-your-interaction-on-a-scale-of-one-to-ten."

"That depends," Jake said. "Can you tell us where the EML *Kalev* was going?"

She checked her papers again, running one finger down a long column of words. "Yes," she said. "Portus. It's—well, it's a port. The city used to sit side-by-side with Ostia Antica, back in the old world, but now it's on the edge of an ever-stretching desert."

"Sand!" Marisol whispered excitedly. "That woman said Christopher was sailing for the sands!"

"So much sand," the Curator lamented. "The location makes no sense. No sense at all! Many ships land there, so Portus is linked to hundreds of destinations, but none stay for long. The port is too isolated. We've tried to correct it over and over—Portus would be much more useful next to Ostia Antica again—but the stones are stubborn."

"Stubborn?" Jake couldn't help but ask.

"When Portus began disappearing from the old world, bricks crumbling and roads wearing away and seawalls sinking beneath the waves, it appeared next to the desert, filling in one stone at a time."

Just like the lighthouse. . . .

"Every time we try to rezone the place, it disappears and builds back up overnight," the Curator explained. "Always next to that darn desert! It's most vexing; it defies order. Sometimes I wonder if lost things don't *want* to be cataloged. OH—" She clapped a hand over her mouth, eyes wide and watery. "Please don't tell anyone I said such a thing! If the Administrator found out . . ."

"Don't worry," Marisol reassured her. "You've been very helpful!"

"A ten out of ten!" Jake added.

The official behind the counter beamed, waving them on to the buoy island, where they could catch a ship to Portus. They might not know where he was heading from there, but Christopher Creaturo was still in their sights, and they weren't far behind him.

This wasn't over yet.

Not by a long shot.

11

MARISOL

THE ANCIENT ROMAN CITY OF PORTUS WAS
BUSTLING.

It was very easy to believe there were a thousand
places you could go from here. A constant stream of ships
sailed into its U-shaped basin: canoes and catamarans,
schooners and pontoons. Marisol even spotted a giant
unicorn inner-tube spinning in their wake. She tried to
see if the Beruna family dinghy had somehow ended up
here too, but there were hundreds of prows and the harbor
itself was over a mile wide. The lighthouse that towered
over its entrance looked more like a chess piece by the
time the cousins reached the docks.

Marisol had to cling to Jake's arm so she wouldn't lose
him in the rush of passengers as they disembarked and
made their way out into a crate-cluttered marketplace.

Here they paused, turning in a slow circle to take in the jumble of stalls—*Socks for sale, never together!* Colors looked bolder to her after she'd been underwater for so long. Smells were stronger too: spices and frying dough sizzled from shop fronts.

"Do you have any coins left?" she asked Jake hopefully.

"No." Her primo shook his head. "The sooner we catch Christopher, the better."

Hunting the rogue was getting expensive. They'd spent the last of their money on the passage here, and even so they'd had to scrub decks to keep the captain happy. He'd looked like one of Port Royal's pirates, right down to the eye patch.

Marisol was happy to put that voyage behind her, though she still wasn't sure what lay ahead. All of the *buzz* that should've been in her fingers was now in her stomach, reminding her that she hadn't eaten anything since the *Baychimo*.

"Maybe Oz could do some begging for us." She looked over at the Tasmanian tiger, who'd stuck as close as a shoe to the cousins' heels. His sandy striped fur blended with the desert air a little too well. "Do you take to-go orders?"

The creature's bark sounded like laughter.

"It was worth asking," Jake consoled her. "Now, let's find a quieter place where we can concentrate."

They wandered closer to the edge of the city, down roads no one needed, since they only led to vast hills of sand. *The ever-stretching desert.* "Do you think Christopher came this way?" Marisol wondered aloud. "Toward the sand?"

"These could be his footprints!" Jake pointed at a set that climbed toward a nearby dune. "If we reach the top, maybe we'll see him!"

Step by step, Marisol followed the footprints. But the longer she studied them, the more she realized that the tracks were all different sizes and shapes, and they were appearing without anyone actually *stepping* in the sands. . . .

"I think these are lost trails, Jake—"

"Careful there!" a voice called out, startling the cousins to a stop.

They both looked up to find a woman in a gleaming helmet that wasn't a helmet at all but a colander. Wild brown hairs sprang through its holes, quivering as if they were living things. The stranger herself stared hard at the ground.

There was nothing there, when Marisol dropped her gaze, except . . . maybe . . . Her eyes went a little funny, and she quickly blinked and looked away. "¿Qué *es* esa cosa?" she muttered.

Jake had the same disoriented expression on his face.

"Sorry, ma'am, we didn't mean to step on anything, uh, important." He paused. "Is that spot important?"

She ignored them.

Marisol wondered whether she should try asking too, or if they should simply back away from this peculiar lady. Then Oz—their furry diplomat—stepped forward to nudge his nose against the woman's leg. She lifted her head, showing them a leathery face.

"I don't have time for— Oh, hello, Oz."

The Tasmanian tiger made a soft whining sound, and she sighed.

"You two, get around the other side of my handcart where it's safe. This here's a thin spot! One wrong step and you'll go POOF!"

Her handcart was filled with an assortment of things: broken dishes, forks and shells, the odd earring. Staring at the stash, Marisol thought it would be at home in any of the market stalls here in Portus, or at Ostia Antica.

Suddenly the sandy ground near the woman's feet began churning.

The grains weren't sinking but *hopping.*

"Come on! Come on!" Her hands wriggled inside fingerless gloves. "Gimme something good to sell!"

The ground shook, and Marisol trembled with it. Remembering the woman's warning, she took a step back, tugging Jake with her.

Several things popped out at once: a quarter, a parakeet, and a bedraggled stuffed bear. The bird took off in a flash of sapphire wings. When the sand solidified, the scavenger picked up the remaining items and tossed them onto her cart.

"Next time it'll be gold!" she said to no one in particular. "Just you wait and see!"

"Does this thin spot connect to the Unknown?" Jake's eyes went bright. "Could it send us back home?"

The woman's head did a nod-shake circle. "Yes. No. Lost things from the old world show up here, but it doesn't work in reverse."

"Then where would we POOF to?" Marisol wondered.

"If your name is recorded in a ledger, you're tethered to the World. The Unknown just spits you back into another thin spot. I ended up all the way over in the Aral Sea once, lost my whole haul to another scavenger! And that cart had a *diamond* in it!"

"Do you find a lot of treasure?" Marisol tried to sound casual, but her heart was beating hard enough to meet her teeth. The shifting sand by their feet and the salty smell of the sea reminded her of the beach house, and thinking of the beach house reminded her that she still hadn't found a way to save it.

Small in the scheme of things.

But big in its own way.

The scavenger shook her head, her colander gleaming in the sun. "Not enough. Never enough. But my luck's about to turn! Just you wait and see!"

Marisol suddenly felt a shiver go through her—hungry, but not hunger.

She stood bolt upright.

Jake's gaze snapped over to her. "Mari, are you okay?" he asked quickly. "You look like you swallowed an electric eel."

In reply, she lifted both hands and wiggled her fingers at him. It was impossible not to grin. "They're back, Jake."

His eyes widened. "The magnet fingers?"

"¡Sí! Maybe it's because we're on dry land, I don't know! Maybe Christopher forgot to concentrate again? But they're tingling. I can feel it." Marisol's hands swiveled toward the nearest dune, where blue sky waved against orange sand. It seemed their first hunch was right! "He went this way!"

"Let's go," Jake said immediately. He looked across at the collector to say goodbye, but she was already leaning down again, muttering to the ground. So he simply nodded, and Marisol took off at a jog up the hill.

———◦•◦———

A couple of hours later, nobody was jogging. The desert's giant undulating slopes reminded Marisol of waves as she and Jake struggled—shin deep—through the sand.

Swimming would be so much easier. They'd only managed to get past three of the huge dunes.

"This way?" Jake asked, pointing toward yet another grueling hill. There was no reason to change direction, but she knew what he really meant: *Are you sure?*

Because if she was wrong, then they were trekking out under the blazing sun for nothing. It was too hot to wear Amelia's jacket, so she'd tied it tight around her waist. Her stomach pinched against the leather. Her hands tugged straight ahead, stronger and stronger with each stride.

"This way," she said firmly.

Her cousin groaned. "I wonder if there's a charm for walking across sand."

"Even if there were we couldn't afford it," Marisol reminded him. "We've almost caught up with Christopher, though. My fingers are burning!"

"So are my calves," Jake muttered.

As they scaled the next set of dunes, Oz fared best out of all of them, his paws leaving tiny golden avalanches as he skipped to the top. Something had gotten the thylacine excited: his ears were stiff as arrows and his nose quivered. He danced on all fours, waiting for the cousins to join him.

"See anything?" she called to their companion.

"Ah-ah-ah!"

Jake paused to wipe his hair out of his eyes. "Does that mean yes or no?"

"I'm still learning the accent," Marisol teased.

Thankfully, it turned out that Oz meant *yes*.

The cousins struggled their way to the crest of the dune, and when they joined their friend, Jake and Marisol found themselves staring over a city.

The place was half swallowed by amber sands. Columns covered in colorful hieroglyphics burst out from the ground, alongside sphinx statues and branches that reminded Marisol of the palm fronds on Folly Beach.

"Wow," Jake breathed, all troubles momentarily forgotten. "This place must be Egyptian. This is *so* cool."

"This is so hot," Marisol replied, dabbing sweat off her forehead, and he laughed.

Oz led the charge snout-first, still snuffling after some scent, and Marisol and Jake ended up rolling down the hill, tumbling to a stop near the edge of the city. Upon closer inspection, it was obvious that it wasn't *all* Egyptian. Medieval castle turrets rose out of open courtyards. Lavish gardens pushed back at the desert, filled with buildings that had stone Chinese dragons crouched on their roofs.

"What is this place?" Jake wobbled dizzily to his feet. "Places, I should say."

The tumble hadn't shaken any sand in Marisol's

hourglass, but it had twisted her necklace. Script flashed through the monocle when she spun it straight, telling her that the gardens had been relocated from Beijing's Old Summer Palace in 1860, and the wider city was called Amarna. Back home it'd been devoured by the Sahara. Here it served as a . . . *centerpiece of the royal collection?*

Marisol kept reading. "I think this is Queen Nefertiti's palace!"

"Really?"

"The monocles haven't been wrong so far," she said. "We should've used them to learn more about that woman in Kitezh. The one Christopher loves. The one who's forgotten everything. . . ."

A strange look drifted over her cousin's face.

"Jake?"

"What?" His eyes snapped back to where they were standing. "Oh, yeah. Sorry. Which way are we supposed to go from here?"

Marisol fought off a frown and focused on her fingers instead. They ended up following Oz, who was following his own nose between sets of dune-throttled pillars, through the palace's wide-open doors.

Queen Nefertiti's court was even more impressive up close. Crowded too. Brightly muraled halls bustled with courtiers—gossiping whispers and shiny sets of jewels.

Silk dresses and embroidered robes and garments from all across history swished past massive statues of Akhenaten. Or so the inscription at the base read.

"There's a lot of crowns here," Jake whispered when they passed a pair of golden-haired princes in velvet sleeves that looked uncomfortably puffy and hot. "Those two definitely aren't Egyptian. Nefertiti must not be the only lost royal. We studied her in school, just like you studied Amelia. She was a pharaoh's wife, but lots of Egyptologists think she became a pharaoh herself when he died. There are no official records, though. History lost track of her."

"I'll bet that's why she's in the World Between Blinks," Marisol said.

Everyone in this palace seemed fancy, flashing with colors and coronets—kings and queens and courtiers from all over the map and every era were mingling. Marisol could have people-watched for hours. *Would* have, if her fingers weren't prickling with pins and needles, if a glimpse of white up ahead hadn't snagged her attention.

It was only another frilly dress, but she just *knew* that Christopher Creaturo was in this building somewhere.

"Do you smell Christopher, Oz?"

The thylacine was certainly tracking something, following his nose past billowy skirts and uniformed staff.

It was all the cousins could do to keep up. They passed through courtyards and garden paths. Oz's whiskers shuddered; his tail stuck straight.

They were close. . . . And when they caught Christopher, perhaps they didn't have to return the ledger to the Curators *straightaway*. Perhaps they could hunt for a small bit of treasure first.

Marisol's heart thrummed as they followed Oz into a vast glowing room. Candles—there were hundreds of them—reflected off walls made of amber. It was like stepping into a fire that didn't burn. Warm and gold and red and rich.

"Oh no." Jake's shoulders slumped. "Oz smelled something all right."

The Tasmanian tiger sat on his hind legs, shamelessly begging for a slice of cake on a servant's silver platter. It *did* look delicious. But that wasn't the point!

"I said Christopher! Not cake!" she scowled.

"You *did* ask him to fetch some food for us," Jake reminded her. "Besides, Oz probably needs a full stomach to concentrate on tracking things he *can't* eat."

"What about my hands, though? They're never wrong, Jake. ¡Nunca!"

It seemed that they were this time. Marisol's fingers felt as fiery as the room around them, yet Christopher was nowhere in sight. She spun around, in hopes that she'd

172

overlooked him, but there was nothing but amber.

Jake touched her shoulder gently. "Don't worry, Mari. We'll figure it out. Right now, maybe Oz has the right idea." He stepped closer to the servant, who was now putting a slice of cake on the ground for the Tasmanian tiger. "Excuse me, sir. Can we have some cake too?"

"Are you guests of Queen Nefertiti?" The man looked the children up and down, and Marisol suddenly felt very *sandy*. Her shorts and sandals and salt-tangled hair couldn't look more out of place. Everyone else touring this room was dressed to the nines.

"We're visitors," Jake replied, in that wriggly not-lie way of his. "*Hungry* visitors."

"In that case, welcome to the Amber Room!" The servant gave a grand wave. "This is one of Her Majesty's favorite finds, and it ranks among the greatest treasures in the World Between Blinks! It vanished from St. Petersburg's Catherine Palace in the old world in 1941, during the thick of the Second World War." His expression grew solemn. "There were Nazis involved. As evil as evil can get."

The cousins followed the servant as he explained all about Peter the Great and his daughter Empress Elizabeth and the half a million amber pieces used to create the room's mosaics back in eighteenth-century Russia. It was a far cry from ancient Egypt. . . . For all the Curators kept trying to catalog everything around them, the World did seem to keep on jumbling itself up.

"This room is unspeakably valuable," the servant droned on. "Some estimates place it at around five hundred million dollars!"

Marisol's thoughts caught on the number. *Five hundred million?* She hadn't realized amber could be worth so much. Though it was very possible her fingers had. They flickered like birthday candles when she paused to study a panel's fragments. Some were tiny—as small as the shells she and Nana used to collect. Queen Nefertiti wouldn't notice if a sliver went missing. . . .

A not-magical itch grew in Marisol's hands. Yes, stealing was wrong . . . but this room was technically already lost. So wasn't this just finders keepers?

She found herself starting to reach out, glancing around to check if anybody was watching, all while imagining her family's response when she told them she could pay for the repairs to Nana's house. "We can keep it!" her mother would say. "No more packing!" Victor would add with a pump of his fist.

Then Jake turned a little and bumped against her, and she snatched her hand back.

Wait a minute.

If she didn't want Jake to know what she was doing, that meant it was wrong. Suddenly she could picture the face he'd make if he realized she'd stolen from their host, and her cheeks heated up in a quick flush.

First she'd led them off track with her magnet fingers, because she couldn't stop thinking about gold/diamonds/fill-in-the-treasure-here, and now she'd very nearly done something she would have been ashamed of. Something her family would have been ashamed of. And Nana? Oh . . . what would Nana say if she were here?

The thought ached in Marisol's chest, right where her heart should be.

"Mari!" Jake hissed, grabbing her hand.

She jerked back as if she'd been stung. "What? I didn't!"

"What?" Her primo shot her a confused look, then nodded toward the door. "Look who's there, you *did* find him!"

Christopher stood on the threshold. Relief crashed over Marisol, almost dumping her on the ground like the waves at the beach that picked you up and gave you a good sandy tumble back to shore. She *had* tracked Christopher Creaturo here!

Hadn't she?

It would be a very big coincidence otherwise, but stranger things had happened since they'd arrived in the World Between Blinks and there was no time left to wonder. The ledger sat open in Christopher's hand. He was wielding that very same ballpoint pen he'd used to scratch out Nessie and the London house and probably the USS *Seawolf* too.

Uh-oh.

"Maybe we can sneak around the edge of the room, get close before he sees us," Jake whispered as he eased back behind a large potted plant. "You go left and I'll go right—"

Before the plan was finished, Christopher's pen struck.

The Amber Room vanished!

Ladies and gentlemen who'd been admiring the painstaking mosaics found themselves staring at air. The servant shrieked, his platter of cakes flying over what was now just a vast stretch of desert. Oz enjoyed the sugary shower—jaws wide open. Everything else was chaos. Shoes stampeding. Guards yelling. Sand flying.

"He's getting away again!" This time when Jake grabbed Marisol, she didn't shrink back.

They ran toward where the door used to be. But so did dozens of other people—they were caught up in a mass of hoop skirts and hysteria, and Marisol lost sight of Christopher almost immediately. Hand in hand with Jake, she plunged in the direction she'd last seen him.

The ground started shaking—same as it had next to

the scavenger—and Marisol looked down to see another crack forming.

There.

Blink.

Gone.

Blink.

There.

The tear stretched from the center of what used to be the Amber Room, through Nefertiti's palace, over the dunes, all the way to the scavenger's thin spot. Many of the courtiers saw it too. They clucked and scattered, sweeping the children away from the crevasse in their silky wave of panic.

"The World is falling apart!"

"The Amber Room is gone!"

"Ack! My wig!"

Marisol's throat felt straw-thin when she pulled out her monocle to get a steadier view of the damage. This crack was just as see-through as the previous ones. Past the sands was another palace—Catherine's, no doubt— where more tourists stood with more cameras, taking pictures of the sudden doubling of amber. The old and new were colliding, the walls twice as thick as they had been, jagged cracks running across them.

Christopher had sent the Amber Room back to Russia.

Jake paused too—monocle to big blue eye. "This tear

looks way bigger than the others, doesn't it?"

"WHO DARES TO STEAL FROM NEFERNEF-ERUATEN NEFERTITI, GREAT OF PRAISES, LADY OF GRACE, SWEET OF LOVE, MOST POWERFUL QUEEN IN THE LAND OF THE LOST?" This voice was thunder and sun, scathing everyone who heard it.

The crowd around Marisol and Jake froze, then dropped to their knees.

Not wanting to stand out, the cousins did too.

Even Oz slunk to his belly when the queen appeared in the doorway.

She looked like a statue brought to life. Her cheekbones were high, and her eyes were rimmed with furious black makeup. Her wig was a deep blue, matching the tall crown that sat atop her head. A serpent reared up near its golden base—Marisol couldn't think of a more perfect animal to match the woman's expression.

"WILL NO ONE SPEAK?" Queen Nefertiti's pleated gown spit sand when she turned. "WHO IS TO ANSWER FOR THIS?"

Marisol's palms went cold and clammy. She was very glad they *weren't* holding the piece of amber she'd been eyeing. . . .

Jake's hand shot up. "Um, we know!"

¿Está loco? Everything inside Marisol shriveled—mummified—when Nefertiti looked at them.

"Do you now? What is your name, boy?" The queen's eyes narrowed, flicking to his hourglass. "Assuming you know it?"

"My name is Jake Beruna, Your—Your Majesty. This is my cousin Marisol Contreras Beruna, and this is our companion, Oz. We've been chasing this man, you see. His name is Christopher Creaturo, and he stole a ledger from the Curators." At least her primo was smart enough to omit *their* helping hands from the story. "He's been crossing items out of the book and sending them back to the, uh, other world! We've been chasing him all over the World Between Blinks, trying to stop him."

"Have you?" the queen asked dubiously. "But you're so tiny and your legs are so short, and the Curators don't often surrender their control. Why would they ask *you* to chase this thief?"

Um . . .

Jake's expression struggled between the truth and anything else. If they admitted it was their fault Christopher had the ledger—and therefore, their fault that Nefertiti's beloved Amber Room was gone—that wouldn't be good. And it certainly wasn't smart to say, "The Curators sent us because they didn't want the Administrator finding out they let someone steal a ledger in the first place." Getting the Curators into trouble might change their minds about sending the cousins home.

Marisol decided on a distraction. It usually worked when her parents asked difficult questions. "Your Majesty, I saw Christopher in the doorway just a minute ago." She sounded much surer than she felt. "If we hurry we can catch him and find a way to get your treasure back."

Queen Nefertiti's nose wrinkled as she considered this, showing off a small bump Marisol hadn't noticed before. "No. Guards!"

This was it! They were going to get thrown into a dungeon to rot for the rest of their immortal lives! If ancient Egypt *had* dungeons . . . Maybe they'd get locked in a tower instead, like those princes in England.

But when men with spears answered the queen's call, she did not have the children whisked away. "Gather the Ninth Roman Legion and the Lost Army of Cambyses and send them searching for this Christopher Creaturo. He has one of the Curators' ledgers in his possession."

"He's dressed like a Curator too!" Jake piped in. "He might even try to pretend to be an official. He's crafty like that."

"We should go with your soldiers to help them!" Marisol added.

"No." Nefertiti's blue wig swayed as she shook her head. "My armies will move faster without children attached. This is a matter best left to grown-ups. Oh—don't look so crestfallen! You'll both be richly rewarded for helping me catch this criminal."

Richly rewarded? Marisol's insides glittered with the possibilities. Diamonds? A crown? Something valuable enough to save the beach house? If Nefertiti *gave* it to them, that was completely different from stealing.

"All we need is the ledger," Jake said quickly. "We're supposed to return it to the Curators personally."

He was being smart, securing their way home. Wasn't that exactly what she'd wanted when she feared she'd let treasure lead her magnet fingers here?

Still, Marisol had to fight the urge to stomp on his foot and shut him up. They could ask for the ledger *and* something shiny, couldn't they?

The queen nodded to Jake. "I'll give you the ledger once the thief is caught and my Amber Room is restored. In the meantime, you shall be my guests of honor: feasting with the rest of the royals and sleeping on the finest silks this side of the Unknown!"

Jake shot Marisol a glance. He looked . . . worried. Christopher was getting away yet again! But, she reasoned, it *would* be nice to let someone else do the chasing for a change. Aside from their nap on the *Baychimo*, the children had been going nonstop. Silk sheets would feel nice on Marisol's aching calves.

"We would be honored," she answered. "Thank you, Your Majesty."

"Yeah," Jake mumbled. "Thanks."

Oz barked his gratitude, a dollop of icing still stuck to his nose.

For now, they were staying.

12

JAKE

NEFERTITI'S COURT KNEW HOW TO PARTY!

That evening was the fanciest feast Jake had ever been to, and he'd attended his fair share of embassy "shindigs" with his mom. Lost royals and nobility and dignitaries from a long stretch of centuries gathered in a high-pillared hall. Trays of exquisite snacks were ferried about by unimpressed servants, while stories of power and foul play were shared across the long tables. Being a royal—particularly a lost one—seemed to involve lots of backstabbing.

Jake and Marisol nibbled on soft, buttery slices of Ansault pear, their eyes wide and ears eager. There was a lot to take in. Names included.

"Nice to meet you!" A gentleman with an Austrian accent and a sloping chin smiled at the cousins. "I'm

Giovanni Nepomuceno Maria Annunziata Giuseppe Giovanni Batista Ferdinando Baldassare Luigi Gonzaga Pietro Alessandrino Zanobi Anton—"

"Really, Johann!" Though the boy who said this looked closer to their age, his face was chiseled. Almost a marble bust, if not for his warm brown skin and tumbling black curls. "They'll fall asleep before you finish!"

The man with the endless name sighed, deflated. "Some people call me Archduke Johann Salvator. Even more call me Johann."

"How can you remember such a long name?" Jake wondered.

"It's mine," the archduke said simply. "To keep it that way, I recite it every morning, noon, and night."

"That sounds like a lot of work." Jake glanced down at his hourglass. The charm felt heavier than usual, so heavy that he wondered one more time if it'd be so bad to let go of a grain. Just one. A teary goodbye to a friend, maybe?

Marco in Italy. Or Silvie in France. Or Freya in Australia.

Then again, he'd had so many. . . .

Johann followed Jake's gaze. "You've got to stay on top of your sands so they don't get dragged down. Or rather, dispatched to the Great Library of Alexandria. That's where the Administrator archives them."

Marisol furrowed her brow. "The Administrator? We've heard that name before, but who *is* the Administrator?"

"He's the first Curator. Their boss." Johann's sloped chin went sharp. "Queen Nefertiti doesn't like him much, and this *is* her court, so we should probably change the subject. Now, I heard you just visited the underwater cities. How were they?"

"Watery." Jake was too distracted tucking his necklace back under his collar to answer properly.

The archduke was undeterred. "I love the water! It was the sea that brought me to the World in the first place! I was sailing near Cape Horn, when my ship was caught in the most incredible storm. Waves thrashed our bow and fog swirled everywhere, though I thought it was odd that the winds didn't tear the clouds apart. When we sailed out the other side, well—later on I learned it hadn't been fog at all, but the Unknown. Was your journey similar?"

"Less dramatic," Marisol said. "We did meet a chicken that lived in a car, though."

She and Jake supplied the details as the statuesque boy tossed Oz pieces of meat seasoned with silphium. The Tasmanian tiger seemed to appreciate the herb's leek-like taste, even going so far as to lick the prince's hands clean. He *was* a prince, as it turned out.

"Alexander Helios," he said politely when Johann prompted him to introduce himself. "Son of Queen Cleopatra and Marc Antony. Also, a friend of Oz."

Queen Cleopatra? Jake tried not to let his jaw drop at yet another big name from history class!

"Oz?" A suntanned man with neatly combed cirrus-cloud hair looked up from his discussion, then laughed. "Oh, I thought you meant Australia. But you were talking to my fellow countryman here." He leaned down to scratch the back of Oz's neck, and the thylacine's tail quivered with pleasure. "Harold Holt," he said. "Australian prime minister. Well, I was before I went for a swim off Cheviot Beach. The surf was so rough that I got myself all tumbled in it, didn't know which way was up or down. Kelp was everywhere. . . . When I finally surfaced, I found myself here!"

Everyone here seemed very eager to share their stories . . . to talk and talk and keep their memories stuck. *Like a starfish to a rock*, the *Baychimo*'s captain had said. It made Jake's lids droop. He fought off a leaden yawn.

This did not go unnoticed by Prime Minister Holt. "You two seem ready for bed," he said.

"We can wait up," Jake protested. "The soldiers will return soon, won't they? I mean, shouldn't they be back by now?"

"Don't you worry!" Alexander Helios waved away his

words. "We are speaking of the best scouts of the Army of Cambyses, and the Ninth Legion of the mighty Roman army."

Marisol eyed the prince thoughtfully. "They must have already gotten lost at least once, or they wouldn't be here."

"Their navigating has improved since then," he promised. "Rest, and let the work be done."

In the end, there was nothing to do but take his advice and wait. The children were shown to their room and brought big beaten-bronze bowls of water that cast rippling candlelight reflections all over the ceiling. They dipped in cloths and scrubbed themselves clean, and then—to Jake's not-so-slight embarrassment—the servants brought a new set of bowls, because the first round of water was dingy gray.

With the exception of Amelia's jacket, which Marisol refused to let out of her sight, the cousins' clothes were taken away to be washed. The white linen robes left in their place were cool and airy—perfect for a desert night.

The bed Queen Nefertiti had provided was enormous, with plenty of room for them both. Its silk sheets were soft enough to melt in. After a moment's consideration, Jake laid the leather jacket across the foot of the mattress for Oz, so their friend could jump onto the slippery silk without sliding off the other side. *Zoom, plop!* Besides, letting their companion sleep on the floor seemed like bad manners.

"I really hope they're back with the ledger when we wake up," Marisol murmured.

"They will be," said Jake, with more confidence than he felt.

Oz settled into his jacket bed with a grunt while Marisol nibbled her lip. "Jake, if she offers us a reward again . . ."

That wasn't what Jake had been expecting. "Huh?"

"She's a queen!" Marisol gestured at their bedchamber's luxuries: incense, ornately carved wood, plush rugs. "A *fancy* queen! She could spare us a diamond or something, and she wouldn't even notice it was gone. We could save Nana's beach house if we had enough treasure like that. Nobody would have to sell the place if there was money for a new roof!"

Jake sighed. "Oh, Mari. . . ."

His cousin's cheeks ruddied. Her eyes flashed. "I—It's hard to concentrate on finding Christopher when there's so much treasure around." She looked down at her hands, voice softening. "It would be nice not to worry."

"Then don't." This came out more harshly than he'd intended, but he was tired. So tired. "Even if we *did* bring back enough money to save the beach house, our parents don't want the trouble of keeping it up. And Nana's not there anymore. Sometimes . . . sometimes you just have to let things go and make a clean break."

Tears stained Marisol's freshly scrubbed face. "A clean break is still broken," she said stiffly. "You think I'm holding on too tight? Well, I think you're giving up too easy, letting go of a place we love! Of a *person* we love!"

That shut him right up. His throat closed, and it was impossible to get words out. Barely possible to get a breath *in*. Perhaps he did give up on things too quickly, before the letting go could hurt. But Marisol hadn't had to leave her life behind like he did. She hadn't said goodbye to her house and her friends and her school over and over again, with everyone promising to keep in touch and everyone knowing they probably wouldn't.

Oz whimpered, curling up as small as possible in the children's silence.

Candles shivered, and Jake didn't know if he'd apologize even if he *could* speak. How could you be sorry for who you were? How could he hold on without getting hurt?

After another quiet moment, Marisol softened, wrapping her arms around Jake's neck and making the front of his robe damp with tears. He returned the hug automatically.

"Oh, Jake," she said, sniffing a little. "I didn't mean

it like that. Just, don't you want to fight for the house? Some of our best memories are there, even *after* Nana. Do you remember the night after her funeral? We lit that big bonfire on the beach, and we all wrote our messages to her on paper lanterns and sent them up to the stars?"

"A bonfire?" Jake blinked into her tousled black hair, his own head giving an uneasy shake. "I—I don't remember that. I think maybe Mom and I must have gone home by then."

"No," Marisol protested, pulling away. "No, you helped me tie the string on my message. You said you learned the knot from a man on a boat in Indonesia!"

Jake stared at her, feeling his heart punch hard at his chest. He *had* learned to tie a knot from a man like that—he could still see his face, the crinkle of his smile, his nimble brown fingers in the sun. But he was sure he'd never taught it to Marisol beside a bonfire on the beach. All their fires at Nana's house had been smaller, for cookouts in the backyard, for one very specific reason.

"The city doesn't allow bonfires on Folly Beach," he reminded his cousin.

"I know. We got special permission from the city council because Nana contributed so much to the community," Marisol said tightly. "The mayor was there! Don't you remember?"

But he didn't.

He *didn't*.

"Jake, I—" Marisol suddenly broke off, her eyes fastened to his necklace.

"What?" Jake whispered.

Marisol reached for his hourglass, pulling it out from under his white linen robe and gently lifting it between them.

A grain of sand had slid from the top and was anchored in the bottom half.

"That's where your memory went," his cousin whispered.

Jake's insides felt cold. He couldn't even tell the memory was gone—would never have known if Marisol hadn't told him. "Oh . . ."

He wasn't sure what else to say. He certainly couldn't tell Marisol that he'd *wanted* to lose a memory, never mind the fact that this was the wrong teary goodbye— he'd wanted to forget the last sight of a friend he'd never see again. Not Nana's memorial.

Jake didn't feel one ounce lighter when he stared at the grain. "I guess it's been archived by the Administrator in the Library of Alexandria," he whispered. "That's what Johann said, right?"

Marisol nodded grimly. "But the Curators told us that their boss wouldn't notice until we lost at least two pieces of sand. We won't be cataloged yet. We still have time to escape this place." She dropped the hourglass, taking his hand in hers. "In the morning we'll have the ledger back. ¡Sólo lo sé!"

The two of them settled down to sleep, but Jake's thoughts whirled for a long, long time after Marisol's breath slowed.

Would the Curators be able to send them home after all of the damage Christopher had caused?

Would Jake's bonfire memory come back when they left the World Between Blinks? Or was it lost forever?

Is this how it would feel, to slowly become more like the woman in the underwater city? *And yet,* a tiny voice buzzed inside his head, *if you could lose all your bad memories so painlessly, wouldn't it be worth giving up a few of the good as well?*

When he finally managed to sleep, his dreams were uneasy.

Trickling in dozens of sand-strewn pieces.

Vanishing back into black.

As if they were never there at all . . .

The next morning, things were even worse.

The bedraggled army scouts limped in after breakfast, and none of the groups had Christopher. Two of the Romans had tried to arrest another Roman scout in the dark, mistaking him for Christopher, and living up to its name, the Lost Army of Cambyses had gotten . . . well, lost.

"There were too many trails!" Jake overheard an officer explaining. "Footprints kept appearing out of nowhere. They led us in zigzags and loop-the-loops, and at one point one of our men was doing the foxtrot!"

Needless to say, they'd returned empty-handed.

Marisol looked like she was on the verge of tears, shoving aside her empty plate and flexing her fingers into fists.

"Can you feel where Christopher went?" Jake asked.

She felt *something.* He could tell by the way Marisol's eyebrows dove together when she glanced at a silver serving platter. It held a box of (delicious) Mayflower Donuts, which had a strange rhyme scrawled on the cardboard.

THE OPTIMIST'S CREED

As you ramble on through life, brother,
Whatever be your goal,
Keep your eye upon the doughnut
And not upon the hole!

Marisol stared at this poem, blinking back tears and clenching her hands. "I don't know," she said finally.

"You do!" Jake assured her. "You've found Christopher

with your magnet fingers twice before."

"But what if this last time was a fluke, and I was really just tracking treasure? We can't afford to go in the wrong direction." Her eyes darted over to his hourglass, their meaning clear.

They were back on the hunt with no time to waste. *Even less*, Jake thought guiltily, *since I chose to forget Nana's bonfire*. He shifted so Marisol couldn't see the fallen grain of sand, his monocle clinking against the timepiece. *Eyes ahead, don't look back.*

"We can't afford to sit here either." They had to keep moving, so Jake stood. "Come on, I have an idea!"

"¿Qué?"

"You'll see!"

He grabbed a cinnamon doughnut to go, tearing off bits for Oz until there was no hole at all. The thylacine followed the cousins' trail of crumbs through several court-yards, up to the top of the highest medieval castle turret. Wind whipped past them, sprinkling Jake's last doughnut piece with more sand than cinnamon. He tossed it to Oz and looked out over the battlements. The Curator was right. It was *ever-stretching*, a three-hundred-sixty-degree view of desert, desert, desert. Plus a small glimpse of *dessert*, though Oz had nearly finished that.

The dunes that had led them to Amarna flattened off just after the swallowed city. Half sand, half sky, all shimmering with heat from here to the farthest horizon.

Marisol shielded her eyes, taking this in. "What are we doing up here, Jake?"

He wasn't *completely* sure. Hopefully his plan would work. . . . "Which way are your fingers pulling?"

Doubt creased Marisol's mouth, but she lifted a finger to the skyline opposite Portus.

"That's just sand. . . ." Jake's heart sank, but he narrowed his eyes and stared as hard as he could. Was there some clue out there he couldn't see? Slowly he traced a path to the horizon, and then . . .

Wait a minute.

Was that . . . ?

Though it was hard to see for sure with the mirage-painted air, Jake thought he saw the rippling golden sand change color at the very edge of the horizon, as if someone had drawn a line with a ruler. On one side was desert, and on the other, a rich, green band.

"Is that a jungle?" Marisol guessed, squinting at the distortion too. "It's the right color."

Here goes nothing. . . . When Jake lifted the monocle to his eye, the desert that had seemed so barren began blooming with script. He spotted a *Lesser Bilby* and a *Bubal Hartebeest*, alongside the quasi-mythical *Lost Ship of the Desert*. While it was tempting to read through the vessel's many exits and reentries into the World Between

195

Blinks, Jake forced his focus past the ghost ship. The monocle seemed to magically track his gaze, telling him that he was looking at *Sections of the Amazon Rainforest circa 1970—NONRESIDENTIAL, EXPLORE AT YOUR OWN RISK.*

"You're right, Mari! It is a jungle—" He stopped short, words all tangled in his throat. The script on his lens had gone red: *Christopher Creaturo, July 4, 1949—WARNING: DO NOT ENGAGE WITHOUT PROPER PERMIT.*

"It's him!" Jake croaked. "It's Christopher!"

The man's white suit was still in their line of sight, but just barely. Without the monocles, there was no way the cousins would have spotted him: smaller than a dust mote and flickering in the heat.

"Where?" Marisol scrambled for her own vision charm, then gasped. "He's *old*! And he's so far away!"

"We need to reach the jungle before he does," Jake said.

"That'd be nice," she ventured. "But Christopher's been on the go since last night. There's no way we can catch up with him."

"Not on foot," he agreed, grinning.

"Then what . . . ?" Now it was *her* turn to grin. "Oh, Jake!" She reached inside the pocket of Amelia's jacket and pulled out the walkie-talkie. "¡Eres un genio!"

"Let's see if it works," Jake replied.

Marisol held the walkie-talkie to her mouth and

pressed the button on its side, staring into the sky as if Amelia might appear at any moment. "Come in, Amelia, come in, Amelia, this is Marisol and Jake! Do you read?"

There was a stretchy, staticky pause, full of nothing but the radio channel's hiss and Oz's high-strung whine. It was only when the thylacine butted Jake in the back of the knees that Jake realized he was holding his breath.

Then, just as he began to worry, the radio crackled to life. "Hey there, friends!" came Amelia's cheerful voice. "Great to hear from you! What's cooking?"

"A *lot*," Marisol replied. "We're at Queen Nefertiti's palace right now. We were wondering if you had time to give us and Oz a lift?"

Again there was the pause, and then Amelia's voice crackled through. "Sure can! There's a landing strip right next to Amarna. I'll be coming in from Roanoke, so I'll see you there in a jiffy! Anything for an adventure! Earhart out!"

Jake swept Marisol up in a hug so tight that she squeaked as her feet came off the ground. "This is it!" he said. "We're finally going to be one step ahead of him. This is the moment the tide turns in our favor, Mari!"

"I hope so!" She hugged him back just as hard. "It's just that, we still don't know exactly where Christopher is going, or why he's sending stuff that was lost in the 1940s back to our world. . . ."

"No," Jake admitted. "But once Amelia flies us to

that jungle, we'll be a step ahead of Christopher. We can find a way to block his path and ask him what he's up to."

Marisol's face turned pensive. "How? Fallen trees? Quicksand? A diversion of doughnuts?"

"That last one just might work," he joked. "Though we'll have to wait and see where we land before we come up with a plan."

His cousin nodded.

"Tranquilo con la ruta," she whispered, mostly to herself.

As the trio headed back down to the palace courtyard, they found that Queen Nefertiti was waiting for them. She reminded Jake—strangely—of water. The way her sapphire crown flowed into her wig, the way that spilled onto her shoulders, the way those flowed into her gown. It was elegant and refreshing and so very different from yesterday's first impression.

"I was hoping to catch you three before you left," she said, her voice like a ripple across a still pond.

"We've got a lead on Christopher Creaturo, and we're going to follow it!" Marisol explained. "We'll do our best to get your Amber Room back."

Queen Nefertiti smiled. "I'm beginning to see why the Curators put their faith in you. It wasn't fair of me to judge your spirit by your outward appearance. Your determination is at least ten times your height!"

"We're not that short for our age. . . ." Jake found

himself fighting not to stand on tiptoe. "And Mari's right. We'll find the ledger. We'll fix everything Christopher broke."

"I know." Nefertiti's hands, which had previously been crossed behind her back, flashed in front of the cousins.

Marisol's gasp could be heard all the way to the ocean.

Jake couldn't believe what he was seeing.

The queen was holding a diamond. A BIG diamond. That kind of jewel wouldn't just fix the Berunas' beach house, it could probably buy the entire island of Folly Beach. Plus some.

Sunlight sprayed into rainbows as Queen Nefertiti offered this treasure to them. "A little Tasmanian tiger told me you were in need of a jewel. This is the Great Mogul Diamond. It's been in my collection for more than three hundred years. Long enough for me to get bored with it. Consider this your preemptive reward for restoring the Amber Room to my palace."

"Oz told you?" Jake shot a startled stare at the thylacine.

His bark sounded a little like a chuckle; his teeth looked very much like a grin.

"In his way," Queen Nefertiti amended. "He also pointed out that I came across as rude yesterday. For that, I hope you'll forgive me."

"¡Bueno!" Marisol's hands shot out. Even cupped

together, they dipped with the diamond's weight. "Muchas gracias, Reina Nefertiti."

"You're very welcome," the monarch replied. "Now go and earn it."

How in the worlds are we going to explain an egg-sized diamond to our parents? Jake wondered. Then again, this was a pleasant problem compared to the rest. They could solve it *after* they caught Christopher, reclaimed the ledger, restored the lost treasures, and found their way back home.

Thirty minutes later, the cousins were waiting down by the airstrip. Prime Minister Harold Holt had helped them raid the kitchens, so they had a backpack stuffed with food, which Oz kept nosing as they stood in the shade of a palm tree. Amelia's plane grew from a liquid dot to a blazing silver bird—large enough to read the NR16020 letters on its left wing. It touched down on the airstrip, rattling to a halt in a filmy cloud of dust.

She jumped out with a buoyant wave, and Jake and Marisol filled the pilot in on their adventures as she refueled.

"This Creaturo's a slippery character, that's for sure," she agreed. "Look, I can take you to the Amazon jungle, but I can't land the plane anywhere close. The sand is too loose and the trees are too thick. What I *can* do is show you how to use parachutes. It's not as hard as you think, and you can aim for a clearing."

"What happens if we don't hit a clearing?" Jake asked.

"Well, it hurts a lot more if you hit a tree on the way down," Amelia admitted. "But you'll be okay, I'm a great teacher. We'll strap Oz onto you, Jake. You're the bigger of the two of you."

The cousins exchanged a very long glance. Jake knew Marisol would punch him if he said out loud that he was worried about her parachuting, but she *was* smaller than he was. Then again, what was it Nefertiti said about height? *Don't judge a spirit by outward appearance. . . .* Marisol might be younger, but that didn't make her any less strong. Any less brave. She was just as much a partner in this adventure as Jake was.

If they were going to jump out of a flying plane, they'd do it together.

With a gulp, Jake nodded.

Amelia's parachuting class involved a lot of jumping off a low wall into a pile of sand that was definitely softer than the ground in the Amazon would be. Jake did his best to pay careful attention, trying not think too much about what would happen if they landed wrong.

Half an hour later they were packed into the back of Amelia's plane, Marisol in front of Jake and Oz sitting on his lap, strapped to his front. The thylacine gave his cheek an encouraging lick as they went *bump-bump-bump-rattle* along the tightly packed sand.

Then, with a stomach-lurching hop, they were up in the air and climbing into the perfect blue sky above the rippling desert.

Next stop, the Amazon jungle.

13

MARISOL

UP, UP, AND AWAY!

Soaring with Amelia Earhart was noisier than Marisol imagined it would be. The *Flying Laboratory*—as Amelia called her silver plane—was LOUD. Even with two wads of cotton stuffed inside her ears, Marisol heard every gear's angry hum. Every screw's fight to stay tight.

Jake tried yelling something, but propellers ate his words as the ground rattled away. Marisol leaned forward to get a better view. All of the Lockheed's passenger windows had been sealed, Amelia explained, for her flight around their old world. The front windows were clear—of course.

Their pilot beamed through the glass as she guided their plane higher and the World Between Blinks became bite-sized. Harbor boats looked like floating leaves. Queen Nefertiti's palace turned into squares and swirls. When Marisol checked through her monocle, she could still see the crack Christopher had caused snaking through anthill dunes. Miles and miles away, the Amazon thickened the horizon with its lush green swathe of trees, cut down in the regular world and reappeared in this one.

Hopefully, they'd reach the jungle before Christopher did.

There was so much to fix.

Marisol glanced back at her cousin. Freckles popped out of Jake's blanched face, and his knuckles whitened around his parachute harness. His hourglass dangled over the chest strap.

Its fallen grain hadn't moved.

One memory. Gone.

After last night's discovery, Marisol had been checking her own timepiece obsessively. There was no change. She and Jake had arrived in the World Between Blinks together. So why were their sands dropping at different speeds? Why did people they met remember all fifteen of their names—*cough, Johann, cough*—while the dancing woman in Kitezh's square couldn't even hold on to one? She'd looked more modern than the Austrian archduke, with her red lipstick and trim skirt.

Timing must not determine how fast the amnesia spread.

Amelia had that theory about how being remembered back home helped some of the lost last longer, and Johann had talked about fighting to *stay on top of your sands*, but studying Jake's charm made Marisol wonder if maybe the opposite could also be true. Maybe some people wanted to forget.

Wanted to *let go*.

The *Flying Laboratory* hit an air pocket, tossing Marisol's stomach like pizza dough. She hated feeling so unsteady. Being calm on the route was way more complicated when it involved cracking worlds and a sad, sad primo.

After another bout of turbulence, she felt for the Mogul Diamond in her pocket, gripping until its facets dented her palm. Holding on to the jewel meant holding on to Nana's beach house.

And all of Nana's memories.

She squeezed the diamond tighter, even tighter, but it didn't feel real. When Queen Nefertiti had placed this treasure in her hands, Marisol hoped they'd go back to a solid, sure state. *North is north. Lost is found. ✕ marks the spot.*

Christopher Creaturo is here.

But she still couldn't tell if her fingers sparkled *down* for her pocket or for the desert below or for some unseen gold mine beneath that. What if the Mogul Diamond wasn't enough? What if Jake was right and their parents would sell Nana's beach house no matter what? What if—

A tap on Marisol's shoulder brought her attention back to the cockpit. Amelia grinned, pointing out the window at a passing pterodactyl.

It would've taken the cousins a long, hot, sandy day to walk to the jungle—over so many dunes—but after only a few minutes Amelia waved them toward the back of the plane. They climbed over old fuel tanks and unlatched the rear door. A wall of cold wind pushed back, smooshing Oz's ears sideways and turning Jake's hair into a helmet.

Trees began dotting the ground below.

And . . . was that a speck of white, trekking across the rippling sand toward the tree line?

Marisol leaned forward to get a better look, but Jake caught her harness.

"I THINK IT'S CHRISTOPHER!" She could feel her lungs and lips shaping the words, but they didn't make it out. "DOWN THERE!"

Jake frowned. The dot was already gone, vanished into the jungle. Below was a thick carpet of green: trees and trees and trees and trees. Golden threads of river tied them all together. It looked just like the stretches of jungle Marisol flew over back home.

Amelia signaled from the cockpit.

It was time to jump.

Jake looked so pale he was almost see-through. Oz wriggled in the boy's harness, eager to get the leap over with. The longer they waited, the farther they'd have to trek back through the Amazon to find Christopher. Marisol gave her cousin a thumbs-up encouragement. He mirrored the gesture and stepped out into thin air.

With another pat to make sure the Mogul Diamond was secure, Marisol threw herself after him.

Skydiving didn't actually feel like diving at all. There was no sudden drop of the stomach, no wild flailing. In fact, Marisol found that if she spread out her arms, they acted like wings, pushing her in any direction she wanted to go.

She flew toward Jake and Oz. Full grin. Her primo's teeth were out too—more of a grimace.

Count to twenty, then deploy your chute! Amelia had instructed.

Marisol found her cord and pulled.

There was a quick snap as the harness dug into her armpits. Jake's pack unfurled too. White fabric billowed everywhere, and they were no longer falling, but floating. The *Flying Laboratory* buzzed past—Amelia waving from the controls—before vanishing back over the horizon.

The trio drifted closer to the jungle, feet and paws dangling. There didn't seem to be much clear landing space below . . . except for the river. A massive creature stood on its bank, drinking. It looked like a guinea pig—if guinea pigs were the size of cows with doglike tails.

Marisol didn't know if there were ancient, extinct species of piranhas or crocodiles in the World Between Blinks, but if there were, they had to be bigger too. Right? Just like the megalodon. . . .

"We should try to land in the trees!" she yelled.

Jake cocked his head. "WHAT?"

"THE TREES!" She pulled the cotton from her ears and shouted again. "AMAZON WATER CAN HAVE LOTS OF TEETH! ¡ES PELIGROSO!"

He nodded, steering away from the water.

It was a brambly landing.

Parachute cords tangled with vines as Marisol found a good branch to balance on. Jake landed in a nearby tree. Thankfully, they weren't too far off the ground and it was an easy climb down, especially for Oz, who stayed strapped into the harness while Jake lowered the thylacine to the jungle floor.

"Fue divertido," Marisol said once all three of them were safely on the ground.

"Fun?" Color was just now returning to Jake's face. "You thought that was fun?"

"More fun than trekking across a wasteland." She brushed bark off her jacket. "Oops, I never gave this back to Amelia. . . ."

The walkie-talkie was still in the pocket, along with the little green jar of smelling salts. And the giant diamond. And the occasional stray lint ball. Below these, Nana's sugar spoon *clinked* against countless other items in the pockets of Marisol's shorts.

No wonder she felt so off balance.

"That's okay," said Jake. "We might need another lift back to the Crystal Palace once we get the ledger from Christopher."

Speaking of . . . "I think I saw him walking into the jungle from the desert!"

"Really?" Jake brightened. "Did you check your vision charm to make sure?"

"No. The plane was too shaky." Confirming Christopher's identity with the monocle would've meant letting go of the Mogul Diamond, and Marisol wasn't about to admit that. "But who else would be walking through the desert in a white suit? If we head back that way we might be able to catch him!"

Her cousin frowned. "Which way *is* that way?"

She thought for a moment, wondering if she dared test her magnet fingers. They hadn't always pointed true since she'd arrived in the World Between Blinks. Could she trust them? It was better to depend on less supernatural senses. They'd spun an awful lot in the sky, but if the river was over there—and it was, she could hear its mighty rush—then the desert had to be in the opposite direction. "Back through these trees."

"Okay!" Jake adjusted their food pack, his face back to its signature *keep going* expression. "Here goes nothing!"

Marisol had been to her own world's version of the Amazon several times. It was a short plane ride from the mountains of La Paz, and a fun getaway from the city's dusty traffic. Mom loved looking at all of the bright flowers, Dad had a fascination with the even brighter birds, and Victor enjoyed making faces at the monkeys.

This jungle was different. Wilder. They didn't have a guide to clear the trail with a machete or to point out different animals along the way. What was it about this place that was so . . . *oh*! In the middle of asking herself the question, Marisol knew. This was a part of the World Between Blinks that wasn't cramped by the Curators' filing systems—a part that grew green and vibrant and every which way.

Marisol loved how *alive* she felt walking through it.

Oz did his best to scout, leading them on the easiest path nose-first. Still, it was slow going. Sweat swirled across their faces, and insects screamed down to buzz in their ears and sting at their skin, and their legs were scratched pink. The sun crept through the leaves as they walked—higher, then lower.

"Are you sure we're going in the right direction?" Jake asked as they paused for their umpteenth water break.

She had been. But—between her unreliable fingers and Jake's memory loss—Marisol wasn't *sure* about anything anymore. She'd never felt more lost than she did at this very moment. Not even when she'd sobbed on the steps of the inside-out lighthouse, with that sassy chicken clucking back.

It'd be easy to cry again, here where stranger, louder birds called and shadows slithered through overhead leaves. But Marisol knew that wasn't what Nana would do.

"We can't give up yet," she said, determined.

Jake flinched. "That's not what I meant."

That's not what *she'd* meant either. Marisol took a long drink, then screwed the cap back onto their canteen. "We're walking away from the sunset, which means the desert is still ahead. We could run into Christopher Creaturo at any minute!"

"What if we've already passed him?" her primo wondered. "It's a big thick jungle, which means our monocles are useless. Are your fingers still pointing straight ahead?"

It was Marisol's turn to flinch. "I'm not a compass, Jake."

"Of course not!" he protested. "Mari, I only meant . . ." But he trailed off. His face wandered too, as if he were deep in thought.

Or, Marisol suddenly feared, *deep in losing one.* Her eyes flicked down to Jake's hourglass. There was still only a single speck of sand at the bottom—too small for what it really was. Had he wanted to forget the bonfire for Nana? That night with all of those memorial lanterns going up in flame over the Atlantic Ocean, constellations just for their grandmother? Marisol had never seen anything so beautiful and sad before, and she would never, *ever* want to forget it.

If Jake had let go of Nana's goodbye first thing, so easily . . .

Well, then, what was next?

Marisol held her breath, but Jake's remaining sand didn't fall.

Her lungs started to burn.

She exhaled slowly. Getting angry wouldn't do them any good. "If we want to get home, we should be calm on the route."

"Huh—?" Her primo blinked. "Sorry, I was watching Oz. What've you got there, bud?"

The Tasmanian tiger had planted himself by a large leaf and was sniffing at its inhabitant: a lumpy, bright orange toad.

"I wouldn't touch that if I were you!" A British voice rang out, clear as a bell. "That amphibian is one of the most poisonous creatures alive!"

Marisol and Jake turned to find a man emerging from the underbrush. He was dressed like an explorer—from his broad-brimmed hat to his worn boots. A crumpled handkerchief fluttered from his hand.

He waved it toward them with a reassuring grin. "It's all right, young travelers! I'm a friend! Are you lost?"

"Yes," Jake answered.

"Isn't everyone lost here?" Marisol pointed out.

The man stroked his dark moustache. "I suppose so. But there are different types of lost, you see. Explorers lose themselves on purpose. The Unknown feeds our bones and fuels our souls. You two, on the other hand, look disoriented. Is there some place I can help you find?"

"We're searching for some*one* actually—" Marisol paused when she realized Oz was still investigating the venomous reptile. "Stop that, Oz! You'll get hurt!"

The newcomer took a closer look. "Ah—I was mistaken. Sometimes I forget which Amazon I'm in. This isn't a golden poison frog but a golden toad. It wouldn't hurt a fly."

"Don't toads eat flies?" Jake asked.

"That they do!" Wrinkles gathered around the man's eyes as he laughed. "You've both got vim and vigor, that's for sure. Colonel Percy Fawcett, at your service."

Introductions were exchanged. Oz wandered over to a cluster of trees, his snout tilted skyward. Marisol was about to explain their search again when she realized exactly what the thylacine was staring at.

One of the trunks was *moving.*

And it had scales.

"Is—wait, what *is* that? A snake?" Her theory about extinct things being bigger looked right: the creature was almost forty feet long. It could swallow an elephant, no problem.

"A Titanoboa cerrejonensis. Amazing to look at, scary to see." Percy backed away from the slithering giant. "Still, I'd rather take my odds out here with these beasts than be chained to some Curator's clipboard. Life is so much bigger beneath the trees . . . plus I have some T-rex repellent back at camp. Come. We'll be safe there."

They didn't have to think twice about following him.

The explorer's camp was tucked into a rare clearing. A fire burned inside a ring of packs and mules. Two younger men crouched by the flames and another sat on a log, while a fourth gentleman carved the letter L into a nearby tree.

"Watch your step!" Percy warned as they followed him through the last of the underbrush, past the woodcarver. "Herr Ludwig Leichhardt here likes to string nets around the perimeter—they kept him safe from beasties in Australia when he was exploring the place."

"We think so anyway. Poor chap's memory has gone

past half-glass!" exclaimed one of the men by the fire, who wore a hat like Percy's and shared the same longish nose. "Who do we have here, Dad?"

"Marisol, Jake, and Oz, meet my son, Jack, and his friend Raleigh, who both joined me on my journey to search for the Lost City of Z!"

Jack and Raleigh were in the middle of sorting through intricate shards of pottery. They paused to nod at the cousins.

Percy Fawcett turned toward the camp's last member. "And this is the intrepid Uemura Naomi, who arrived in the World after summiting Mount McKinley."

Naomi was a middle-aged Japanese man in a red flannel shirt. So far, all the explorers seemed to be men. Perhaps, Marisol mused, lady explorers were too clever to get lost?

He bowed his head in greeting and edged over on his log, offering the cousins a seat. "Welcome, travelers!" His voice was musically deep. "Please call me Naomi. What brings you to Amazonia?"

The T-rex repellent Percy started spraying around the campsite made the whole place smell like peppermint.

"Well . . ." Jake pinched his nostrils. Everything he said sounded sucked through a straw. "It's a long story."

"Always better than a short one." Jack Fawcett grinned.

Marisol and Jake took turns telling their tale, and

even though she'd lived the adventure, it was strange to hear. Drowned cities, a desert queen, and prehistoric monsters? Mom and Dad would *never* believe this. Victor would probably pee his pants with laughter.

The explorers, however, seemed rapt. Except for Herr Leichhardt, who was busy carving a second L onto a second tree.

"So now we're trying to get back the stolen ledger so we can go home," Marisol said.

"Home?" Percy seemed stunned. "Whyever would you want to do that?"

Jack broke in, smiling at his father's surprise. "Not everyone's like you, Dad. You were always more at home in uncharted jungle than in England. Truly, it was the World Between Blinks calling you."

"That it was," his friend Raleigh agreed. "There were always rumors about the Lost City of Z—stories about a piece of pottery someone found deep in the Amazon, about a trace of a building left behind, about piles of treasure beyond counting. Legends that sent men searching the jungle. They always returned empty-handed."

"And now we know why," Jack concluded. "The Lost City of Z had already disappeared on the other side of the Unknown by then. We strove so hard to find it that we slipped through too."

"It's just upriver," Percy said, his eyes shining with all the gold he could not see. "For now, anyway. The Lost

City of Z is more beautiful than anything the imagination could conjure."

"What do you mean, it's upriver *for now*?" Jake asked.

"It refuses to stay still," replied Percy. "Here one day, gone the next."

"Oh, just like Portus." Jake glanced at Marisol. "It keeps moving back to where it wants to be, no matter what the Curators do."

"Just so, my lad," Percy agreed, pleased. "The city doesn't want to be in any one place. It wants to stay lost, and that suits us right down to the ground. The joy is in the chase, you know! We love nothing better than to hunt for it!"

"Really, who'd want to find it properly anyway?" Jack touched the brim of his hat, which looked as if it had been on his head for *quite* some time. "What would you do then? Grow corn? Raise chickens? Miss home?" He shook off this thought. "Once we laid eyes on Dad's city for the first time, we knew there was no going back. We belong here."

Marisol swallowed. This sounded similar to what Jake had said on the ocean floor: *You say the lostness pulls you. I think it follows me, and this time it finally caught up. Like . . . like I belong here, or something.*

What if they *were* in the World Between Blinks because of Jake?

What if he wanted to stay here too?

217

Her cousin leaned close to the fire, drawn in by the explorers' words.

She fought the urge to pull him back. "Aren't any of you sad, being lost?"

Raleigh and the Fawcetts shook their heads. Herr Leichhardt kept hacking away at the trunk.

Naomi picked at his flannel shirt, thoughtful. "Sad?" he asked. "No. Not sad. This is the biggest adventure any of us could ever undertake! Meeting such fascinating people and seeing such strange sights. I, for one, have made it my mission to explore every part of this world."

"It *has* been an adventure," Marisol replied. "But we still want to go home to our family."

Oz, who'd been resting by their log, cried out in warning. Branches snapped. All five explorers whirled around, brandishing whatever they had on hand—pottery shards and the can of T-rex repellent and a pocket knife.

There was another crack.

Then . . .

Thwip!

"By golly!" Jack Fawcett tipped up his hat and squinted into the emerald jungle. Howls erupted from the leaves. "I think Herr Leichhardt's trap actually caught something!"

The German explorer stood by his chiseled initial, looking vaguely surprised. "A dingo?"

"Dingoes don't exist here, mate," Raleigh reminded him. "It could be a dire wolf, though."

"Or a demon duck of doom," Percy said. "It sounds squawky enough."

"I AM NOT A FOWL!"

Marisol's heart forgot to keep beating.

She knew that voice.

So did Jake. Her cousin sprang to his feet and ran for the trees. Marisol followed with the rest of the camp, halting beneath a giant net that looked like it belonged in a scene from an adventure movie.

There, swinging alongside several vines, was Christopher Creaturo.

"LET ME DOWN!" He was upside down, arms and legs poking through at odd angles, unable to see who he was shouting at. "PLEASE!"

Percy Fawcett's head moved in circles, taking stock of the man. "What is a Curator doing so deep in the unzoned zone? With a ledger, no less."

"He's not a Curator!" Marisol and Jake said, almost in unison.

Christopher looked more like a castaway now, anyhow. His suit was less white after a night in the desert and a day in the jungle. His face was red from twisting against the ropes. His expression went limp as soon as he spotted the cousins.

"Oh, hello. Marisol. Jake," he said meekly. "How—how did you get here so fast?" The ledger was already mashed to his chest, but Christopher repositioned to hug the book even tighter. "Ah, those were your parachutes. . . . You jumped out of an airplane to beat me. I shouldn't be surprised. You're both Berunas, through and through. I—I don't suppose you'd like to free me from this net?"

"Why should we?" Jake crossed his arms. "All you've done since the Aral Sea is run away from us!"

"Wait, is this the chap who tricked you?" Percy asked.

"¡Sí!" Marisol's answer burned. "He made us steal the ledger! And he's been using it steal *other* things, like Queen Nefertiti's Amber Room! He's been creating cracks in the Unknown!"

"Cracks?" Christopher frowned.

"Um, yeah," Jake told him. "You're ripping the fabric between the worlds every time you send an object back through the Unknown. The Curators said you could destroy everything."

"Really?" Christopher had a dizzy, almost-sick look on his face, even though the net was swinging less. "Oops."

"*Oops?*" Marisol yelled. "That's all you have to say for yourself?"

"Sounds more like an evil plan than an accident to me," Colonel Fawcett interjected. "What exactly are you

220

up to, my not-so-good fellow? And why have you dragged these poor children into your schemes?"

"I'm not evil," Christopher protested. "And I wasn't trying to *steal* the Amber Room, or any of the other entries I crossed out. Those were test runs to make sure I could safely send my one true love back home. I'm trying to save her, you see."

"But if you're not evil, then why did you trap Jake and me here? We want to return home too!"

"I'm sorry." It was difficult to tell if Christopher was red from embarrassment or because he'd been hanging upside down for so long. "I didn't know the Curators would be so cross with you. I only brought you here because—"

He didn't get a syllable further—both the cousins and all of the explorers raised their voices at once, their words twisting together like a many-headed monster.

"How did you—?"

"My not-so-good sir, you cannot—"

"It's not possible to—"

"What do you mean *brought us here*?"

"How could you—?"

"You can't—"

"What do you mean *BROUGHT US HERE*?"

"I—" Christopher shrank from the clamor of voices, causing his net to twist again. "You have to understand, I desperately needed help. Those of us who've been cataloged by a Curator can't enter the repositories—there was no way I could get an old ledger on my own. I needed someone who'd arrived here recently. So I snuck into the record room where they keep the current ledger, and wrote your names in."

"You wrote their names in?" Percy Fawcett demanded. "Nobody has ever *brought* anybody to the World Between Blinks. Everybody knows the only way here is to slip through the Unknown by accident!"

"I've spent a long time hunting for a way," Christopher replied. "I wouldn't have done it if I'd had *any* other choice. My sister, Lucy, agreed to help me, but she was too frail by the time I had a plan in place. Aside from you two there was no one else in our family who could make the trip so easily—"

"Wait a second," Jake interrupted. "*Our* family?"

Lucy. That was Nana's name. Marisol had heard it said a thousand times, and she'd seen it written down with the middle initial as well: Lucy *C.* Beruna.

The jungle's light shifted as Marisol finally saw Christopher Creaturo for the first time. Still-life. Black and white. An exact match to the wartime photograph in the beach house hallway. Where he stood beside Nana and Papa and the dancing woman from Kitezh—his one true love.

"You—" she whispered. "You're Nana's brother."

14

JAKE

A LONG, PRICKLY SILENCE FOLLOWED.

Percy was the one to break it, his accent punching through the clearing's chorus of insects. "Nana? Who is Nana?"

"Our grandmother," Jake answered, his head whirling.

"You are their great-uncle, sir?" Percy's gaze swiveled back up to Christopher. "If that's the case, this is a poor show indeed."

Christopher squirmed against the ropes. "You must understand," he said, almost pleading. "This is my last chance. My Hazel has faded, and soon I will fade too. Soon I'll forget her and lose her forever."

The look Jake and Marisol exchanged was crammed with a hundred questions, all of them wordless. Marisol didn't speak, but Jake knew by the way her mouth had softened that she was willing to listen to Christopher. His cousin had the biggest heart of anyone he'd ever met, and the break in Christopher's voice *was* hard to hear. And he *was*—somehow, distantly—their long-lost relative.

Still, Jake wasn't feeling very forgiving.

"We have a *lot* of questions," he told his great-uncle.

"Starting with, who's Hazel?" Marisol planted her hands on her hips. All stern. "Is she the lady we met underwater?"

Christopher managed a small nod. "She doesn't remember me, but I visit her anyway."

"This conversation might take a while," Naomi observed. "Perhaps we should let Mr. Creaturo down before too much blood rushes to his head?"

"Yes, please," their great-uncle croaked.

"It's up to the children," Percy decided. "What say you, Marisol and Jake?"

Marisol scrunched her nose. Then nodded. "Bueno."

"But only if he promises not to run anymore," Jake added.

The vow was made. Herr Leichhardt cut the rope with his pocketknife and lowered Christopher to the jungle's loamy floor. He lay there for several seconds, letting his face become a less beet-like shade, before picking up the book and following them to camp.

"I'll make some tea," Jack Fawcett volunteered as everyone settled by the fire.

"Good idea, son!" said Percy. "Everything's better with tea."

A smile flickered across Christopher's face. "That's what Lucy used to say."

Nana *had* said that, usually when she was pouring sweet tea into glasses tall enough to last through two or three stories. By *the end* Jake was down to ice cubes, wanting more. But that wasn't possible now—his grandmother was gone, the tea would be hot, and the idea that Christopher Creaturo was Nana's brother was just too weird to swallow.

"How do we know you're telling the truth?" he asked. "You've lied to us before. . . ."

"I can do better than tell," said Christopher eagerly, digging in his pocket. "Let me show you my story." He produced a miniature flashlight and began to peel off his jacket. "We'll need to hang this up," he instructed. "Stretch it out like a projection screen."

Jack's friend Raleigh stepped forward, taking the coat from him and pegging it up on the explorers' makeshift clothesline. Several mismatched socks fell off to make room, which Oz dutifully collected as chew toys.

"This," said Christopher, brandishing the flashlight, "is called an Illuminator. Curators use it to examine archived memories; shine it through a grain of sand and the scene comes to life!"

It felt as if the Illuminator's light was beaming straight through Jake—gutting and glowing. If the Curators could use this tool to examine specific memories, then that meant they could tell one memory from another.

Perhaps there was a way to leave behind his worst memories—the goodbyes, the hurts—while keeping the ones he liked.

"Where did you get that?" he asked, thinking of what Archduke Johann had told them about missing memories. "The Library of Alexandria?"

"I imagine that's where it came from," Christopher said, in a vague sort of way that made Jake think that whoever had taken the Illuminator hadn't asked for the Curators' permission first.

Their great-uncle took off his necklace. Now that its hourglass wasn't concealed by his shirt, Jake could see that much of the sand had fallen. Forgotten. Christopher flicked on the Illuminator and held it against the time-piece. Light shot through the top granules, landing on the white surface his jacket provided.

Jack Fawcett handed out cups of tea as an image appeared on the fabric, colors dancing to life in a quick swirl, then resolving into the most familiar view of Jake's life.

"Nana's beach house!" Marisol cried. "But who are those people?"

Their beloved porch was populated by strangers—women in bright cotton dresses and men in light gray suits and hats. Christopher among them. Music with a strange, scratchy quality floated out from the picture. It was coming from a record player. The laughing people all held glasses of golden, sparkling champagne, and as Jake watched, they clinked them together. "Cheers!"

One woman turned toward them, smiling, and instantly Jake recognized her poppy-red lipstick. Another woman with curling auburn hair and merry eyes twined her arm through Hazel's. She reminded Jake of Mom and Aunt Cara, and her lips twitched like Uncle Todd's did when he was about to tell you a good joke.

And then he knew who she was. "That's Nana," he breathed.

"That's my sister, Lucy." Christopher's eyes creased tight, as if to hold back tears. "She and Hazel were best friends, which is how we met. But this isn't the memory I'm looking for."

He clicked the Illuminator, and the scene whirled away, replaced with a crystal-blue lake at the foot of a jagged mountain. A group stood on the pebbly shore, shrieking with laughter as they pulled off their coats. They were going to swim, Jake thought. Did they have their suits on underneath?

"Avert your eyes, children!" Christopher fumbled for the switch on the Illuminator. "Wrong memory!"

Jake heard Naomi laugh behind him and try to turn it into a cough as the scene shifted again. And again, and again.

Hazel was in every one of Christopher's memories, and Nana was in many of them too. Then came a memory that did not arrive in a flurry of color or laughter. Instead, the jacket was stained with brutal browns and dark greens, white-that-was-no-longer-white, and the occasional slash of red.

"Ah," said Percy sadly, from behind Jake. "This sight I know well. This is war."

"This is how I lost her." Christopher's voice sank like a boot in mud. There was so much of it on the screen. "Come, it's perfectly safe. We can't touch the memory, and the memory can't touch us. Believe me, if there were a way to change that, I would've found it by now."

He held out his hand to Marisol, and she slipped her fingers into his larger, rougher ones. Jake set his tea down on the ground and grabbed her other hand, and to his right, he felt Percy join hands with him as well.

Oz watched the human chain form, too busy gnawing on a sock to tag along.

"Don't let go," Christopher warned. "I'm not entirely

sure what would happen if we did."

And so saying, he walked toward the dirty jacket pegged to the washline, towing the children and explorers with him. When he reached the screen, Jake's vision flickered, trying to properly see something that didn't make sense. Somehow, Christopher took one more step and walked straight into the picture on the jacket.

As soon as he did, they were all inside the scene. Jake clung to Marisol's and Percy's hands—*DON'T LET GO*. He didn't dare. Not this time. At least his head was free to move, twisting sharply to take in their surroundings.

"This is a field hospital," Percy said. "We must be near a battlefield, just behind the front lines."

They were in what looked like a huge barn, lined with row after row after row of low beds, mostly pieces of canvas slung across thin metal frames. Jake had slept on a bed just like this when he went camping in the Outback with his mom. It hadn't been very comfortable.

But the young soldiers on the cots looked like they had other things to worry about. Most of the patients wore bandages as dingy as Christopher's clothes. Some slept, some stared at the ceiling, some called out. Their cries sounded like ghosts. Women hurried up and down the aisles, all dressed in khaki—some wore dresses, others trousers, one had on a leather flight jacket with a sheepskin collar that reminded Jake of Amelia's.

Nobody seemed to notice the impossible sight of six men and two children—for even Herr Leichhardt had come—holding hands as they walked through the hospital. Christopher found them a place against the barn wall and nodded at a spot just in front of him. "They'll be here in a moment," he said.

Jake didn't have time to ask who—he knew the answer as soon as he saw them. Bandages spilled over Hazel's arms while she bustled in their direction. Another, much younger version of Christopher, dressed neatly in his army uniform, trailed behind her. It was the Christopher that belonged back in this time.

"It's your break," she said to him over her shoulder. "Go sit down, get something to eat. Your unit will be expecting you back soon enough."

"I'm exactly where I want to be," he protested.

"Where's that?" Her poppy-red lips crimped into a laugh. "A hospital in the middle of France?"

"Wherever you are," he answered simply. "Can I help you carry those?"

Hazel stopped in front of the line of apparently invisible observers from the World Between Blinks, turning to face Christopher.

"Oh, love." The laughter drained from her voice, until she sounded so, so tired. "We're in the middle of a war. How can you sound so hopeful?"

"Hope is all we have," he said. "I'll never give it up. I couldn't. Not when you're standing right in front of me."

"There's so much pain here," she murmured. "These men have lost their health, their hope, their dreams."

"Time will bring those things back in new ways," he insisted.

But Hazel shook her head, diamond-bright tears welling up in her eyes. "So much loss," she said. "It clings to me like a cloud, Christopher."

He opened his mouth to reply, but his eyes went wide, and he seemed to lose his words.

Jake felt his own breath flee his lungs, as though he'd been punched. Hazel was fading right in front of them, tears rolling down her cheeks as she became fainter and fainter, until she was translucent. And then she was gone.

Christopher blinked at the spot where she had been, then dashed to the next aisle and grabbed a nurse by the shoulders, swinging her around to face him.

"Hazel!" he cried. "She just vanished, she vanished right in front of my eyes!"

The nurse blinked at him. "Who?"

Jake heard the *click* of the Illuminator switching off, and abruptly they were back in the Amazon clearing. Oz whuffed a *welcome back* between bites of sock. Their tea was still hot, seeping steam into the jungle's damp air, and after the chill of a French battlefield this warmth was a relief. So was the change in soundtrack—instead of distant artillery, a much softer chorus of birds, animals, and insects rushed back in at Jake. Hums, clicks, whirrs, and cries. Cries not too different from the ghost soldiers . . .

"Are you all right, lad?" Percy squeezed his hand. "War is never easy to see."

Jake's shaking fingers felt as flimsy as Hazel's. He understood why she vanished . . . why it was easier to just slip away. "I'm fine."

He pulled his hand from Percy's.

He didn't let go of Marisol, though.

"¿Qué pasó?" his cousin asked. "What happened after that?"

Their own Christopher, who now looked tired and worn thin, tucked the Illuminator away in his pocket.

"Hazel was simply gone," he said quietly. "She was so loving, so sensitive, that the loss around her became too much. Nobody nearby even seemed to notice, though I found out later that her family did. So did my sister, Lucy. Hazel went down in the records as missing in action. I devoted myself to finding her, and after the war I searched everywhere."

"Where do you even begin a search like that?" Raleigh tugged at the brim of his hat, anxious.

"Lucy helped me," Christopher said. "She was always very gifted at finding things. I used to tease her that she had magnet fingers. We followed the trail of hints and clues all over the world. If you know where to look, down the backs of libraries and on the highest shelves of very old bookstores, you can find records of the World Between Blinks. Eventually I found my way here."

"How?" Jake whispered.

Christopher gave him a small sad smile. "I loved Hazel too much. I wouldn't let her go, and by chasing something that was lost for so long, I became lost myself."

Jake saw the explorers around them nod. It was just the way they had come to the World too.

Percy stooped to retrieve his cup of tea from where he had set it on the ground. "Listen, old chap," he said. "You have my deepest sympathy, but you haven't explained why you pulled these children into your search."

Christopher nodded. "Lucy—Jake and Marisol's Nana—never gave up on me. Even after I ended up in the World too. She used her magnet fingers to find thin spots in the Unknown. She called them 'doors,' but we could only ever talk to each other through the space—I wasn't able to travel back home."

It was just like the scavenger had explained: *Lost things from the old world show up here, but it doesn't work in reverse.*

"Lucy always took care to stay on her side, so she wouldn't become trapped like me. She took care to document everything too. She told me she kept maps at home, and I know she marked the sites on them."

"X marks the spot," Marisol whispered.

Jake pictured his grandmother's curling ᐵCs, inked over all the places on the map she'd told him there was treasure to be found. He could practically feel the dry creases of the paper beneath his fingertips, smell the musty-but-comforting scent that always seemed to come from old books.

"Not X," he said slowly. "C.C. For Christopher Creaturo." He released Marisol's hand and dropped to a crouch. In the damp earth beside his mug, he traced out the swooping curves of back-to-back Cs. Put together like that, they looked just like an X.

He glanced up at Marisol, whose hand had retreated to her pocket. Probably wrapped tight around the Great Mogul Diamond.

"Nana always did say brothers are treasures." Her lips twitched—like Uncle Todd's, like Nana's. "It makes a lot more sense if she was talking about someone other than Victor."

Christopher let out a soft sigh. "She talked about you two, the last few years. It was so hard to watch her growing old when I never did, but I loved to hear about the life she lived, with all of her many adventures. And I loved learning about the new generation of Berunas growing up to continue that tradition. She talked about your sense of adventure, about . . . the things about you

234

that might help you make the trip."

What did that mean? Marisol's magnet fingers? Jake's own cloud of lostness that stuck to him, as Hazel's had clung to her? His insides swirled like a dancer's—around and around—and even though it wasn't his fault they were in the World Between Blinks, it could easily be his fault that they stayed. They could be cataloged and trapped forever. All he had to do was let go of one more memory, let one of his hurts or farewells just drift away. . . .

His hand turned into a fist.

His stomach became a bowling ball.

"Why didn't you just *tell* us?" he burst out. "You could have *asked* us to help you!"

"I was going to," Christopher promised. "But the Curators arrived before I expected them to catch up, and I had to run or they'd have taken the ledger with Hazel's name inside. I can't save her without this book. It's my very last chance. . . ."

"Sure," said Marisol, her eyes narrowing. "But then you *kept* running away from us."

"I didn't know what they'd told you. I didn't know if I could trust you to help after"—their great-uncle faltered—"after my lies."

Everyone studied him in silence. Oz dropped his jawful of yarn. Marisol crossed her arms. Colonel Percy Fawcett cleared his throat in the most British way possible.

Even Herr Leichhardt turned from where he was carving his latest L into a tree.

"I could have handled it better. . . ." Christopher shifted his weight from foot to foot.

Go on, go on, the insects chirped.

"I'm sorry," he said.

Jake exhaled slowly, and he felt like he was breathing out the worry and the tension that had been settling into his bones, growing with every thump of his heart over the last few days.

He looked across at Marisol, and she nodded. "Te perdonamos."

"We forgive you," Jake repeated.

"But we still need to get home," she added.

"They will be worrying about you by now," Christopher admitted. "Even though we don't age, time passes here just as it does back at home. I saw that when I managed to communicate with Lucy—she grew older, but I never did. If you've been in the World for days, then you've been missing at home for days."

Jake's heart started thumping all over again. His mom would be completely freaking out. So would Aunt Cara and Uncle Mache, and everyone, come to that. . . .

Percy took a sip of his tea. "You will have been gone for the better part of a century, Mr. Creaturo. Are you sure you wish to return with Hazel to the modern world?"

"Yes." Christopher sounded like a soldier when he answered. Dogged. Determined. "I have a plan."

"Well," said Jake. "We're going to need a bunch of plans to get everything we need to get ourselves home. And they're all going to have to be *good*."

15

MARISOL

THERE WAS A LOT TO DO.

To escape the World Between Blinks with everyone and everything intact they'd need to collect a very long list of items. Ledger entries mostly. Sure, Christopher Creaturo had the volume with Hazel's record inside, but there were three other names that needed to be crossed out as well: Jake's, Marisol's, and of course his own.

"Yours should be easy enough," he told the cousins around the campfire. "The Curators keep their most recent records in the Public Record Office of Ireland—the one that burned down in 1922. Security is much laxer there than at the Crystal Palace. Cataloged citizens of the World can enter without triggering any alarms."

"Is that how you managed to write Marisol and me into a ledger?" Jake asked.

"That's right." Christopher still looked somewhat

shamefaced about the situation. "I put on a white suit and walked right in with a pen."

Marisol's stomach dropped. "But the Curators said that if we were officially cataloged, we had to stay here forever. Did you catalog us?"

"No, no," Christopher hastened to reassure her. "Cataloging requires much more detail, and at least forty-seven different forms being filled out. The red tape is a nightmare. This is . . . a shortcut. After I wrote you into the current ledger's entries, I took the page with me, since it was always my intention to send you back home with Hazel. I left that paper with her for safekeeping."

"Will she *remember* to keep it safe?" Marisol didn't mean to sound mean, but the woman they'd met in Kitezh had had the attention span of a goldfish.

"It's folded into her jacket pocket. She won't even realize it's there. . . ." Christopher glanced at his own hourglass. "Good thing *I* remembered. The sands have been slipping away faster and faster since Lucy died. I'm not exactly sure why, but that's the reason I was desperate enough to write your names down. I knew I was running out of time."

Jake was getting fidgety on his log. "So that's how you get us home," he said. "By crossing out our names from the page you hid with Hazel, and crossing out *her* name from the ledger you already had us steal for you."

"Yes," Christopher said slowly. "But there's more to it.

I don't want to send Hazel back to the old world without her memories, so—"

"Our friend Johann told us the fallen sands are archived in the Library of Alexandria." Her primo leaned forward eagerly. "Do you think there's a way to get to them?"

"I hope so," their great-uncle replied. "The Administrator makes sure the Curators save everything. Problem is, he doesn't like giving stuff back."

"Hoarder," muttered Raleigh.

"It's a rather selfish system," his friend Jack agreed.

Christopher nodded. "We'll have to be quick and clever about it, but if we can get into the Library of Alexandria's memory archives without being detected, we should be able to fill our hourglasses back to the top."

"I'll do it," Jake said, without hesitation.

Marisol blinked at him. For someone who had said he wished he could shed his memories, it was a surprise to hear Jake wanting to save someone else's for them. Perhaps he'd changed his mind once he'd forgotten the bonfire for Nana.

Maybe he didn't want to be lost after all.

The thought made Marisol breathe more freely, even though there was still so much to worry about. Missing memories, Hazel, the ripped-out record page . . . It was a ton of ground to cover, especially on foot. But there was one thing Christopher had hurried past.

"What about your ledger entry?" Marisol studied her great-uncle. The longer they talked, the more glimpses of brotherly treasure she uncovered. His chin dimple matched Uncle Matt's, and he laughed the way their grandmother used to.

His sadness was also like Nana's: a V appeared between their brows, their blue eyes went deep, deep, deep. "I was hoping my name would be in this book." He nodded at Hazel's ledger. "But the Curators' records are chronological, and I arrived here several years after Hazel did. It took me decades to figure out where her volume was shelved. . . . I'm afraid trying to track the book down now would be a lengthy lost cause."

"I can find it!" Marisol wiggled her own magnet fingers and explained, "I can find anything, same as Nana!"

It wouldn't hurt to find the Great Mogul Diamond's entry either. If Marisol didn't cross it out, then she couldn't take the jewel home, which meant adiós beach house! After seeing the porch party inside Christopher's memories, the place seemed more important than ever.

Jake tapped at his hourglass with a frown. "We might not have time to go back to the Crystal Palace before Christopher's sand falls through. Plus it could be dangerous. What about the alarms?"

"Alarms won't be a problem for us. We still haven't

been cataloged," she pointed out to her primo. "But you can sneak into the library. I'll go to the Crystal Palace by myself. Not alone!" she amended after seeing the look on his face. "I'll ask Amelia for a ride! And we can pick Hazel up from the underwater cities on the way! That's two birds with one stone!"

Three, really. Marisol's knuckles brushed the diamond when she pulled the walkie-talkie from her pocket. "We can meet up when you guys are finished at the Library of Alexandria. We'll fix the cracks Christopher made, and then we'll go home!"

"It makes sense." Their great-uncle smiled. "Lucy always suspected you inherited her powers. She'd be proud that you're using them."

Marisol smiled back. For the first time in several days, she was happy. Hopeful.

Just like the Curators, they could find a way to save everything.

Leaving Jake—and Oz, and Christopher, and the rest of the explorers—behind in the jungle felt strange. And, if Marisol was being completely honest, kind of scary. She'd never *really* felt lost with her cousin beside her. Jake's steady hand and sturdy grin made everything okay, even when it really, really wasn't.

Marisol liked having him in arm's reach.

But this was the route she had to take: back to the edge of the desert, and an hour's hike later, onto Amelia's airplane, which found a strip between the dunes to land on. Together, the two of them flew to a phantom island that had appeared above the underwater cities. After a quick dive to Kitezh, where Curator Horace waved them straight through customs after Marisol's promise of a perfect ten rating, they managed to get Hazel on board the *Flying Laboratory* too.

"I thought you said this was a laboratory!" Hazel climbed inside the plane with a confused expression. "I don't see any microscopes or test tubes or bubbling smoke."

"I should hope not," Amelia muttered.

Then it was back to the scene of the crime, where this entire mess began. . . .

The Crystal Palace glittered beneath the late-afternoon sky, almost as bright as the bling in Marisol's pocket. She didn't dare admire the real jewel up here. What if Hazel accidentally opened the rear hatch thinking it led to a bathroom and Marisol had to drop her treasure to keep the woman from falling? This wasn't as far-fetched as it sounded. Christopher's true love was adrift now that she'd left the ocean behind: unbuckling her seat belt, wandering from wall to wall, touching levers and buttons and requiring constant attention.

Even after Amelia landed the plane in a field behind the Crystal Palace they had to keep an eye on Hazel. The *Flying Laboratory*'s shiny surface helped, distracting the nurse with her own reflection.

"I like that lipstick." She waved at herself. "Where did you get it?"

Amelia pulled down her goggles to study the Curators' storehouse. They were close enough to see the shelves through the windows—and the many, many white-clad officials tending them.

"I've never been part of a heist before," the pilot said excitedly.

Marisol wasn't exactly an expert either, but she was in charge. First things first—collect the easiest ledger entry. She turned to Hazel. "Is there a piece of paper in your jacket pocket?"

The nurse looked more solid out of the water, her colors crisper. Concentration gathered inside her eyebrows as she rooted around the old-fashioned uniform. These were the same clothes she'd been lost in, Marisol realized. The same type of outfit Nana wore such a very long time ago.

"Aha!" Hazel cried out in triumph, producing a folded page.

The paper crinkled just like Nana's maps when Marisol opened it. Sure enough, their names were inked at the top:

Marisol Contreras Beruna
Jake Beruna
Kraken

She pointed out the final entry as Hazel and Amelia leaned in over her shoulders. "That's how Christopher distracted the Curators and got them to leave the Crystal Palace last time."

"He set a *kraken* free?" Amelia whistled. "Hot dog, I'd have paid to see that."

"Who did?" Hazel pursed her oh-so-red lips.

"Chris-to-pher," Marisol enunciated.

The nurse fished out her necklace, pointing to a set of dog tags. "The dancing man told me this was my name. . . ."

It was CREATURO CHRISTOPHER J flashing on the steel. He must've given Hazel his dog tags to help keep their love from fading. There was a second set beneath her great-uncle's ID: CLIVE HAZEL S.

"No, no." Marisol pointed to the other letters. "Christopher is the dancing man. You're Hazel."

"Hazel," the nurse repeated. "I like that name. It fits so much better than Christopher. Hazel. HazelHazel-Hazel." She glanced back at her airplane reflection. "Oh, hello! I'm Hazel! What's your name?"

Marisol's stomach tightened. So did her fingers—though she tried not to crush the paper. Seeing Jake lose a memory was hard enough, but this was extra awful. It helped her understand why Christopher had risked so much.

She cleared her throat and looked back at the Crystal Palace.

Still swarming.

"We'll need another decoy to clear out the Curators so I can slip inside," Marisol said to Amelia.

"Hmm." The pilot squinted thoughtfully. "And we're all out of krakens."

"We need a different stunt this time. . . ." Marisol trailed off.

Amelia's eyes brightened. "Stunt! Gee whiz! That's it, Marisol! You leave the distracting to me and the *Flying Laboratory*. Though"—the pilot glanced toward the plane's tail, where Hazel kept waving at herself—"it'd probably be best if she stayed here. Aerobatic flying requires a tight seat belt."

Marisol hung back in the gardens, exactly where she and Jake hid only a few days before. It was Hazel hunched next to her now, both of them watching the silver dot that was Amelia's airplane.

"When the people in white suits come out of the building, I'm going to sneak in." Marisol clutched the back of Hazel's jacket—hard. "You can't follow me."

"Why not?"

"These ledgers are off limits to citizens of the World Between Blinks. You've been cataloged, so an alarm will sound if you try to enter the building." Hazel looked like she'd already forgotten the start of the conversation, so Marisol doubled back. "Only I can go inside. You have to stay here, or you'll set off an alarm."

"Oh." Her companion looked crestfallen. "That wouldn't be good."

"I need you to stay outside and keep watch," Marisol instructed. "Make sure the Curators are distracted and I don't get caught. Do you think you can do that?"

Hazel nodded.

"Bueno."

Across the harbor, the Lockheed took a sudden dive. Marisol's heart swerved with it—back and forth—as she watched white smoke plume from its tail.

Was Amelia Earhart about to crash?

No!

The plane pulled up well before the city's hodgepodge buildings. The smoke had disappeared too, starting again when the *Flying Laboratory* made a giant loop. . . . An O, Marisol realized.

"She's skywriting!" she whispered to Hazel. "That'll get the Curators' attention for sure!"

SOS. Amelia's final letters were perfect and urgent. There was only one problem: the Curators inside the

Crystal Palace didn't notice the clouds. Their noses were stuck deep in their books. So deep, that Marisol maybe didn't even need a distraction to slip in. . . .

But before she could make a new plan, Hazel acted on the old one.

The nurse slipped free from her jacket and leaped across the garden, rapping against the palace's glass panes. "Yoo-hoo! Look, Curators! There's writing in the sky!"

Startled, the officials looked up. Monocles dropped, books shut. White suits began filing to the door.

"Is that supposed to spell *sauce*?"

"Come now, don't you know your acronyms? Those clouds say *save our souls*."

"Whose souls? The clouds?"

"Actually, SOS isn't an acronym. It's a Morse code distress signal—"

"That sounds serious. Boss, you'd better come and look at this!"

As the Curators milled and debated and rated the danger from one to ten, Hazel shot a big ol' wink toward the bush where Marisol was hiding. *Smooth.* At least the World's caretakers were moving now. Half of the officials whipped out their clipboards and began to trickle down the hill.

The other half stayed.

Maybe the Curators had learned their lesson after the first break-in, or maybe Amelia's skywriting just wasn't monstrous enough. Whatever the reason, the rest of the Curators shrugged and went back to shelving.

Marisol felt her lungs squeeze dry. There were still too many eyes. Climbing the overhead trees wouldn't work this time around.

What in the worlds was she going to do?

"Yoo-hoo!" Hazel ran to the other side of the massive building, smudged her face against the glass, and started blowing giant raspberries. It was easy to see why she'd been Nana's friend. . . . Marisol could imagine her grandmother doing the exact same thing in an otherworldly emergency.

Nana would also, probably, actually flex her magnet fingers.

Marisol took a deep breath and channeled everything into a single wish: *I need to find the best way to Christopher's ledger . . . and then the Great Mogul Diamond's.*

Her hand moved to point out a spare shelving cart—*yes, perfect!* The cart had two shelves for holding books, one above the other, and was mounted on a set of wheels. There was room between those shelves for a girl, if she made herself small.

Marisol dashed over and climbed inside, using Hazel's jacket as cover when she curled onto the cart's lower level. Fabric was much less noticeable against the books than elbows and knees. Also, the leftover Curators were too mesmerized by the nurse's window faces to notice.

Now came the *really* tricky part: moving without being seen.

Hazel couldn't make pig noses forever, and some of the bookkeepers were already back to their tasks. Marisol peered out beneath the jacket, scooting the cart forward with her arms when the coast was clear. Whenever it wasn't, she retreated like a turtle into its shell. White pants strolled by. Marisol held her breath and counted to sesenta before inching out again.

One foot. Stop!

Two feet. Stop!

Forget turtle. She was as slow as a snail.

It took forever to reach the shelf that held Christopher's ledger. The book was on the bottom, thank goodness! Her fingers turned into fireworks when she grabbed the volume, flipping through pages to make sure she had the right entry.

Sure enough, her great-uncle's name was there.

Marisol swallowed when she read the date beside it.

Christopher Creaturo had entered the World Between Blinks on July 4, 1949.

The Great Mogul Diamond had vanished a long, long time before that. Hundreds of years, according to Queen Nefertiti. If the Curators' records really were kept chronologically, that meant the next shelf was too far away to wheel to.

Should she get out and make a run for it?

Before Marisol could decide, another flash of white caused her to shrink into a ball. There was some orange in the mix too—bright, flaming hair.

It was Red Bun.

The strictest, meanest of the Curators who'd sent them on this quest in the first place was standing right there, her hair still pulled back so tight the sight made Marisol's eyes water.

"What is an east wing cart doing all the way over here?" The Curator walked right up to the cart, grunting. "Min-jun! Do we have to review the filing systems again?"

"I didn't do this." Marisol recognized the soft, kind voice of the man who'd given her and Jake the money and the monocles.

"So the cart sprouted legs and walked here by itself, did it?" Red Bun sighed. "Never mind. Take it back to where it belongs. Please and thank you."

Marisol hugged Christopher's ledger to her chest— roly-poly style—as Min-jun pushed her back the way she came. They zoomed past rows and rows of records and dozens and dozens of feet. Min-jun didn't stop by the entrance where she'd found the cart, either. He kept wheeling well into the east wing.

Toward the next ledger. Yesssss!

Marisol couldn't reach out yet, but the tingling in her

fingers confirmed she was close. Min-jun parked the cart and gave it a pat.

"Stay put!" he said, before returning to his other shelving duties.

She counted to sixty again. Her fingernails burned.

She was so, so close.

When the coast was clear, Marisol steered down two more aisles. *¡Aquí!* The book her fingers picked looked much older than Christopher's tome. Its leather was cracked, and for a second she feared the pages would crumble when she opened them.

"Please be here, diamond! ¡Por favor!" Marisol whispered as she flipped through entries from 1747. There! *The Great Mogul Diamond.* Her insides went all sparkly when she read it.

Now her family could keep the beach house!

Now everything was perfect.

The feeling lasted as long as it took Marisol to hide the second ledger under her jacket. Then it trembled, along with the rest of the Crystal Palace's glass, rattled by a high wail: *WARNING! UNAUTHORIZED SUBJECT HAS ENTERED THE PREMISES AT THE SOUTH TRANSEPT. CHAOS COULD ENSUE! PLEASE TAKE NECESSARY PRECAUTIONS.*

She peered past the shelves to see Curators flocking to the building's central fountains. Hazel, who was greeting her reflection in the water, hardly even noticed the frenzy. Or the alarm she'd triggered.

"Arms up!" the closest Curator—Droopy Moustache—yelled. "Please identify yourself!"

Hazel blinked. Obviously, she'd forgotten Marisol's warning.

Along with everything else.

Red Bun glared through her monocle. "This is one Hazel Clive. She slipped through the Unknown on January 12, 1945. Data suggests she spends most of her time in Kitezh."

"So what is she doing here?" Min-jun wondered.

"What indeed!" exclaimed Droopy Moustache.

"I . . ." Hazel frowned, scraping through dust-mote memories. "I'm helping a friend. I think."

"Friend?" Red Bun's eyebrows shot up.

Min-jun glanced over his shoulder, straight at the shelves Marisol was spying through. She dropped back behind some books. Her stomach followed.

What a gigantic mess. . . .

"Oh dear." Hazel's voice rang hollow. "I'm not sure I was supposed to tell you that."

"This alarm is giving me a headache," Red Bun complained. "Min-jun, escort this resident into the gardens, will you? We can question her better out there. The rest of you! Sweep the shelves! Leave no page unturned!"

Blow on a dandelion and its seeds will find more directions than a compass. The Curators exploded just as fast. Spilling everywhere.

If Marisol stayed put, she'd get caught for sure.

The east entrance wasn't far, but it was difficult to run with *two* ledgers. Marisol nearly dropped both books as she rushed through the doors and dove into the garden. Crawling through the bushes wasn't much easier. Gravel bit her knees and twigs snarled her hair. Her arms ached, holding on to so much.

How was she supposed to rescue Hazel too?

Min-jun, Red Bun, and Droopy Moustache had the nurse cornered by a Maui Ruta Tree—or, as the brass plaque read, the MELICOPE HALEAKALAE, 1919, HAWAIIAN ISLANDS. Hazel danced over its roots, squirming at the Curators' many questions.

"What is your friend doing?"

"Where is your friend now?"

"Do you know who was flying that airplane?"

Hazel shook her head over and over until she looked dizzy.

"We might have to consult her hourglass in the Great Library of Alexandria," Droopy Moustache said.

No! Marisol grit her teeth to keep from crying out. If that happened, Jake and the others could get caught too! She had to find a way to divert the Curators. Things were desperate enough to call in a backup kraken! Marisol rifled through her pockets, on the off chance that they held a pen.

They didn't.

There was only one thing she could part with. . . .

Only one thing the Curators might chase.

Marisol's fist froze around the Great Mogul Diamond—knuckles burning. She'd wanted to hold on to so much, so tightly. She'd wanted to hold on to the beach house, hold on to the crowded bookcases and the splashy wallpaper and the porch lined with conch shells and sharks' teeth.

She'd wanted to hold on to the sun-warmed water from the garden hose, splashing over her bare feet to wash off the sand, and the chatter around the breakfast table as everyone planned their day's adventures.

But what Marisol was really trying to hold on to was her family's togetherness, and you couldn't keep that in your hand any more than you could catch a puff of smoke from the Berunas' backyard cookouts.

You couldn't use a particular thing or a certain place to make your life just the way you wanted.

But you could hold on to *love*.

Christopher had been fighting for decades with everything he had to hold on to Hazel.

You could hold on to the things that made you *you*.

The explorers still chased the horizon and all of its

new discoveries, but they didn't mind whether they had *stuff.*

And in the end, *stuff*—even big things, like the beach house—wasn't what made you happy.

For a moment Marisol thought of the scavenger with the colander on her head, barely looking up as she waited, waited, waited for the next piece of treasure to emerge from that thin spot, wanting more, always more, but it was not enough.

It was never enough.

And suddenly Marisol knew the beach house wasn't what mattered. Nana had filled the place with shark's teeth and photos of adventures, but each of those things had been carefully chosen, and the real treasure had been the stories Nana had told over a glass of sweet iced tea. The way she'd laughed and put her wrinkled hands over theirs and said *te amo* with a slight Southern twang . . .

Love was worth more than the things that reminded you of it.

Goose bumps shivered across Marisol's magnet fingers. Her grandmother wasn't gone—not all the way—because pieces of Nana lived on through her. Through her gift of finding what was lost, through her adventurous spirit, through her love for her family.

She knew exactly what her grandmother would do, because *brothers are treasures* and Hazel was Christopher's heart. Nana's oldest friend was way more valuable than some creaky, leaking beach house.

It was time to let go.

Eyes ahead, don't look back! She threw the diamond as hard as she could. It sailed over the Curators' heads—twinkling like a star against the early-evening light. Hazel *oooooooh*ed. Droopy Moustache cupped his hands and stumbled over bushes trying to catch it. Red Bun followed.

The ledgers in Marisol's arms slipped as she ran toward Hazel—good thing there was no need to carry both books anymore. She tossed the oldest copy to a very stunned Min-jun.

"Here you go! I'll rate you ten out of ten if you don't tell!"

The kindly Curator caught the book. And smiled.

"C'mon!" Marisol used her newly freed hand to grab Hazel's. "¡Vamos!"

Together they started to run.

16

JAKE

LUDWIG LEICHHARDT TURNED OUT TO BE *VERY* USEFUL.

The German explorer hadn't lost *all* of his memories yet, and now that they were doing something he was interested in, he'd come back to life. On their journey to the Library of Alexandria, where the memory hourglasses were stored, he talked more and more, his words coming first in ripples, and then in great gushing waves.

Just now, the whole group behind Operation Hourglass—Jake, Oz, Christopher, and the explorers—were crouched in a hutong, which turned out to be a narrow Chinese street bordered with bright red doors and brighter, redder lanterns. Somewhere in the old world, its stones had been demolished to make way for shinier buildings. Now, the alley sat just a couple of blocks from the library itself.

"I came to see the library shortly after my arrival in the World!" Leichhardt was bubbling as he scratched out a map in the dirt, tapping each room with a stick. "I studied at the universities of Göttingen and Berlin back home, you know, and I wrote books. I wanted to see the greatest library the world had ever known." He was visibly excited—he'd even trimmed his beard in preparation for the trip.

Jake was just as excited, anticipation fizzing inside him like a Fourth of July sparkler. He'd get back Hazel's and Christopher's memories, of course. But there was much more to it. . . . Christopher's Illuminator, which could be used to shine specific sand scenes back to life, *must* mean there was a way to tell the memories apart. And that meant that for all the memories he took from the library, he might just leave a few behind there as well.

So many goodbyes to so many friends.

Or the last time he saw Nana, with her veins too blue in her skin and her smile so weak, and Jake couldn't breathe for remembering it now, but the sight was too stark to forget on his own, and he wished he could just—

Percy nudged his shoulder. "Jake, old chap! Are you with us?"

"I'm in." He looked back down at the dust-drawn map. His nerves crackled like a live wire. "What do we have to do?"

After a long look at the library's layout, it was decided

that Leichhardt, Percy, Raleigh, and Oz would head inside with Jake. Naomi and Jack would wait outside with Christopher.

"One last thing," Percy said before they left the hutong. "If we succeed and send you four back to the old world—then I believe we explorers must swear an oath of secrecy. If word got out that it's possible to return, too many people would try it, and heaven only knows what things or places they might bring with them. It could be a disaster."

"You're right." Jack's eyes widened. "If this works, we'll have to keep it to ourselves. Our secret."

"We must swear," Leichhardt agreed.

And so they did, shaking hands to seal the oath. And then Jake, Leichhardt, Percy, and Raleigh left the others behind, making their way along the streets toward the library, Oz trotting ahead of them to lead the way.

The Library of Alexandria itself stole Jake's breath away—though that also could've been because there were so many stairs leading to the main courtyard. Here the building wrapped around a reflecting pool, which made the structure seem taller than its three stories. People from every era of history hurried across the plaza like ants on an anthill, caught up in the important business of learning.

Jake felt slightly disappointed, watching them come and go. He'd been prepared for a much more daring entrance. "I thought we had to climb in through a window. . . ."

"The library is open to the public," Leichhardt replied. "But the hourglass archives are a special collection. For those, a permit is required. Or, in our case, burgling skills. Come! Let us thieve!"

Leichhardt strolled through the front door with immense confidence for someone who was about to rob the place. Jake, Percy, and Raleigh followed, with Oz last of all.

"Good afternoon," said the Curator stationed at the entrance. "And welcome to the Library of Alexandria. We hope you'll take a moment to rate your experience when you leave. Oh, hello, Oz!"

Oz yipped a hello, and Jake said nothing, staying on the far side of Percy, in case he was recognized. But it didn't take long for their new surroundings to distract him from his worries. Leichhardt's map—while accurate— simply hadn't captured the library's scope. It was *huge*!

There were rooms for eating and talking, for studying and attending lectures. Everything was lit by bold golden sunshine, which burst through open windows that were cut into the stone, without any glass. Statues of Greek and Egyptian gods watched over the aisles. An inscription above the shelves told Jake that this was: *The place of the cure of the soul.*

But more than anything, what he noticed was . . .

"Gad, that's a lot of books," Percy said, craning his neck to look around.

Leichhardt nodded enthusiastically. "These aren't the original papyri—scrolls, I mean—that would have been in the library. Or at least, not all of them. Most of history's missing texts are here: works by Cicero, the lost notes of Da Vinci and Nikola Tesla. They have Hemingway's earliest stories too! The papers were in a suitcase that was stolen from a train station, did you know? This happened after I came to the World, but I've heard . . ." He took in Jake's confused expression and laughed. "Ah, this is wasted on the young. Jake, they have the unfinished Pratchett novels here! One day you'll wish you had stopped to read them."

Jake's eyes fell on a large poster pinned to the wall outside a lecture theater. "Well, I've sure heard of Shakespeare," he offered. "But his plays exist in our world."

"Not this one." Raleigh's hat nearly fell off as he peeked into the performance. "They're acting out *The History of Cardenio.* Too bad we don't have time to pop in and watch!"

"What's that up ahead?" Percy asked. "I see more Curators."

Leichhardt was all business once again. "That's the acquisitions department," he said. "Back in the old world, works were brought there to see if they were worthy of inclusion in the library. Here, it holds the hourglass repos-itories."

A pair of Curators was standing guard, though the sign above their heads did most of the warning for them:

RESTRICTED AREA, PERMIT REQUIRED
FRAGILE MEMORIES, HANDLE WITH CARE

Jake's heart threatened to break his own hourglass—*thump, thump, crack!*—as the little group approached. This was where they'd find out if their plan would work. It wasn't much of a plan, but there was only one way into the repositories. Well, two, but the Curators were unlikely to let them just stroll through the front door.

Leichhardt and Percy charged up to the two guards, full of firework greetings.

"Good afternoon!" Leichhardt cried. "I have a list of seventeen queries. I have alphabetized them!"

"I require your attention," Percy said loudly, coming to stand between his Curator and Jake, Raleigh, and Oz. "I have forty-three suggestions for the improvement of the library."

Meanwhile, Raleigh and Jake edged over to the nearest great open window. Jake stuck his head out and swallowed hard at what he saw. Their recon had been right. There was a ledge outside, but it looked a lot smaller than it had from the ground. Three whole stories ago!

"Good luck, old chap," Raleigh whispered, helping him climb out the window, and holding on until Jake had his balance.

He shuffled along the ledge—*eyes ahead, don't look back OR DOWN!*—trying desperately not to think about how much air there was to fall through. Marisol was so much better at climbing things, but Jake had to be the one to do this—he was the only person who could sift through the memories he wanted to leave behind.

He fought off the thought of Nana in that hospital bed and looked back toward the window. Raleigh was lifting out Oz, who didn't seem the least bit worried that Tasmanian tigers did not have wings. The animal balanced just fine, giving his human companion an encouraging little wuff. After a deep breath, Jake kept on shuffling. It was about twenty feet to the next window, which would be inside the hourglass repository.

Fifteen feet, shuffle shuffle.

Ten feet, shuffle shuffle, careful steps.

A playful breeze snatched at his shirt, ruffling his hair. "Oh, Oz," he murmured. "This had better be worth it."

Oz placed one careful paw in front of the other, tail trembling with excitement.

Five feet, just a few more steps.

Jake was careful not to relax as he got closer. His

fingertips were sweating when they gripped the window-sill. Oz mimicked the position and hopped onto his hind legs, but the thylacine needed opposable thumbs even more than a set of feathers.

"*Ah-ah?*" he pleaded, batting those liquid dark eyes.

"You're lucky you're so cute!"

"*Ah-ah!*"

Jake clung to the sill with one hand, and with the other, he grabbed at Oz's back legs, giving the creature a heave. Nails scrabbled, fur flew. A tawny striped rump disappeared through the window, landing with an audible thump on the other side.

Jake hoisted himself through after Oz, the stone scraping his palms raw. When he straightened up, he was faced with shelves of hourglasses. Shelves on shelves on endless shelves. Christopher's words rang in his head. *They're chronological. Every hourglass is arranged by the date its owner arrived. Follow the dates on the shelves and you'll be fine.*

The shelves nearest Jake were centuries old, and almost every hourglass had a clear top and a full bottom. He raced through the aisles, counting down the years in a whisper. Hazel's came first, the top completely emptied, the bottom stacked high with sand.

Next came Christopher's, with only a third of the grains left at the top. How hard it must've been for him to hold on to his memories, and to Hazel. He must love her very much, and Nana must have helped him remember this long. Wherever Jake's grandmother was, she'd be smiling, knowing that he and Marisol were helping her brother. Finishing this story for her . . .

Jake thought about the explorers as he ran along the shelves once more, but Percy and his crew had been very clear: they didn't want Marisol to steal their ledgers, and they did not want Jake to bring their hourglasses out. They were enjoying their expeditions in the World Between Blinks, and they had no desire to return home with Christopher, Hazel, Jake, and Marisol. There was still too much to see here.

But suddenly the urge to turn back struck him. He didn't have time to think—he simply whirled around and hurried to the 1840s. There, toward the end of the shelves, sat Ludwig Leichhardt's hourglass. Very few grains remained up at the top.

Jake flipped the timepiece upside down, giving it a shake to start the sand flowing in the opposite direction. He didn't dare wait long, but by the time he turned the hourglass right side up and placed it back on the shelf, Leichhardt had at least half his memories restored. It seemed a pity for him to lose so much of his past, and a good thank-you, to give some back.

Oz made a low noise in the back of his throat, and

Jake nodded. "Gotta keep moving," he agreed softly, and they turned toward the most recent shelves. The cousins' hourglasses were almost the last, his with just one grain of sand at the bottom, Marisol's with none at all.

Jake picked them up carefully, considering. . . .

He couldn't just shake his hourglass to send the sand through quicker—he might lose the wrong memories again. He needed the correct tool—something like Christopher's Illuminator. There had to be more here, right? How else would the Curators examine this collection? If Jake could find one and use it to single out some of his worst memories, then he could leave those pieces of sand on the shelf and be on his way. Carefree.

Happy.

Jake's thoughts were already in the courtyard where Christopher was waiting, and beyond that to the olive tree by the Aral Sea, where Marisol and Hazel had agreed to meet up with them.

Perhaps that was why he didn't hear any footsteps.

When Jake rounded the end of the aisle to search for an Illuminator, he crashed straight into a Curator in a starched white suit.

The official was a silver-haired man with a pale, puffy face, thin lips, and a pointed chin, and he immediately reminded Jake of a turtle without its shell. The man's eyebrows, though . . . they were the most impressive pair

Jake had ever seen. They looked like caterpillars who dreamed of becoming scarves—thick and pale.

They wiggled extra wide when the Curator spotted the four hourglasses clutched to Jake's chest, and Jake stumbled back, putting some distance between them.

"Ah." Big Brow's voice dipped as deep as a cello's. "You must be Jake Beruna."

"What?" Jake took another step back, and Oz made a soft, unfriendly noise. "How do you know my name?"

"You're a new arrival," the man said, tilting his head to study Jake like he was an interesting sort of puzzle. "My Curators tried to keep your existence from me. That was foolish."

Jake tried to calm his mind, considering the man's words. "*Your* Curators," he repeated, horror creeping over him. "Then you must be . . ."

"The Administrator," the man finished his sentence for him. "Indeed."

An ice-water chill dripped down Jake's spine. The Administrator could properly catalog him and Marisol. He could trap them in the World Between Blinks forever, and Christopher and Hazel too! *Why* had he lingered?

But the Administrator sounded more conversational than hostile. "I'm not surprised you found your way here."

"Oh?" said Jake, playing for time. "Why's that?"

"You are drawn to these memories. Or rather to the

forgetting," the man explained. "There is a great deal of lostness around you, Jake. You are a boy who *wants* to be lost."

Jake felt like someone had sat on his chest, as all the things he'd lost came rushing at him, all at once. His father, his friends, the places he'd lived. Some of them had disappeared for their own reasons, but a lot of them he knew he'd pushed away before he could lose them. Because he didn't want to miss people or places—it hurt too much. It was like he always said: *eyes ahead, don't look back.*

"I understand," said the Administrator quietly. "How painful it can be. How heavy. Life is full of loss, and sometimes it's too much to carry around with you." His hand went to his necklace, and Jake saw that the man didn't have any hourglass at all. No sand. Nothing. "Many of my Curators don't realize this—they cling to their memories like coins or stamps or cards. But you, Jake Beruna. You feel the pull of this place. You could be truly happy here. Light and free. I could see to it that nothing would hurt you ever again."

Jake's mouth opened, then closed again. The Administrator made the Curators sound like Marisol, determined to hold on to things. But he sounded like Jake too, that tiny, inner whisper that wondered if it would be easier to dance like a ghost beneath the sea or sail in the salt spray above.

The Administrator *understood*, in a way so many others didn't. He wasn't urging Jake to keep his chin up, to find the positives, to look forward to the next good thing.

If this man had truly found a way to take away the unhappiness that came with losing the things you loved . . . Well . . .

Wasn't it at least worth asking about?

"How?" The question ached in his throat.

"Let me help you. Give me those hourglasses." The Administrator pointed at the stolen charms. "I can move all of the memories in yours to the bottom so you'll never have to miss anyone, or anything, ever again. Nothing will be able to drag you down!"

"But . . ." Jake's mouth went dry. "But I don't want to lose *all* of the sand! There are memories of Nana in there! Of—of . . . of picnics in Paris with my mom! Of bushwalking in Australia! Of my cousins, my family, of the beach house!"

The Administrator frowned, his caterpillar eyebrows clashing together like they wanted to fight. "A memory is a memory, Jake. They all weigh on you."

Jake shook his head. "Those memories are what make . . ." He trailed off as the realization hit him squarely. "They're what make me into me."

And then he saw. There was no such thing as an all-good or all-bad memory. The picnic in Paris had been

270

delicious, but ants had gotten into the pastries. The bush-walk in Australia had been beautiful, but it had finished up with them tired and sweaty, sunburned and dotted with bug bites. The beach house was home, but it came with the memory of losing his grandmother. Even the last time he'd seen Nana, she had grabbed Jake's hand and whispered, *I love you*, and how could he ever stand to forget those words, just to forget she'd been sick?

Like the salt of peanut butter and the sweetness of chocolate, it was one that made the other taste so good. Enjoying the cool shade of a tree only felt so wonderful because you'd felt the heat of the sun first.

"They're all good memories," Jake said slowly. "And they're all bad memories. They're both. Maybe some of them are amazing, or some of them are awful, but that's how you get the sun and the shade. The bad is how you know the good when you see it."

Beside him, Oz made a chuffing sound that Jake thought might just be agreement.

"Let me take them away," the Administrator said, taking a slow step forward.

"I miss Nana so much," Jake whispered. "But that's because of how much love we had. I miss my friends when we move, but it's because we did so many great things together. The sadness is the peanut butter to the chocolate of happiness."

"What? What do snacks have to do with it?" the Administrator demanded, his tone growing annoyed.

"They go together," Jake said simply. "And sometimes it's hard, but that's okay."

He could see the beach house in front of him, its walls held up by his grandmother's many photos and maps. He could hear all of the stories she'd shared—pointing out different frames with a laugh. *Did I ever tell you about that time . . . ?* Sometimes the memories were happy, and other times they were sad, but they were all there.

Even the picture of Christopher and Hazel.

"Memories aren't supposed to drag you down," he realized. "They're supposed to come along for the ride! Even the ones that hurt. My cousin says you have to be calm on the route, and that's right. Not every memory needs to stay with you, but you can't just leave them all behind. Even when the route is tough. I'd rather keep my memories, thanks."

The Administrator studied him for a long moment, blinking slowly. There wasn't any sign on his face that he understood what Jake meant. Even a little bit. Eventually, he sighed. "I was hoping to avoid this, but I cannot allow you to remove any memories from the repository."

And with no more warning than that, he lunged at Jake, arms outstretched, grabbing for the hourglasses. Oz threw himself forward and tangled with the Administrator's legs, causing the man to stumble into a set of shelves.

For a heart-skipping second, they wobbled.

And then the entire aisle of hourglasses came crashing down.

Glass and memories sprayed everywhere.

"NO!" The Administrator was on his hands and knees, trying to scoop sand into his palms. "NO! NO! NO!"

Jake didn't stick around to help. There was no point bothering with windows anymore. Holding tight to the hourglasses, he ran straight for the door, bursting back into the main library with Oz at his heels.

The guards were surprised, to say the least.

The explorers were only slightly more prepared— with twitchy legs and decoy hourglasses hidden in their jackets.

"Good luck!" Percy clapped Jake on the shoulder and turned to run. "You've been most helpful!" he called to his Curator as he bolted along the hallway, pulling his hourglass from his jacket and lifting it high above his head.

"Thank you, Jake! Enjoy your next adventure!" shouted Leichhardt, who took off in the other direction.

"This way, Curators!" yelled Raleigh, running along a narrow passageway, waving his hourglass in the air.

The explorers were laying down three other trails for the Curators to follow, creating as much confusion as possible by waving their hourglasses about, forcing the

Curators to chase them in case they were real.

Jake wished he had time to say one more goodbye to his friends, but they were already off enjoying this newest adventure.

"Thank-you-for-your-visit!" a dazed Curator called from the doorway, as the Administrator bellowed his frustration and elbowed his way past. "Please-rate-the-service-you-have-received-on-a-scale-of-OOF!"

Jake and Oz bolted down the staircases, nearly slipping on the polished marble, and he could hear the clatter of footsteps behind them. He rushed past two ladies in curled silver wigs that could've doubled as beehives, and then dodged around a man in a tuxedo. The last few steps almost caused him to do the splits.

When they reached the bottom, Jake and Oz ducked behind the statue of a stern-looking goddess, and they both stood there, panting, as two Curators hurried past, disappearing into some papyrus-stuffed shelves.

The coast was clear.

It was now or never!

Marble scribbled under claws and sneakers as they made a break for the front door. "Ten!" Jake shouted, before the exiting Curator could ask the usual survey question. "Definitely ten!"

"Thank you!" the official called after him, sounding delighted.

But Jake was already halfway down the steps to the

courtyard, where Christopher, Jack, and Naomi were holding the reins of . . . What the heck were those? The two animals looked like zebras at the front and horses down the back, brown-and-white stripes on their heads and shoulders, solid brown rumps bringing up the, uh, rear.

As Christopher mounted one bareback, it tossed its head and pranced in place, making a sound like *kwa-ha-ha!*

Jack was waiting to boost Jake up onto his, and he grinned when he read the question on the boy's face. "Quaggas! They're from Africa. Relatives of a zebra. Aren't they something?"

Naomi gave him a nod, then hurried toward the library's main entrance, managing to collide squarely with the Administrator, who was just running out. As the Administrator desperately tried to duck around Naomi, the Japanese explorer bowed courteously, then bowed again, apologizing profusely for the collision, and delaying him a vital ten seconds.

"Safe journey, mates!" cried Jack, and slapped both quaggas on the butt. With Oz racing ahead of them, Jake and his great-uncle galloped out of the courtyard.

17

MARISOL

THE ARAL SEA WAS STILL MONSTERLESS.

Marisol sat by its shore, trying not to worry as the sun sank low, lower, lowest. Amelia's emergency clouds had scattered, so the sky and its mirror were both smooth, except where Hazel kept leaning in to see her own reflection.

"Hello!" Marisol's heart skipped every time the woman greeted herself. "Hello there!"

She looked back over her shoulder at the St. Helena olive tree. Jake and Christopher still hadn't arrived and even though they hadn't set a firm time, the Crystal Palace was on fire again—catching the sunset and spitting rays back. Ember orange everywhere. It felt so close. It felt too late.

Her hourglass had lost a single grain of sand.

Marisol held the timepiece between her fingers, counting the missing memory over and over. *What if Jake had gotten caught? What if all their plans fell through? What if Hazel never really learned her name? What if they never got to go home? Victor would probably love being an only child. . . .*

Each thought made Marisol squeeze tighter, until her fist ached. Until she realized that this was the *bad* kind of holding on . . . The kind that kept her from being alive, enjoying a gorgeous sunset by a lost sea in a world with just enough magic to make happy endings possible.

Just as she slipped her necklace back into her shirt, four silhouettes appeared. Sharp black, clean cut. Against the neon sky they were all elbows and shoulders and one very happy tail.

"Hey there!" The accent was unmistakably Amelia's. "Look who I found trotting down the Via Hadriana! Well, walking really. Those poor quaggas were running out of steam. . . ."

"Jake!" Marisol dashed toward her cousin. "¡Estás bien!"

His hug smelled like sand and old books. "¡Sí! I'm okay! It looks like you are too." He sounded relieved. "Did you have any trouble getting the ledger?"

Um . . .

At the sight of the newcomers, Hazel had stopped splashing. She wore her pleasant poppy smile as Christopher waded into the water, arms stretched for an embrace.

"Hazel! My love!"

"Hello!" The nurse held out her hand. "It's nice to meet you."

A heartbroken look stole over their great-uncle's face. It knew just where to fit—right around the chin dimple, clinging to his golden eyelashes. This wasn't the first time Christopher had worn such sadness.

Hopefully, though, it would be the last.

"We had a few close calls, but we got Christopher's ledger," she told her cousin. "Did you guys grab the hourglasses?"

Jake grinned and began pulling out much larger versions of the charms around their necks. One at a time, he set them on the ground, making sure the name plaques read upside down:

Jake Beruna. Hazel Clive. Marisol Contreras Beruna. Christopher Creaturo.

Gravity got to work.

Sand started to sift. Memories began to return.

"Oh!" Hers was from Nana's last visit to Bolivia—they'd eaten picana at midnight on Christmas Eve, letting the spicy chicken, beef, and corn simmer on their tongues while they sang carols.

"The bonfire!" Jake exclaimed at the same time; his

face lighting up with memories of the flames. "You're right, Mari! I wrote Nana a letter on that lantern and let it float up to the stars—I can't believe I forgot!"

Marisol wanted to cry—happy tears, as well as sad—when she looked back at the couple standing in the sea. Their reflections rippled, not quite meeting, as Hazel kept trying to introduce herself.

"Hello! My name is Hazel Susan Clive—" She gasped, hands clasping over her mouth. Her eyes widened. Fuller. "I—I remember my name!"

"Haven't we told her like twelve times?" Amelia wondered.

Christopher stood, waiting.

Hazel's eyelashes fluttered, her stare getting more and more crowded. It was like seeing someone's soul poured back into their body. Thought by thought. Story by story. Until . . .

"Christopher?" It dawned on her face and in her voice. "Oh my stars and garters! Christopher Jacob Creaturo!!! You found me!"

"Hazel . . ." was all he could say.

She threw herself into Christopher's open arms. They spun together in the water. Their joy was almost too pure to look at, brighter than the burned-out stars in the sky above. When they kissed, Marisol knew that everything—even giving up the Great Mogul Diamond—had been worth it.

Jake made an *ew* face. Amelia clapped. Oz gave a husky, triumphant bark, which then turned into something of a growl. . . . The thylacine's hackles rose as his snout pointed back at the olive tree.

Leaning against its trunk was a Curator.

Marisol felt every season at once—summer heat, ice in her veins, the dread of lengthening nights—before she realized that it wasn't just any old official. It was Min-jun. There was a frown on his normally kind face, but that might've been to keep the monocle set in his eye.

"Ah!" Jake yelled. Then, seeing past the glass. "Oh!"

"Hola, Min-jun."

"Hola, Marisol. Hello, Jake." He pushed himself off the tree, scanning through the scene through his monocle. "What creatures of habit you are! Not only did you return to the scene of the crime to commit the same crime, but you repeated your rendezvous too!"

"You didn't tell the others, did you?" There were no more silhouettes on the horizon, but Marisol had to be sure.

"And risk my perfect rating?" Min-jun shook his head. "No. But I'm afraid it's only a matter of time before they show up. They're still very upset. You've made a terrible mess of things." He stared straight at Christopher. "Cracks everywhere! Fissures forever!"

Hazel frowned. "Cracks? What cracks? Christopher, what did you do?"

280

"I broke the world for you," he answered softly. "But don't worry, love. We're going to fix everything and return home, where we can keep our memories."

The Curator's gaze flitted from the reversed hourglasses to Hazel. No doubt he was seeing how much more of her there was now. "Sometimes Curators get too carried away with cataloging. The memory repository isn't a very fair system, is it?"

Marisol and Jake answered at the same time. "No!"

"People need their memories, even the painful ones," her primo went on. "It's what makes them *them*. If Amelia forgot how to fly, she'd still be Amelia Earhart, but she wouldn't be *the* Amelia Earhart anymore, would she?"

The pilot scuffed some sand with her boot. "Huh. I hadn't thought about it like that before."

"Me neither," Min-jun admitted.

"I don't want to forget how to fly! I can't! Then I'd have to walk everywhere or . . . or . . . sail!" Amelia looked flustered—curls licked out from under her cap. Her shoulders hunched.

Marisol peeled off the borrowed jacket and handed it back to their friend. "Don't worry. You're *the* Amelia Earhart. No one in my world is forgetting you any time soon. I know *I* won't."

"Thanks, pal!" she sniffed.

"You could also file a complaint with the Administrator," Min-jun suggested. "Though he'll be more amenable to changes once the worlds aren't in danger of ending."

"I think it might be a stretch, even then," Jake said with a guilty sort of look.

"In that case . . . I'll have to think about it," Min-jun said quietly.

"You and me both," Amelia added.

Marisol cleared her throat. "Speaking of the end of the world . . ."

The page filled with Christopher Creaturo's illegal entries was still in her pocket. She handed it to her great-uncle, careful not to let it fall into the water. Christopher stepped out of the Aral Sea, hand in hand with Hazel, and even though he had to let go to pull out his ballpoint pen, their shoulders kept touching.

"Here," Min-jun offered up the fountain pen from his necklace. "You'd better use this one."

"Are they charmed to do something special?" Marisol wondered.

"They make anyone's handwriting legible. *Nothing* is worse than a form you can't read! I mean, except for the collapse of the Unknown," Min-jun admitted. "And eternal amnesia."

"I'd like to use it next, to fill out a complaint card," Amelia said.

But there was a lot to rewrite first. Christopher scrawled a new monster's name beneath the kraken—and suddenly Nessie was back in her twilight sea, swirling the last dregs of sunset with her fins.

"What about the building in London?" Jake reminded their great-uncle.

"The ones destroyed during the Blitz, yes . . ." A scribble. "There. They should be back in the World Between Blinks now."

"And the Amber Room!" Marisol added. After all, it wasn't Nefertiti's fault that Marisol had ditched their reward.

"Done! You see!" Christopher returned the pen and page to Min-jun. "It's all fixed! Everything's back where it should be."

"Except for us," said Jake.

The monocle was in Min-jun's eye again. He squinted at the entries, then out toward the Loch Ness Monster, who was celebrating her return with underwater cartwheels. "It looks satisfactory, but I'm afraid I need a stamp of approval to cross out entries. Especially ones from the 1940s, as yours are."

Even though Min-jun was a helpful Curator, he was still a Curator, and for a moment, it seemed red tape would keep Christopher, Hazel, and the cousins tied here anyway.

Then Amelia stepped forward.

"Well, I don't need a stamp!" she declared. "These

kids deserve to go home, by golly! So do the lovebirds."

Min-jun didn't stop her from taking the stationery. He didn't stop her from opening the other ledgers either. All four names sat out on display, waiting for the strike-through.

This was it.

Time to say goodbye.

They thanked Min-jun for not tattling on them. They hugged Amelia, then Hazel, then Christopher, who promised that they'd meet again on the other side of the Unknown. The hardest farewell was the one Marisol couldn't say.

Oz sat on his hind legs—same as he had at the Frost Fair, when he first came snapping for their gingerbread. His ears lay flat, and there was a sad, sad whimper behind his teeth.

"I wish we could take you with us, Oz." She laughed at the thought of bringing an extinct animal back to the beach house. *Look, Mom and Dad! Can we keep him? ¿Por favor? I promise I'll pick up his poop!*

"Me too." Jake knelt down to hug the thylacine.

"Ah-ah!"

Marisol joined the huddle. "Thank you for being the best Tasmanian tiger I've ever met," she said, her voice thick.

"Ah-ah-ah!" Oz licked them so hard their eyelashes stuck to their eyelids. *"Ah!"*

Min-jun cleared his throat. "I don't mean to rush, but I think my colleagues will be here soon." Sure enough, there was a long, pale line of suits marching out of the city; clipboards ready to categorize Nessie's reappearance. "It might be best if you start disappearing!"

"On it!" Amelia flourished the fountain pen like a wand. "Don't worry, Oz and I will stick together! Goodbye, Hazel Clive! Goodbye, Christopher Creaturo!"

It was strange, watching someone vanish without smoke or a sound effect. Not even a *poof!* The lovebirds were just there and gone, between blinks. Back to . . . somewhere.

"Where will the Unknown send us?" Marisol reached for Jake's hand. "Back to the lighthouse?"

Min-jun paused. Considering. "I think you'll find yourselves exactly where you're supposed to be. The opposite of lost."

Her cousin disappeared, and Marisol was holding just air, just air. In the distance she could hear the Curators squabbling about whether to use Form 1091a or Form 1091b for the Loch Ness Monster's reprocessing. Hopefully Min-jun and Amelia wouldn't get in *too* much trouble.

"Bye, kiddo!" The famous pilot winked at her. "Maybe I'll see you around."

The pen struck.

Marisol loved the air around the ocean.

At night, in the summer, it almost felt like perfume. Or a lullaby, depending on how chatty the cicadas were. Tonight, the critters gave those extinct Amazon insects a run for their money. *Welcome back!* they screamed out of the marsh. *You have some explaining to do!*

She and Jake stood at the end of Nana's dock—no boat, no excuses. Good thing they didn't need either of those things right away. The backyard sat empty. Lawn chairs yawned at shadows and the grill had that lumpy black smell that meant it hadn't been used since the last thunderstorm.

"Where is everybody?" Jake wondered.

"Out looking for us." There were two cars in the driveway, and a light shining through the kitchen window. "We've been missing for three days!"

"Oh, yeah. . . ."

Neither cousin moved. Marisol kept staring at the house—realizing just how many shingles peeled off at the gable. It *did* need a lot of work. She hadn't seen it before.

The constellations above made shapes she recognized. Treasure chest jewels: twinkling and twinkling. "I wonder where Hazel and Christopher ended up."

"France, maybe?"

"I hope they're together."

"Me too."

"I already miss Oz."

"Me too." Jake's face looked softer in the moonlight. And . . . was that a tear shining by his eyelash? Marisol reached out and grabbed her primo's hand again.

"What are we going to tell our family?" she asked.

"The truth, I guess."

"Sorry, we got sucked into a world where everything lost ends up and we couldn't get back until we tracked down an evil villain who turned out not to be very evil at all but our great-uncle Christopher Creaturo, although we wouldn't have caught him without the help of our new best friend Amelia Earhart and a Tasmanian tiger named Oz." Marisol paused for a breath. "Also, did you know that T-rexes hate the smell of peppermint?"

Really? the cicadas chirped back.

Jake couldn't help but grin. "Maybe not the *whole* truth. We'll tell them our boat got swept away and we were trapped inside the lighthouse. Which is technically what happened."

"I'll let you do the talking," Marisol decided. "Are you ready?"

Another light had switched on inside. And another, on the back porch.

"I think so." He swallowed. "You?"

"Whatever's waiting for us in there can't be any scarier than a megalodon. Or cannibal rats. Or a Titanoboa. Or Red Bun. Or the Administrator."

In fact, it was Victor who stepped out onto the porch.

The floodlights slanted so his hair looked like kraken tentacles. He paused at the top step, trying to decide whether or not he was imagining the figures at the end of the dock.

"Mari? Jake?" *Blink, blink.* "Mari! Jake!" He came hurtling down the steps to throw his arms around Marisol, lifting her clean off her feet. She squeaked a protest, then went silent as he squished all the air out of her, his arms a warm, strong band around her body. "We were so scared, we . . ."

But then Victor seemed to remember that he was too mature for hugs like this, and he set her down on her feet, clearing his throat.

"We're back," Jake supplied helpfully, pushing his hands deep into his pockets.

"You two are in sooooo much trouble," Victor said, then tipped his head back to raise his voice to a shout. "Moooooom!!! I found them!!!"

More lights flicked on. The creaky old beach house announced every relative's footstep. Marisol heard their names shouted and sobbed. The twins—Veronica and Angeline—even put away their "eye phones" to join in. As the rest of the stampede descended, she hugged her grumbling brother one more time. Tighter than tight.

It was good to be home.

18

JAKE

JAKE SPENT THE WEEK MAKING NEW MEMORIES.

He'd raced along the beach with his cousins, feeling the sand that was just sand stick between his toes, and plunged into the salty waves, thankful that he didn't have to worry about mega sharks. They'd played tag up and down the shore, dug networks of giant holes, and Jake had tried to teach the family how to play cricket, which he'd learned in Australia, though nobody—even Jake—really understood the rules.

Things were almost returning to normal.

Almost.

Their first night back had been a long one. He and Marisol stumbled through an explanation for their parents about getting stranded out at the Morris Island Light. About hitching a lift back from a pair of mysterious kayakers. About living off the picnic they'd taken with them. It wasn't a very good story, even the second time around when they'd repeated it to officers with bright badges and coffee breath. Marisol turned roja in both cheeks. Jake kept waiting for the police to crumple up their notepads, to tell him to tell the truth.

But the Unknown wasn't done with the Beruna cousins yet.

At least, that's what it felt like, when the authorities left and their parents finally tucked them into bed. Jake wondered if maybe, somehow, shreds of magic had followed them back from the World Between Blinks, a little lostness that attached to their family, washing away the memory of how worried they'd been. It was less than a day before nobody spoke of their absence at all.

The only signs that Jake and Marisol had disappeared were their necklaces. All of the charms' charm was gone. The magnifying glasses showed nothing new, scrolls stayed scrolls, and their hourglasses obeyed the normal laws of gravity, no matter how many times the cousins snuck away to test them. Up and down, up and down. They turned the timers in Nana's attic, summoning the World with whispers.

"I wonder what Oz is doing right now."

"Eating. Or flying with Amelia," Marisol guessed. "Or both. I wonder what happened at Nefertiti's court when the Amber Room reappeared. . . ."

They wondered and wondered and wondered. Most of the imagining was fun, but every time Jake saw a ✕ marking on one of Nana's maps, he couldn't help worrying about Christopher. Had Hazel and their great-uncle made it back safely? If so, why hadn't they texted? Or telegraphed?

Or . . . something.

But then, one afternoon, Jake made his way up from the beach, Marisol at his side, his cousins Victor, Veronica, and Angeline trying their best to avoid burrs. As the five of them paused in the front yard to hose the sand off their bare feet, Victor squinted up at the porch.

"Hey, who's that?" he said.

There were two extra adults sitting with their parents—a man and a woman. They had their backs to the children, and they wore sunhats that hid even their hair. Jake couldn't see their faces, but a tiny thrill of hope shot through him, and his heart threw in an extra beat.

Marisol looked electric too. "Jake, do you think . . . ?"

"Maybe," he said quickly.

She grinned, salt-static hair flying everywhere as she seized Jake's hand and dragged him up the porch steps.

"Oh, there you are!" his mom greeted them with a smile. "We have visitors."

And then the visitors turned around.

Oblivious to the way Jake and Marisol froze in the screen door, the other cousins piling up in behind them, his mother continued. "Children, this is Christopher and Hazel Creaturo. Christopher is our . . ."

"Second cousin, I believe," Christopher supplied. "Three times removed. Or maybe four." He looked exactly as he had in the World Between Blinks, except that he wasn't wearing white anymore. Now, he was clad in a pair of jeans and a green shirt.

Aunt Cara's smile was identical to Mom's. "Can you believe they found us on one of those genealogy websites? You know, the ones where you send in a sample, and they tell you what countries you're from, and match you up with other people who are related to you. Who knew Nana had even done that? But it would've been just like her to try something new."

Christopher was all courtesy, paying no particular attention to Jake and Marisol. "This place was listed under 'Beruna' in the phone book. We just thought we'd drop by on the off chance someone was home," he said. "We're driving down the East Coast for our honeymoon."

"It's a pleasure to meet you all." Hazel's lipstick was a different color—more coral than red—which made her look like a stranger when she smiled at the cousins.

In fact, there was no hint of recognition in either adult's gaze when they met Jake's eyes and shook his

292

hand. Had there been a problem with the hourglasses? Had the Unknown stolen their World Between Blinks memories? Had they forgotten who Jake and Marisol were?

Jake's thoughts chased each other in a worried circle, but they were interrupted when Uncle Todd stuck his head out the door from the house. "Pierre and I are making shrimp and grits for lunch! It'll be ready in fifteen. Can some of you kids please set the table?"

Jake was about to burst with questions, so he spoke up quickly, before anyone could volunteer him to wrangle napkins and cups of juice. "If there's a few minutes left, maybe Christopher and Hazel would like to see the beach," he offered, using his best We Have Company voice. The one Mom liked him to use when they were at fancy foreign embassy receptions.

He was rewarded with a smile. "That's very polite of you, Jake," she said. "Why don't you take them down, just quickly?"

"I'll come too," Marisol piped up, still holding tight to Jake's hand—and he was still holding tight to hers.

And so, his stomach full of butterflies that were doing acrobatics to rival anything Amelia could pull off, Jake and his cousin led their visitors across the street, onto a path lined with palm fronds and vines. Green swallowed them.

The moment they could no longer see the house, Christopher let out a whoop and grabbed Jake's hands, pulling him free of Marisol to spin him in a circle. Hazel threw her arms around Marisol, lifting her clean off her feet.

"We did it!" crowed Christopher. "We all made it!"

"You . . ." Jake stumbled, staring up at his great-uncle. "You remember us?"

"Of course!" said Hazel. "We've been dying to be sure you made it back as well. We're sorry it took us a whole week to get here. Christopher left bank accounts set up for when we returned, but it took a little while to access the funds and get emergency passports. Then we had to learn how to book flights on the World Wide Web using little plastic cards instead of money. My, but things have changed!"

"The old house hasn't, though." Christopher gazed back in the direction of their family, a smile tugging at one corner of his mouth.

Marisol was grinning too, giddy with happiness, and Jake felt like he'd put down a weight he hadn't known he was carrying.

"It's so good to see you," Marisol said. "It was beginning to all feel . . ."

". . . like we'd imagined it," Jake finished when she trailed off. "Though we knew we didn't."

"If we have our way, you'll be seeing a lot more of us," Christopher replied. "Your parents were just telling us that they're not sure they can keep Lucy's house, what with the cost of repairs. Especially since they only visit once or twice a year."

The weight started to settle back onto Jake's shoulders, pressing them down and winding his muscles taut. But then he realized Hazel was beaming—pink lips smiling under her retro sunhat.

"The repairs will be expensive," she said. "But it just so happens, we have a lot of money. Those bank accounts have been growing since the 1940s. We've been telling the grown ups how excited we are to discover relatives, since Christopher hasn't got any other family. Well, except me, now."

Jake and Marisol waited, their breath balanced on a knife's edge of hope as the newlyweds exchanged a warm glance. Christopher's dimples showed as he continued.

"We'll wait another few days, and then we'll suggest that perhaps *we* could buy the house—and keep it as a summer meeting place for the whole family, of course."

"We'll always be waiting here for you," Hazel said.

"¿En serio?" gasped Marisol. "Are you serious?"

"Very." Their great-uncle nodded, taking Hazel's hand in his. "There's nothing we'd love more."

Jake swallowed hard. He'd finally learned not to leave

everything behind, but with the heaviness of knowing this might be their last summer here, he'd been wondering if it was a lesson he'd been smart to learn. And he knew Marisol had willingly sacrificed the Great Mogul Diamond to get them all home, but that she'd been secretly aching over the coming end of their time at the beach house. He'd seen her whispering to the map-covered walls when she thought nobody was looking.

Sometimes you hold on to things.

Sometimes you lose them.

And sometimes, just sometimes, you had to let go of something so you could find it again.

Jake studied Christopher's and Hazel's knotted fingers, testing this new idea. "So . . . we'll see you next summer?"

"That you will," Christopher said. "Hopefully it'll be a quieter vacation than this one has been."

They walked until they reached the end of the path, and stood on the beach together, staring out at the Morris Island Light, where it had all begun. Where they'd slipped through to the World and begun their wild quest to find their way home.

"Maybe next time will be a quieter vacation," agreed Jake, though he had the funniest feeling. . . .

He blinked, then blinked again, and for an instant in between, he thought he saw land stretching out to the

Light, a house with an old car for a chicken coop sitting beside it. But of course, with that second blink, it was gone.

At least for now.

THE WORLD BETWEEN BLINKS IS ALWAYS THERE.

It is everywhere and it is nowhere.

But most children—the ones who can see—glimpse it at the end of a very good book. They turn to the final page, they read those six solid letters, they study the blank page beyond. There, in the white without words, the story keeps going, sailing across oceans and trekking through jungles and bargaining with queens, strong enough to appear in dreams. Strong enough to let you imagine what was. What could be . . .

THE END

Or is it?
Safe travels, dear reader.

CURATORS' FILES

Dear Reader!

Here are some catalog entries on just a few of the things you'll find in the World Between Blinks. But you'll note that in these pages many more have been mentioned. . . . Perhaps you might like to write a catalog entry or two of your own? There's always more work to do!

CHAPTER TWO

Name: Morris Island Light

Entry into WBB: Ongoing

Notes: While the Morris Island Light itself has only partially entered the World Between Blinks, stubbornly splitting itself between two places at once, its surroundings have appeared here. Due to intense coastal erosion back in the old world, this includes the land upon which the lighthouse used to stand, its keeper's cottage, and even a Model T Ford motor car, which serves as a chicken coop. Note, the chicken will peck, approach with caution!

CHAPTER THREE

Name: Theodosia Burr Alston

Entry into WBB: January 3, 1813

Notes: She is the daughter of US vice president Aaron Burr (who also happens to be the villain of a popular Broadway musical). She arrived here aboard the *Patriot*, which never did reach New York City—its original destination. History considers Theodosia lost with the schooner's crew, but really they're sailing around the World Between Blinks on a mission to find foundlings.

CHAPTER FOUR

Name: Pterodactylus

Entry into WBB: 136 million years ago. Give or take.

Notes: Not a dinosaur. Do not misclassify. Pterosaurs flew Earth's skies during the Valanginian age, long before there were humans to see them. Current relations remain tenuous: *KEEP OUT OF RESIDENTIAL ZONES*.

Name: The Crystal Palace

Entry into WBB: November 30, 1936

Notes: Built in London to house the Great Exhibition of 1851, this all-glass building was the first of its kind. Trees grew beneath its translucent ceilings. When it mysteriously caught fire, a hundred thousand people gathered to watch it burn. Among them? Future Prime Minister Winston Churchill, who declared, "This is the end of an age."

CHAPTER FIVE

Name: St. Helena Olive

Entry into WBB: December 2003

Notes: Native to the tropical island of St. Helena in the South Atlantic Ocean. Despite the tree's name, it has no relation to the true olive, and alas, no olives.

Name: Aral Sea

Entry into WBB: Ongoing (1960s–Present)

Notes: With 26,300 square miles of water, the Aral Sea was once the fourth-largest *lake* on Earth. (Confusing, we know. Earth's record keepers need labeling lessons!) Over 90 percent of that is now in the World Between Blinks. The rest remains between Kazakhstan and Uzbekistan.

Name: The Loch Ness Monster (aka Nessie)

Entry into WBB: December 10, 1944

Notes: *Quasi-mythical.* Can something be lost if it's never found? Legends about the Loch Ness Monster have existed since AD 565, when Saint Columba reportedly ordered a great water beast not to attack a man swimming across the River Ness. There have been hundreds of unconfirmed monster sightings since, and some think that Nessie could be a plesiosaur. They are wrong. Not a dinosaur. Do not misclassify.

CHAPTER SIX

Name: Ostia Antica

Entry into WBB: Extended (AD 476—ninth century)

Notes: Ostia Antica served as Rome's main port in AD 100, receiving shipments from as far away as Alexandria, Egypt. After the Roman Empire fell, this bustling city faded away due to repeated pirate sackings (the scalawags!) and the silting of the Tiber River. If visiting, keep an eye out for the many excellent statues of wrestlers, the celebrities of their day!

Name: George Washington's Dentures (Top Half)

Entry into WBB: July 19, 1981

Notes: The first president of the United States of America wore false teeth, which were made of everything from ivory to gold to other people's pearly whites. The dentures were—presumably—stolen from the National Museum of American History. Half of them made their way back. The other half? Here.

Name: Amelia "Meeley" Mary Earhart

Entry into WBB: July 2, 1937

Notes: In 1932, Amelia became the first woman to fly solo across the Atlantic Ocean, which made her the most famous aviator on Earth. She loved nicknaming her airplanes: the *Canary*, the *Little Red Bus*, and finally, the *Flying Laboratory*, which she tried circling the globe with. This Lockheed Electra 10-E plane flew her from Miami to New Guinea but took a detour over the Pacific Ocean. Instead of landing on Howland Island, as planned, Amelia and her navigator, Fred Noonan, appeared in the World Between Blinks, where she currently runs a taxi service.

CHAPTER SEVEN
Name: Frost Fair
Entry into WBB: February 5, 1814
Notes: During the Little Ice Age (1300–1870), the river Thames froze over twenty-four times. Londoners set up vendor booths over the ice, which housed everything from coffee houses and souvenir shops to acrobats and sword swallowers. At the final Frost Fair in 1814, the ice was thick enough for an elephant to walk across it! How do we know? An elephant actually did!

Name: Kaparunina/Thylacine/Tasmanian tiger
Entry into WBB: September 7, 1936
Notes: These carnivorous marsupials look (and act!) like a strange combination of tiger, wolf, and kangaroo. They *yawn* in the face of danger and make a variety of

interesting sounds to communicate. The last Tasmanian tiger on Earth lived at the Hobart Zoo and was a female named Benjamin. (Exactly who *is* responsible for labeling back there?)

Name: Glenn Miller

Entry into WBB: December 15, 1944

Notes: This bandleader produced more top hits during his career than Elvis or the Beatles! While flying over the English Channel to entertain US troops in France during World War II, Glenn's plane entered the World Between Blinks. He didn't let this stop his concert tour. Currently performing at the Hanging Gardens of Babylon.

Name: The Globe Theatre

Entry into WBB: June 29, 1613

Notes: Built in London in 1599, this playhouse served as a performance venue for William Shakespeare's plays. A large fire brought it to the World Between Blinks, where the Bard's lost works (such as *Love's Labour's Won* and *The History of Cardenio*) are still performed.

CHAPTER EIGHT

Name: SS *Baychimo*

Entry into WBB: Entries, actually. The "Ghost Ship of the Arctic" wouldn't stay lost until 1969.

Notes: This steel-hulled cargo steamer became

trapped in packed ice in 1931. After the *Baychimo*'s crew abandoned the ship, it began drifting around the Unknown for decades, sighted in both Alaska and the World Between Blinks, refusing to anchor in either. Most vexing.

Name: Megalodon

Entry into WBB: 3.6 million years ago. Give or take.

Notes: This mega shark can grow up to sixty feet long, with teeth that measure close to seven inches. *KEEP OUT OF RESIDENTIAL ZONES AT ALL COSTS.*

Name: Bessie Hyde

Entry into WBB: November 1928

Notes: Bessie and her husband, Glen, went rafting down the Colorado River for their honeymoon, braving the Grand Canyon's rapids before slipping through the Unknown. Their boat didn't make the journey with them, and it was found downriver fully intact, supplies still inside. She currently crews the SS *Baychimo.*

Name: MV *Lyubov Orlova*

Entry into WBB: March 23, 2013

Notes: After serving many years as a cruise ship in both the Arctic and Antarctic, the *Lyubov Orlova* was taken to a salvage yard. Its towing line broke on the journey, and the ship drifted free in international waters, causing panic in the United Kingdom due to a rumor that it was infested with cannibal rats. Unfortunately for us, that rumor was true. *WARNING! DO NOT BOARD IF YOU WANT TO KEEP YOUR FINGERS, NOSE, AND TOES!*

CHAPTER NINE

Name: USS *Seawolf* (SS-197)

Entry into WBB: October 4, 1944

Notes: This Sargo-class submarine was deployed in the Pacific during World War II. The Americans believed it was sunk by friendly fire, but the truth is, many, many things get lost during war.

Name: Kitezh

Entry into WBB: Thirteenth century. Give or take.

Notes: *Quasi-mythical.* This legendary city is said to have sunk beneath Lake Svetloyar in Central Russia. Known for its white-stoned, golden-domed churches, Kitezh was attacked by Tatars in 1238. Because the inhabitants had no battlements to protect them, they began to pray. Water miraculously burst out of the ground and swallowed the city. True or not, it ended up in the World Between Blinks.

Name: Wanaku

Entry into WBB: A thousand years ago. Give or take.

Notes: This ancient, pre-Incan city was the home of the Tiwanaku people before being submerged in Lake

Titicaca. Traces of the civilization still lie beneath the water in the old world, between Bolivia and Peru, including its temple. But we've got the best bits here.

Name: The Great Barrier Reef
Entry into WBB: Ongoing (1980–present)
Notes: The largest reef system on Earth has started appearing in the World Between Blinks because oceans are getting too hot for the coral, bleaching them.

Name: Kronosaurus
Entry into WBB: 100 million years ago. Give or take.
Notes: Not a dinosaur. Do not misclassify. This prehistoric sea beast is the largest of the pliosaurs with three-inch-long teeth and a thirty-six-foot-long body. *KEEP OUT OF RESIDENTIAL ZONES TO AVOID MASS CHAOS AND INCIDENTAL PAPERWORK!*

Name: Tusoteuthis
Entry into WBB: 72 million years ago. Give or take.
Notes: This is a very, very, very big squid. Eleven-foot-long tentacles bring the creature's complete length to thirty-six feet. Don't even try and shake hands with it.

CHAPTER TEN

Name: Port Royal

Entry into WBB: 11:43am, June 7, 1692

Notes: This city was (and still is) scalawag central! Pirates made Port Royal their port of call, and they were joined in the alehouses by flocks of wild parrots. Some even say Blackbeard befriended a howler monkey here. (They also say he named it Jefferson.) Two-thirds of the port was sucked into the ocean during an earthquake. Despite this, the pirates (and their parrots) have not stopped their revelries.

Name: EML *Kalev*

Entry into WBB: October 29, 1941

Notes: This Estonian submarine was taken over by the Soviet Navy during World War II. It slipped through the Unknown during its second patrol.

CHAPTER ELEVEN

Name: Portus

Entry into WBB: Extended (fourth–fifth century, give or take)

Notes: A major port of the ancient world, Portus had it all. A lighthouse, a canal linking it to nearby Ostia Antica (not that it'll stay near Ostia, where we keep putting it, oh no), a magnificent sea wall, a safe harbor, and a direct road to Rome. If the river mouth hadn't silted up, it might still be in the old world.

Name: Neferneferuaten Nefertiti, Great of Praises, Lady of Grace, Sweet of Love, Most Powerful Queen in the Land of the Lost

Entry into WBB: 1330 BC. Give or take.

Notes: This queen was the wife of Pharaoh Akhenaten, who established a new capital in Amarna and decreed that the Egyptians would worship only one god: Aten. When the pharaoh died, Amarna was abandoned and swallowed by the desert. Queen Nefertiti vanished from historical records, possibly to become a pharaoh herself? She remains tight-lipped on the matter. *WARNING: CURATES HER OWN COLLECTIONS AND RESISTS ZONING PROPOSALS.*

Name: Gardens of the Old Summer Palace

Entry into WBB: October 18, 1860

Notes: Built for the Qianlong Emperor of the Qing dynasty in China, this "Garden of Gardens" is filled with lakes, bridges, pavilions, and other elegant structures. British troops burned it into the Unknown during the Second Opium War. Despite the fact that gardens *cannot bloom* in deserts, Queen Nefertiti insists on keeping this in Amarna, citing a royalty clause. Our last attempt at negotiating with her ended poorly. For us.

Name: The Amber Room

Entry into WBB: Extended (1941–1945)

Notes: This room in Russia's Catherine Palace was considered the "Eighth Wonder of the World." Its panels' mosaics are made with over 350 shades of amber and many are backed with gold foil—radiating a warm glow when candles are lit. Looting Nazis took the Amber Room apart in 1941, and by the time World War II ended four years later, all trace of the treasure was lost.

Name: The Ninth Roman Legion

Entry into WBB: AD 120

Notes: Known as the Legio IX Hispana, this legion fought in the Roman Army for over two hundred years, then vanished from historical records without explanation.

Name: The Army of Cambyses

Entry into WBB: 524 BC

Notes: *Quasi-mythical.* According to the Greek historian Herodotus, the Persian king Cambyses II sent an army of fifty thousand soldiers through the Sahara, but they didn't reach their destination, nor did they ever return home. Legend has it that the desert swallowed them. They continue to march alongside the Ninth Roman Legion at Queen Nefertiti's pleasure.

CHAPTER TWELVE

Name: Giovanni Nepomuceno Maria Annunziata Giuseppe Giovanni Batista Ferdinando Baldassare Luigi Gonzaga Pietro Alessandrino Zanobi Antonino (also known as Archduke Johann Salvator and/or John Orth)

Entry into WBB: July 12, 1890

Notes: This archduke had an impressive *fifteen* names, but shortened this to a much more manageable two when he renounced his title in 1889. Johann married an opera dancer named Ludmilla "Milli" Stubel, and the two sailed to South America in 1890. They vanished on the journey.

Name: Alexander Helios

Entry into WBB: 31 BC. Give or take.

Notes: After his parents, Cleopatra and Mark Antony, were defeated by Octavian (later known as Caesar Augustus) in 31 BC, ten-year-old Alexander Helios was taken to Rome with his twin sister. He disappeared from historical records shortly after. Due to the boy's youth and Egyptian affinities, Queen Nefertiti has taken a shine to him.

Name: Harold Holt

Entry into WBB: December 17, 1967

Notes: The seventeenth prime minister of Australia

loved the ocean and was a very strong swimmer, so it was considered strange when he vanished off the Victoria coast during a morning swim. Conspiracy theories abound: he was abducted by aliens, he boarded a Chinese submarine. None have correctly guessed that he ended up in the World Between Blinks.

Name: The Great Mogul Diamond
Entry into WBB: 1747
Notes: As a raw stone, this diamond weighed in at 737 carats, the largest ever to be mined in India. Unfortunately, the lapidary who cut it did a poor job, reducing the jewel to 280 carats. It was looted by Nadir Shah when he invaded Delhi, then lost altogether after the Persian ruler was assassinated.

Name: The Amazon Rainforest
Entry into WBB: Ongoing (1960s–Present)
Notes: Earth is losing the Amazon rainforest due to a number of factors: farming, cattle ranchers, fires, the demand for hardwood supplies, and even highways. It continues to appear in the World Between Blinks at an alarming rate. Cataloging a rainforest is no easy task!

CHAPTER THIRTEEN

Name: Phoberomys Pattersoni
Entry into WBB: 8 million years ago. Give or take.

Notes: To the casual observer, this animal looks like a giant guinea pig. And we mean GIANT. It measures 9.8 ft (3 m) long, and weighs between 550 and 1,540 lbs (250–700 kg). It used to live in the Orinoco River delta in the old world's South America, and still prefers to stay in the Amazon. *THREAT LEVEL TO RESIDENTIAL ZONES IS LOW. (Unless it sits on you.)*

Name: Golden Toad
Entry into WBB: May 15, 1989
Notes: These brightly colored amphibians hail from Costa Rica's Monteverde Cloud Forest Reserve. Their habitat there was tiny—only 1.5 sq miles (4 sq kms). They have *much* more room to hop in the World Between Blinks!

Name: Titanoboa
Entry into WBB: 58 million years ago. Give or take.
Notes: These snakes grow up to 45 ft (12.8 m) long and weigh up to 2,500 lbs. (1,135 kg). They once lived in what is now northeastern Colombia, and still prefer the Amazon. Thank goodness. *KEEP OUT OF RESIDENTIAL ZONES LEST THEY ACT AS LETHAL SCARVES.*

Name: The Lost City of Z
Entry into WBB: Unknown. City constantly relocates, in defiance of all cataloging attempts. We are unclear when it first appeared in the World Between Blinks.

Notes: *Quasi-mythical.* The legend is fueled by Manuscript 512 in Rio de Janeiro's National Library, which claims that a Portuguese expedition stumbled upon a wondrous city in the jungle, one that Amazonian tribes described as "enormously rich in gold." Since the early twentieth century, explorers have been searching for the Lost City of Z, though only a handful have succeeded in finding it inside the World Between Blinks, losing themselves in the process. See *Colonel Percy Fawcett (and company).*

Name: Colonel Percy Fawcett (and company)
Entry into WBB: May 29, 1925
Notes: This English explorer spent much of his adult life searching for the Lost City of Z. His seventh and final attempt took place in 1925, when the fifty-seven-year-old traveled into the Amazon rainforest with his twenty-two-year-old son, Jack Fawcett, and Jack's best friend, Raleigh Rimell.

Name: Friedrich Wilhelm Ludwig Leichhardt
Entry into WBB: April 3, 1848
Notes: This German naturalist and explorer frequently carved Ls into trees to mark his path. He was last seen setting off on his third expedition of Australia from the Darling Downs in Queensland. The journey took him into the World Between Blinks instead.

Name: Uemura Naomi

Entry into WBB: February 14, 1984

Notes: This Japanese explorer became famous for his solo expeditions. He was the first person to reach the North Pole by himself, the first to raft alone down the Amazon, and the first to climb Denali without a team. He would have been the first Japanese man to summit Mount Everest, but he stepped aside to allow his elder that honor. The forty-three-year-old vanished while descending Denali during a winter storm.

CHAPTER FIFTEEN

Name: Public Record Office of Ireland

Entry into WBB: June 30, 1922

Notes: This building—along with most of the records inside—was lost in the Irish civil war. The Irish Republican Army used the record office as their munition block, and during the fires of the Battle of Dublin, the place exploded. Oops.

Name: Library of Alexandria

Entry into WBB: Extended (48 BC–AD 270)

Notes: This was the largest library of the ancient world—any ships that passed through Alexandria's port had to surrender their books so the library could copy them. At its height, the place held almost half a million scrolls. Alas, as we learned in the previous entry, wars and libraries don't mix well. When Julius Caesar attacked Alexandria in 48 BC, he started one of the many fires that initiated the collection's transition into the World Between Blinks.

Name: Sir Terry Pratchett's unfinished novels
Entry into WBB: August 25, 2017
Notes: Beloved and bestselling author Sir Terry Pratchett wrote over seventy novels, but he left some unfinished at the time of his death. In accordance with his wishes, his computer's hard drive was destroyed by means of being run over by a steamroller (which was called Lord Jericho). Those lost works now reside in the World Between Blinks, where residents are enjoying them very much, but rather wishing they had endings.

CHAPTER SIXTEEN
Name: Quagga
Entry into WBB: August 12, 1883
Notes: These beauties are a subspecies of zebra and have the stripes to show it! Their call is a *kwa-ha* sound, and despite the double G in their name, their name is pronounced the same way. Am making this note to help other Curators avoid looking foolish in social situations.

CHAPTER SEVENTEEN

Name: Via Hadriana

Entry into WBB: Ongoing

Notes: This was an ancient Roman road built at the order of Emperor Hadrian in AD 137, running from the Nile River to the Red Sea. Time and sand have brought most of this highway through the Unknown, but some traces linger in its original location, making its entry "ongoing."

ACKNOWLEDGMENTS

Writing a book requires assistance and support from so many people, but this one in particular took an army of experts. A heartfelt gracias to Marcelo Contreras and Cara Strauss Contreras for lending us not only their names but their linguistic and cultural expertise. Their incredibly generous help in bringing Marisol's branch of the family to life was irreplaceable, as was their assistance with navigating the nuances of Bolivian Spanish. To those Spanish-speaking readers who might wonder why a turn of phrase seems unfamiliar, the colloquial variations found in Bolivian Spanish are the answer.

Thank you to the Tasmanian Aboriginal Centre for assistance with and permission to use *palawa kani*, the language of Tasmanian Aborigines, as we added Oz the kaparunina to the World Between Blinks.

Our other experts included Soraya Een Hajji, P. M. Freestone, and Yulin Zhuang—to these generous friends as well as others not named here, many, many thanks.

To our friends who offered early critique, Megan Shepherd and Shannon Messenger, thank you! Any errors that remain, despite the best efforts of our advisers and readers, are of course our own.

We are so grateful both to and for our amazing editor, Andrew Eliopulos. Your enthusiasm for the world we created has been unflagging. Your insightful and nuanced questions helped us gently draw out the best in this book and in the journey of holding on and letting go that Jake and Marisol take together. We are so grateful as well to Bria Ragin for her smarts, support, and editorial feedback; to Rosemary Brosnan for her leadership; to Jill Amack for patient and thoughtful fact-checking and copy editing (and for laughing at our jokes); to Kevin Keele for our gorgeous cover art and Cat San Juan for our cover design; to Jon Howard, our managing editor; to Robby Imfeld and his team in marketing and Andrea Pappenheimer and her team in sales. To Suzanne Murphy and Jean McGinley, thank you for making us a part of the family. We could go on forever with the Harper thank-yous—to the teams in sales, marketing, production, design, publicity, and more, we appreciate everything you do for us so very much. Many, many thanks also to the wonderful team at Harper Oz. We'd be . . . lost without you.

This book began when our wonderful literary agent, Tracey Adams, told us about an island that had appeared overnight, the result of sand bars shifting with the tides. Soon it would be lost again, but just for a moment a new place full of driftwood and sharks' teeth was there to explore. The idea of a lost place, a place that you could only see sometimes, took hold, and several months later we surprised her with a manuscript. Tracey—you are endlessly patient, good-humored, and supportive, and we love working with you. We're so grateful to have you, Josh, Cathy, and Stephen on our side!

From Ryan, personal thanks to Kate Armstrong, Corrie Wang, Roshani Chokshi, Megan Shepherd, Laini Taylor (who had many encouraging things to say after she heard us brainstorming this book in the castle kitchen), and the rest of the château crew: Jim Di Bartolo, Katherine Webber, Alywn Hamilton, Laure Eve. The Strauss family. The Graudin family. Raiden. David and Sabriel—all of my love, always. *Soli Deo Gloria.*

From Amie, personal thanks to Meg Spooner, Jay Kristoff, Marie Lu, Leigh Bardugo, Michelle Dennis, Kacey Smith, Nic Crowhurst, Soraya Een Hajji, P. M. Freestone, Kate Irving, Lili Wilkinson, Nic Hayes, Ellie Marney, Liz Barr, Eliza Tiernan, Kate Armstrong, the Roti Boti gang, and my Aussie retreat crew. The Kaufman family. The Cousins family. Jack. Brendan and Pip—I would brave anything to find you.

From both of us, undying thanks to the readers,

reviewers, librarians, teachers, and booksellers who share our stories with the world. You changed our lives first as readers, and now as authors.

And finally . . . thank *you*, for picking up this book and journeying to the World Between Blinks with us. We'll see you in the sequel!

Read on for a sneak peek at the first book in
New York Times bestselling author Amie Kaufman's
electrifying fantasy series, ELEMENTALS!

RAYNA WAS CONFIDENTLY LEADING THEM IN the wrong direction. Anders hurried through the crowd after her, ducking as a woman nearly sideswiped him with a basket of glistening fish. The stink washed over him like a cloud, and then he swerved away, leaving it behind as they ran through a stone arch.

"Rayna, we're—"

She was already turning the corner and running out across Helstustrat, nipping in front of a pair of chestnut ponies that were hauling a wagon full of barrels over the cobblestones. Anders jogged from one foot to the other, waiting as they rumbled past, then took off after his twin sister again. "Rayna!"

She could hear him—he knew that when she flashed a quick grin over her shoulder, white teeth gleaming in her brown face. But she didn't slow down, her thick black braid bouncing as she jogged. He was stuck trying to catch up again. This *always* happened.

"Rayna," he tried, one final time, just as they rounded the corner to see the roadblock ahead, manned by guards clad in gray woolen uniforms. Without breaking stride, Rayna whirled back the way they'd come, grabbing Anders by the arm and yanking him with her around the corner. His heart thumping at the close shave, he leaned back against the cool stone wall.

"Guards," she said, tugging her coat straight.

"I know! They're on every street on the north side of the city," he told her. "Checking everyone who comes through."

Her gaze flicked back toward the corner. "Was there another dragon sighting? Or are they just doing extra patrols before the Ulfar Trials?"

"There was a dragon in the sky just last night," he replied. "I heard them talking about it in the tavern when we were climbing down from the roof first thing." He didn't point out that Rayna had missed that information because she'd been too busy telling him their plans for the day. "They said they saw it breathe fire and everything."

That silenced even Rayna for a moment. Dragons had been gone from Holbard for ten years now, but lately they had been seen in the sky overhead. Anders and Rayna had seen one themselves six months before, on the night of the last equinox celebrations.

It had breathed pure white fire as it circled above the city, then vanished into the darkness. An hour later, a set of stables in the north of the city was ablaze with the ferocious, white-and-gold dragonsfire that was almost impossible to put out, leaping from place to place faster and fiercer than normal flames.

By the time the buildings had been reduced to ashes, the dragon was gone, and with it the son of the family that lived above the stables. Dragons always took children, the stories said. The weak, the sick, and the defenseless.

"Maybe the guards think the dragon from last night could still be spying in the city, hiding in human form," Anders said. "Or planning to start a fire."

Rayna snorted. "What, and they think if they ask people, they're just going to admit they knew where a dragon was but decided not to tell anyone?"

He nodded, lowering his voice to do his best impression of an upstanding citizen. "Yes, Guard, in fact I hide scorch dragons on my roof, because I want to be roasted alive and I don't believe in public safety. I feel a little bit guilty about it, and I've been meaning to confess to somebody, but I wasn't sure who would want to know."

"At least you'd be warm." She giggled, kicking at a slushy, melting pile of snow.

He returned to his own voice, her giggle helping chase away his own nerves, as he had hoped it would. "You never know if you don't ask." But though he smiled along with her, even the words put a twitch between his shoulder blades. *Scorch dragons.* They were the one thing every person in Holbard knew to fear, whether they were locals or traders from across the sea. There were new rumors every day that dragons were near the city again. Rumors they'd burned a farmhouse to the ground just last week, the farmer's family still inside.

"How far south do we have to go to dodge the guards?" Rayna asked, jolting him from that thought. It went without saying that they'd avoid them. Guards asked questions like "Where are your parents?" and other inconvenient things related to adult supervision.

"At least ten streets," he replied. "A couple of them were in wolf form, and I think they smell it if you're worried."

"*Ten streets*? That doubles the distance to Trellig Square! Anders, if you knew we were going the wrong way, why didn't you stop me?" She was all indignation, hands on hips.

"Well, I—" But he gave up before he started. Maybe

he *should* have tried harder. It sort of *was* his fault they'd come so far the wrong way. "I'm sorry," he settled on. But she was already moving again, heading south.

"We'll go over the rooftops."

He was tall and gangly to her short and strong—though the twins shared the same black curls and warm brown skin, in almost every other way they were different. So being taller, Anders boosted Rayna up until she could grab the guttering and haul herself onto the nearest roof. Then he scrambled onto a barrel and climbed after her.

When he straightened up, he could see the rooftop meadows of Holbard spread out before them. Each square of grass was at least twenty houses long and twenty wide, rising and falling with the pitch and slope of the roofs.

The rooftops were covered in bright patches of wild-flowers, red fentills tucked down in the gullies, yellow-and-white flameflowers bobbing in the breeze on the slopes, as well as the occasional herb garden, where some-one had a window big enough to climb out and tend to their plants.

Thanks to the street children of Holbard, wherever there was only an alleyway between two stretches of grass, rather than a wide street, a plank of wood was almost always propped in place to serve as a bridge. You could travel half the city up here without ever needing to set foot on the ground.